Betrayal

Clare L. Roberts studied Art and Drama at Cheshire College and went on to get a first class honour's degree in English Literature at the University of Western Australia, was awarded a Commonwealth Scholarship but returned to England for post graduate studies at Somerville College Oxford, then spent several years teaching English, Classics and Art. 2012/13 were devoted to the Master of Writing degree at Warwick University including three months in Milan working with Tim Parks at the University there. *Betrayal* is a story of family, evil, the power of love and creativity and the strength of the human spirit.

Betrayal

Clare L. Roberts

Arena Books

First published in 2021 by Arena Books

Arena Books
6 Southgate Green
Bury St. Edmunds
IP33 2BL

www.arenabooks.co.uk

*Distributed in America by Ingram International, One Ingram Blvd., P.O. Box 3006,
La Vergne, TN 37086-1985, USA.*

Clare L. Roberts
Betrayal

British Library cataloguing in Publication Data. A Catalogue record
for this book is available from the British Library.

ISBN-13   978-1-911593-83-6

BIC classifications:- FA, FF, 1DST.

Cover design
by Jason Anscomb

Typeset in
Times New Roman

1

'Merda!

The old cherry branch sprang away beyond the reach of her secateurs. Oriana edged up another rung, head in a cage of twigs and branches.

'I'll get you, bastardo.'

She leaned over a thick limb, caught the branch, positioned the blades and forced them closed. It hinged gripping the secateurs, dragging her and the ladder down from branch to branch in a tangle of dark serrated leaves.

Hard clay and spiky grass thumped the air from her lungs. She couldn't breathe. There was a loud miaow and her lungs filled. She turned her head searching tunnels of cut branches for the cat. A small black nose nudged her head.

'Baffina.'

She laughed into unblinking golden eyes and tried to move but her leg was stuck in the ladder. She rolled over awkwardly, freed herself and sat up.

'Thank goodness I'm still in one piece.'

She swept heavy hair from her face and stroked the cat's sleek black head.

'You think I'm here to play?'

Oriana struggled up and rubbed her shin.

'I'm glad you're the only one to see that. They'd tell me I'm crazy, I shouldn't be doing it, ma eccola.' She spread her arms toward the tree. It looked slimmer, brighter, light as a girl.

'Better now? You'll be rid of your leaves before long. More fruit next year, eh?'

Even trimmed it was still too big for the narrow plot, it dominated the end of her long narrow garden, leaving only enough light for a few spring bulbs and lilies but Oriana loved its deep pink blossom in Spring and the plump, juicy red fruit. She loaded the prunings into a wheelbarrow and stacked them in the far corner by the railway line. When the last branch landed above her head she surveyed the pile with satisfaction, *'Makings of a good bonfire.'* Oriana loved bonfires, twice a year as a child her father had burned rubbish on the patch of land behind their garage and her excitement grew with the mound, the higher the better – the magic of fire, crackling and hissing, its hypnotic flames – yellow, red, blue – devouring mountains into dust.

Her wild side was tamed when she married a solicitor, a townie whose only outdoor pleasure was the sea. Dario could sit all day watching the ocean but its monotonous surges and endless bleakness sent Oriana inside herself to a core of isolation where she plumbed the depths of loneliness and futility, the impossibility of knowing another or being known. Sometimes it came at concerts and, in the middle of an auditorium surrounded by people, she would feel alone. It was only her art and her children that kept her away from that chasm.

The sun was at its height but autumn mellowed its intensity. She limped under a persimmon tree full of red and orange fruit past her ravaged vegetable plot with its row of shrivelled tomato plants staked to support their heavy fruit. A couple of glossy purple aubergines and a few gnarled peppers were all that remained of the rest.

A fluffy, grey cat jumped down from the roof of a little shed. She scooped him up.

'Lunch time, Burrichio?'

The passing rush of a high-speed train thwacked the garden. She stopped, surprised, 'Is that the time? The 12.10 to Pavia. It *is* lunch time.'

A green-eyed tortoiseshell cat insinuated itself around her legs. 'How's Tancreda? Hungry? Pity sardines don't grow on trees, eh?'

She gathered bowls under the overhanging vines of her mossy patio and filled them with cooked heart from an old 'fridge in the garage then leant against her shed letting the sun's warmth ease her jarred body while she watched the cats' feeding ritual – Baffina checked each bowl before settling to eat, Tancreda gobbled whole chunks of heart as if starved while Burrichio crouched and ate steadily oblivious of the world around him.

Muted sounds of cooking came from neighbouring kitchens and birds chattered and squabbled around feeders in the persimmon tree. Oriana heaved herself up and picked a couple of ripe fruits, bit into their warm flesh and sucked the pulp.

'Bene,' she rubbed her fingers on her jeans. 'Now, to work.'

With a sack truck she trundled a heavy bag of clay from the garage along the uneven path to her studio at the far end of the barn behind the garage. Leaves and sticks were heaped in front of its bleached wood door and grass had grown between the paving stones. The key turned but the door stuck. She rammed it with her shoulder until it juddered and scraped over concrete carrying her with it into the cool, still interior.

For a moment she stood motionless overcome by the strangeness of what had been her world for a quarter of a century then the smell of dry earth, captured sunshine and the pale patina of clay dust on benches and pots, her big friendly kiln and smooth shiny wheel at the end of the room reassured her. She was home, the place where she was most herself. She trundled the sack of clay to the sink and looked for a place to start.

Light flooded onto shelves of bowls, platters and chalices in a variety of glazes – turquoise, yellow or bright blue, mottled and shiny, carefully patterned or simple and plain – her experiments over the years. The earth and all it supplied was her medium and her fascination showed in little crystal caves of every hue arranged on benches beside ammonites and a sheep's skull. At the end of the room behind her wheel stood two rugged stone faces, big totemic figures by a great acanthus leaf hollowed to make the bowl of a fountain as well as a long, low curved and looped figure without end or beginning set on a plinth. She caressed its smooth surface feeling guilty, *two years ago, Battista's annual exhibition, I was always there. Poor Battista I let him down and he never complained, I lost impetus, deadlines had no meaning. So much time; melted, dissolved, gone. All those calls, opportunities denied, for what?*

Oriana unhooked one of Dario's old shirts from the door, slipped it over her jeans and sweatshirt and trundled her precious load over to a deep bin by the sink. A honey coloured jug full of wooden spatulas, looped wires and little sponges on sticks stood by the taps and, from a shelf above, a spiky dragon with a droopy wing and big, sad eyes looked down at her.

'I'd forgotten about you, I shouldn't have left you all this time should I?' She whispered reaching up for Pietro's dragon. At eight years old Pietro was the youngest of Oriana's five grandchildren and the closest, they were friends. Grandchildren were life's blood to her, more each day as they grew and drew her into their lives.

Her bag was packed ready to take over to the farm when Isabella's labour started for her sixth. Oriana hadn't expected her eldest daughter to become an earth mother but one child followed another and they all looked after each other on the farm. She checked the pocket of her jeans for her mobile. *Last time I hope, enough is enough.* She put the dragon back between two wobbly pots, one with a sunflower lid the other with a hen, the early work of Pietro's twin sisters.

She lifted the heavy sack and emptied its contents into the bin: clay – cool, dark, malleable – the smell of clean earth. She kneaded and squeezed the dark red mass forcing free a heavy chunk from the depths of the bin excitement rising, she knew what she wanted to make of this little mound of earth and here in the studio she was master. The clay made no demands, no promises, she knew its limitations, its possibilities.

She dropped it on the bench and pummelled it with the sides of her fists until it yielded under their warmth. *At last I can make you mine again.* She picked it up and threw it down hard, peeled it free and hurled it down again and again to crush the air from its body – the repeated slap and scream stinging the studio back to life. Grief that had gnawed at her for over a year had crystallised into a mission. She didn't know why or how but she had to build Dario's image now that the tide of anger at his death was ebbing.

She took a length of wire and sliced the firm, finely toned clay into pieces and started to roll long, thin snakes, quickly, urgently. *Twenty years I waited.* She took a thin wooden board and laid lines of clay along its length. *Promises – no, you never made them. I made them to myself – one day....* She joined soft earth tails around the board in an oval like an amphitheatre for his shoulders.

Why has it taken me so long to come back in here? Her strong hands smelled of earth. *My head was a blasted plain littered with lost possibilities.* She laid lines of clay one on top of another. Line by line shoulders rose from the board as she conjured his presence.

Dario, my Dario, the warmth of your body next to mine, your chest to lay my head on, thigh to rest my knee, reassuring bulwark of warm flesh, I miss that. She curved round a shoulder, along the back smearing together the coils. *Which of your faces should I choose? Old? Young? Solicitor? Husband? Father?* Her eyes narrowed, tiny lines gathered at the sides. *Difficult to pull one thread from the tangle of our lives – find a steady picture – the true face of Dario?* Her fingers deftly pressed and pinched then smoothed another coil into position. *He changed, we all change, truth changes. Truth can only be grasped when all's done and over but between you and me it was cut off and I was left stranded.*

She stopped, a rope of clay hanging from her hand, looking at the shallow wall around the board. *A whole lifetime, forty years, which you is mine? Dario the lawyer dominated our lives and took over Emilio, absorbing him into the practice, father and son, hand and glove, as it was always meant to be. I don't want to resurrect the lawyer but he has to be in there, I have to capture the man the world knew as well as my husband.* Her hand dropped to the bench.

I don't know where to begin. I can't do it. How can I get to the heart of you – quintessence of Dario? Not possible, no one can see into another's heart and soul. No image can capture all of you. She laid the coil down but her fingers lingered on its warmth. *Perhaps I didn't know who you were, only what I wanted you to be. This is my way to find you and end the confusion, to lay you, us to rest so that I can find myself.* She attached the coil to the growing wall. *Easy to model your handsome face but I want more than your flesh and bone. I want to see the man who grew from the boy who chose me, the boy I loved.*

It's not impossible – get on with it, just do it – let the clay show you the way, remember Ionesco, 'Once you begin things come easily enough.' She built the walls higher. *Your shoulders – wide enough to curve round mine, your strong arms: my refuge. The first wild months after meeting when we clung together in gardens shrill with cicadas and held each other tight in cool back streets.*

Coil by coil the structure rose – shoulders bulking up from the board – the kiln, bins, even the walls rolled away before the gathering wave of him in her mind sifting memory for all her Darios. *The tall student who pushed his Fiat into Papa's garage; dirty, sweating, cursing until you saw me in frayed shorts rubbing my oily hands on a cloth – the surprise on your face, your frown melted, you raked your fingers through your hair and stared. I was mistress then.* Slowly she shook her head. *Long ago, too far back, the thin and frantic you, too much to do, too much to prove and young faces don't show character, the effects of the daily battle with life. Move on twenty years? After four children and a couple of house moves you were mellower, less gaunt, gathering 'gravitas' with success.*

She caressed the closing curve over the top of his shoulder. *The shoulders of a tall man, narrow, but strong.* She remembered him picking her up like a bale of hay when they took the first two children on a farm holiday. He had stacked bales up in the loft to hide the two of them and they had made love while the children were 'helping' around the farm. *I'd forgotten about that, before we had Lucia and Angelo.* She stopped to survey the shallow wall on the board. *You changed, I suppose I changed too, a mother is only half a wife, I thought parenthood would connect us deeper but it didn't. I balanced children and studio and you set up the practice. Poor Dario, you missed so much of their growing up and they lost out too, especially Angelo. You were absorbed in your world of important cases and meetings when he arrived, a world I was excluded from, the other Dario; inscrutable, smart and efficient.*

The shallow wall of clay looked anonymous. *Are they too thin? Should they curve forward? You didn't stoop in spite of your height. I wish I knew where I'm headed, what kind of a man I want to commemorate. So many parts you played, which one should I choose? Which you is mine? There is so little left to grasp of my Dario, so little to hang onto – your back as you headed for the door each morning. We lost each other somewhere along the way, talk became chat; polite, superficial. You stayed the same to me as in our early days when we shared so much. I let routine take over and we drifted apart so the man at the funeral was a stranger with tributes I didn't understand from men I didn't like. Why? How?*

Forget that, remember the man you knew. She checked the domes over each arm. They were equal. *This is going to be bigger than I thought. On into the man, the character.* Shorter thinner lengths of clay filled the gap between the shoulders leaving an empty circle in the middle. Oriana turned the board round and fitted the first coil onto the back of the neck then worked up into the base of the skull, widening behind the ears, imagining her arms up round the back of his neck, hanging from it, running her fingers between its tiny divide up to the bulge at the base of the skull.

She shook the curtain of hair from her face, turned the bust round and coiled down from the back of the head to the front, forming a dip in the middle of the neck for the throat below the jaw then stopped.

Shirt and tie or polo neck sweater? Sweater, it has to be our Dario, Sunday Dario, the family man. She picked up a wooden scalpel and carefully split the top of the circle leaving the thicker, inside layer for the neck, the outer for the collar of his sweater. With the pads of her fingers she softened the top of the sweater rolling it over all the way round then cut it in a palm's width down to complete the collar. She etched its rib while the clay was still moist, her mind searching recent times for pictures of him realising how little he confided in her how little they opened up to each other like she did with her friends. *Perhaps men don't need friends, clients aren't friends. He didn't even need me like that, why not? Thank God I had my work to lose myself in.* Bending close to his neck she sketched in lines of knitted stitches breathing in the smell of earth and stone, the atmosphere of the studio, her own private world, free from the clutter, clamour and frustrations of family life, free from the loneliness of filling an empty core.

The rib of the sweater was patterned. She sprinkled water over the shoulders and worked on its seams making a slight fold between sleeve and chest. Her fingers moved purposefully, pressing, pushing at the clay then, from the shelf of children's models and pots, she took a square of Hessian and rubbed the surface of the sweater so it softened to the texture of wool. The shoulders and neck in the sweater looked comfortable, human. She was glad to be back, glad to lose herself creating again.

A flush of red bled through the screen of passion fruit leaves at the tiny window and made her realise that the sun was sliding away. She ran a square of hessian under the tap and roughened the surface softening it to the texture of wool then draped it over the bust to keep it moist. She straightened up and stretched her back satisfied. The darkening studio was alive again, focused around the draped figure.

As she crossed to the house she realised how tired she was. Her legs ached. She ran a hot bath and soaked in foam letting her mind drift with the steam. The 'phone rang.

'Dannazione! No, no, no.' She slid on the cold lino as she reached for a robe to go dripping down the wooden stairs.

'Signora Rossi?'

'Si.'

'I would like to speak to your son.'

'Which son?'

'Signor Angelo.'

'He's not here.'

'That's unfortunate, please tell him Vincenzio called. '

'D'accordo.'

'It's a matter of some importance, Signora.'

'I'll let him know, Signor Vincenzio.'

'Avitabile, Signora Rossi, Vincenzio Avitabile.'

The line went dead. Oriana shook her head and shivered, standing in a puddle. 'Who on earth?' There was something strange – the voice? Or was it the accent? She ran upstairs to the warmth of the steamy bathroom and rubbed herself down wondering what it was all about.

While she chopped tomatoes and oregano waiting for the linguine to boil she lost herself in *La Traviata*, singing 'Ah si ben mio' along with the tenor, full throated, abandoned to the tide of music and emotion. Burrichio insinuated himself around her legs and Baffina watched from a shelf full of plants. The telephone trilled again. She stopped mid note. 'Manache!'

'Ciao,' she snapped.

'Signora Rossi?'

'Si.'

'May I speak to Angelo please?'

'He's not at home.'

'Do you know when he'll be in?'

'He won't.'

'Won't?'

'He hasn't lived here for the past six months.'

Silence.

Oriana relented, 'Should I tell him you called?'

'Si, si, per favore, it's Luisa, Luisa Peroni.'

Angelo? All of a sudden in demand, where is he hiding, why? The only loose cannon in the family, the eternal optimist, my hanger on and I haven't seen him in weeks. Why didn't I notice? I've been too wrapped up in Isabella and the baby.

She put the phone down and retraced her steps to the kitchen deep in thought.

So Angelo's cut himself adrift, fine if it weren't for the phone calls, mainly the first, I'm used to the girls – he's far too good looking and easy going for his own good. He seemed all right last time he came, enjoyed his Stufato and torta. He seemed a bit quiet while we were doing his washing – no more romances, wild schemes or expensive gadgets – I thought his new apartment was settling him down. He was so delighted with it. Perhaps I was wrong. He didn't mention either of those names.

She remembered him picking up a photo of him and Lucia holding hands on the beach, studying it for a long time, saying he missed her. As the two youngest they had always been close, sometimes in league against Emilio and Isabella, often feral up in the hills, running along hedges, dangling their legs in the river. *They were as thick as thieves those two. She kept him out of trouble, pity she can't do that any more.*

It humbled Oriana to have a daughter called to God and confused her too. It was difficult to understand a spiritual calling powerful enough to make your carefree daughter surrender herself and all her life to it. Only Lucia could do that.

She poured herself a glass of Orvieto, drained the linguine, topped it with the sauce and a drizzle of olive oil, loaded her fork and filled her mouth with warm, comforting pasta deep in thought. Baffina watched from her perch high on the shelf, finally Oriana looked into her golden eyes and said, 'what about a day in town tomorrow, little panther? Is it time for a visit? Shall I surprise Angelo?'

With that settled she took a deep draught of wine and realised how hungry she was. The pasta was good.

2

Amber light filtered through her yellow linen curtains. *Damn, I didn't close the shutters.* The distant rush of a train changed to a rumble and rattled to a stop beneath her window followed by a long hiss, doors banging and voices. *'That must be the 8.10. I'm late.'* She opened the window and watched the train curving on to Milan. Muffled sounds of morning drifted from neighbouring gardens: chattering starlings, dogs, hens, rattling pots and smoky voices and, in the background, the continual drone of traffic.

On the wall opposite her bed there was a print of Botticelli's Madonna and Child. Dario had bought it for her when she had Emilio, because she thought he looked like the baby in the painting.

Emilio was rounded, golden and content – everything was easy with him, at school he was earnest, ambitious, their 'professor' – he never thought of anything but following his father into the law firm, 'Rossi e Figlio'. Oriana slid navy blue pants from a hanger.

If only Angelo were more like him, I wish he could find his way, settle down to a career. He's wasting his time as a waiter. She took a white silk blouse from a drawer. *Perhaps I should talk to Emilio, he knows people, he might be able to help. He's head of the family now.* She fastened the last button and looked at the print for reassurance then slung a leather handbag over her shoulder and ran downstairs.

The little station platform was as familiar as her sitting room. From her seat on the train she watched fields give way to factories, trading complexes and warehouses, followed by houses, offices and apartment blocks.

Oriana was looking forward to seeing Angelo, he was still her baby, he had a lot of growing up to do but he was always good company – kind and generous, open to everything so his life was a kaleidoscope, a different pattern of bright colours for every shake of fate –she never knew what was next. *What's he been up to? Luisa Peroni? He isn't ready for responsibility. I hope he realises it. As for the other – Avitabile,? New to me, never heard of him. I didn't like the sound of him, his voice was too old and formal for a social call but waiters don't get business calls.*

In Milan she joined the purposeful throng hurrying along the platform to the forecourt and funnelling out onto the pavement. Oriana knew every nook and cranny of the city, tram tracks, bus routes and metro stations, long streets and busy squares, people always on the move. She ducked into back alleys threading her way to the cafe where Angelo worked.

In the narrow street ahead two men were unloading boxes onto the pavement from a truck holding up an old blue van. The frustrated driver was sounding his horn and throwing his arms about. From a third storey window a pale face with mascara'd eyes and deep red lipstick leaned out to yell, 'State zitto, cazzo!' Oriana smiled at the sign returned by the van driver. The two called up to the woman to sign for the supplies and the window slammed shut. On the other side of the street a couple of students with backpacks jostled along the narrow pavement eating Paninis .

Two men emerged from a doorway in the next block, one in an expensive silver suit with a cream shirt open at the neck revealing a tanned chest and gold chain. His head was bowed listening to an older man in a dark blue suit who had an arm around his shoulder. Suddenly the younger shrugged away from the older man's grasp and turned to face him. They stopped and Oriana saw their profiles. She recognised the high forehead, straight nose and the black onyx ring on the little finger of the man in the blue suit. With a warm rush of delight she ran forward calling, 'Emilio!' But they were walking on.

He had taken hold of the arm of the younger man and was frog marching him down the street while the younger shook his head from side to side. Oriana quickened her step and followed, they turned into another street, their pace slowed and Emilio let go of his arm. Oriana trotted to catch up and watched as they turned another corner but when she arrived they had disappeared. Desolate for a moment she stopped and looked up at the austere grey stone office blocks and crumbling warehouses with tubular steel cages full of boxes blocking their windows wondering which had swallowed them. The excitement of the chase gone, she shrugged,*'Va bene, he is busy and I'm getting side tracked. It's Angelo I am here to see.'*

She carried on her way to the bar where he worked. The door was open, the black and white lino wet.

'Signora Rossi.'

The proprietor removed a thin cigarette from his mouth and bent over her hand. She could see his scalp between greasy strands of black hair.

'Signor Grimaldi.'

She looked behind the padded plastic counter and scanned the empty tables with their split formica and aluminium chairs.

'Is Angelo on his break?'

'Break?'

'I can't see him.'

'He's not been here for a month.'

Nonplussed she stared into his face. He stubbed his cigarette into an aluminium ashtray screeching it along the counter.

Less certain she asked, 'Do you know where he is?'

Signor Grimaldi shrugged,' I think he said something about Andromeda.'

'Andromeda? Where's that?'

'Piazza Tommaseo via Vincenzo Monti past XX Settembre.'

'Grazie.'

She stepped out into the light, walked out of sight of the bar and tapped Angelo's number into her 'phone. It burred distantly, she let it carry on, visualising him collecting a tray of drinks and serving them before answering or swimming up to consciousness in his bed and scrambling to the 'phone, or perhaps in a cafe getting himself a coffee and carrying it to a table to answer.

Answer phone; irritated, she spoke, 'Buongiorno, mama here, where are you? Call me.'

Determined to find him and curious to know more about Andromeda, she followed signor Grimaldi's directions. She was annoyed that Angelo had left his job without telling her. He always confided in her; 'Don't tell daddy but...' How many times had she heard that? Now she had heard nothing for weeks, there must be something wrong. Her pace quickened. She found Via Vicenzo Monti and, half way up a couple of expensively dressed men turned out of Via XX Settembre, friends of Dario. They recognised her and stopped. She always felt at a disadvantage with Dario's wealthy clients as if they knew something she didn't. He had spent a lot of time with them, unlikely company though they seemed to her yet in some ways they all had the same stamp – 'Townies, wealthy business men.'

'Signora Rossi, charmed to see you,' said the first, his navy blue coat tailored carefully around his solid middle, bowing his full head of scented grey hair as he grasped her hand. Their unctuous courtesy made her feel uneasy.

'How are you?' asked the other, taller, slimmer, in a grey cashmere coat and blue silk tie with a copy of *Corriere Della Sera* under his arm.

'Well, thank you, how are you?'

'Getting old,' replied the first circling his cigar in the air with a wry smile. She caught a glimpse of his gold Rolex and wondered what time it was.

'It's been a while,' she said.

'The funeral wasn't it? So sorry, the years slip by.'

'Two and a half years,' she replied.

'Two and a half years.' He tapped the ash from his cigar. 'How are the family?'

'All well, thank you. Still growing, Isabella is expecting any day.'

'Congratulations.'

'Grazie.

'Great lawyer, good family, sad loss for us all,' said the other rolling up his paper.

'If you need anything anytime, let me know,' said the first.

'Thank you, buon giorno.'

'Buon giorno.' They bowed their heads and backed away.

They seemed like ghosts of a dim and distant past, she dismissed them from her mind, preoccupied with Angelo.

Andromeda stood out from its ancient stone neighbours with its red door and black noticeboards framed in chrome. It shrieked modernity while the tall, distinguished old buildings around seemed to have settled back on their haunches to watch fads come and go. The place was silent, eerie, the red door blank. The notice boards held photographs of girls gyrating, arms aloft, jewellery glittering and boys, heads down, hair spiked or coloured, shoulders bent dancing as if alone. Spotlights isolated small areas of the dance floor with lurid intensity and the photographs trapped them. It looked grotesque to Oriana. 'Some difference to Contadini,' she muttered to herself but she could see the attraction; upmarket, glamorous and young. She tried the 'phone again, still no answer, *'If he's working late at night he'll be fast asleep,'* she reasoned.

Oriana wasn't going home until she had seen him so the day lay ahead, entirely her own. She walked purposefully back toward the centre. She loved Milan, it had been the beacon of her growing up; trips in with her dad collecting car parts, the scene of her romances, friendships and her career as an artist and finally, the sun of her married life; dances and dinners, shopping with children, the vibrancy of a big city – always something going on – stages in the piazza, scaffolding, spotlights, loud speakers and always the grandeur of the Duomo. She walked down Via Ludovico Ariosto to Piazzale Francesco Baracca without thinking and found herself among the cane chairs and white metal, glass topped tables of what used to be a favourite meeting place over a quarter of a century ago, cafe Santa Maria the name was the same, it hadn't changed much. She crossed scuffed pine boards and ordered a coffee. Greenery spread from pots all around. She took her coffee onto the pavement to make the most of the dwindling autumn sun and listened to the conversation at a table just inside.

"They want silver for the price of tin, I'm tired of churning out bead earrings when I can make works of art – pendants and bracelets but they take weeks and people don't want to pay for craftsmanship, things they can keep, pass on.'

'No, they pick up a notebook, turn it over say they love the marbling, run their fingers over the vellum, see the price and put it down.'

'Nothing changes,' thought Oriana.

'Oriana!'

She swung round, 'Elena!' She rose and hugged the soft full figure in a long purple skirt and blue flowered tunic. They kissed.

'You haven't changed a bit.' Elena said nervously pegging her frizzy grey hair behind an ear. Oriana noticed that her nails were chipped and the skin of her hands was thin and dry.

'Are you still working?' She asked looking down into Elena's round face, skin a little greyer, features a little droopier but still the same pretty Elena. The waiter put Oriana's coffee on the table.

'Can't afford to give it up but then don't know what I'd do if I did.' Elena looked over to the table inside and waved to the two artists then sat with Oriana.

How are Clara and Giuseppe?' asked Oriana.

'Grown and flown, thank goodness. No Mammismo in our house,' she laughed.

'Partner?' asked Oriana.

Elena shook her head, 'I'm better off without, friends of both sexes fine, lovers – too complicated. I like to please myself and concentrate on my work. It's never easy for a woman to get on with a man around to please, they say they understand but it stops when you can't listen to their troubles, feed them up or sex them happy. Dario was different, he left you to it, didn't he? Even converted half the barn into a studio for you. What a man.'

'Keep me occupied and out of the way,' he said,' Oriana laughed.

'He would do anything for you, sad loss, I'm sorry.'

'It was good of you to come to the funeral. It was tough, bit of a blank now, I seemed to be shrouded in grey cloud for ages,' Oriana said, 'but life moves on.'

'Are you working?' asked Elena.

Oriana nodded, 'More for myself davvero, it's good to lose myself in it, I am doing a bust at the moment. I tried sculpting a while ago, limestone mainly, I enjoyed that.'

'I bet it's good, you've got talent.'

'Listen who's talking, your pots are beautiful.'

'Tourist fodder to keep the wolf from the door. I can't raise anything as perfect as you, your strong hands could stretch clay paper thin, tall and elegant.'

'Sometimes,' Oriana shrugged, 'They're what they are, I am glad you liked them, there haven't been many recently.'

'Do it if it makes you happy. I know you, it was always family first, they've grown and flown, it's your time now.'

'If I can smooth their path, help along the way, I don't mind. They're good kids.' Oriana's 'phone buzzed in her handbag, she excused herself.

'Mama? '

'Angelo.'

'I have to collect drink from Pavia for the club. I won't be back until 18.30. Will you still be around?

'Si, si, I'll see you in front of Vittorio Emmanuelle at 18.30?' She closed the phone and slipped it back into her bag.

Chairs were scraping the boards, Elena's friends were leaving,

'Oriana, ti presenti Mario.'

Slightly shorter than her, Mario looked neat in his tight dark denims and white sweatshirt, with a thin black leather briefcase under his arm. His hair was grey hair at the temples and perfectly cut. He swept his eyes down her long blue trousers, silver buckled belt and up over her open white silk blouse. His chest seemed to swell as he took her hand and kissed it, briefly, punctiliously. She almost expected him to click his heels, she supressed a smile.

'Buongiorno,' she said.

'And Susanna,' said Elena indicating a willowy figure in jeans and boy's white shirt with hair cropped in short tufts. She wore big silver hoops and several silver studs along her ears.

'Ciao,' said Oriana, smiling into the solemn young face. 'I like your bracelet, may I have a look?' Susanna slipped it off and handed it to Oriana. Two delicately engraved silver snakes twined together biting each other's tails. 'It's beautifully done, it must have taken forever,' Oriana said returning it. The girl nodded and slid it back into place. She had an intricate seahorse tattoo at the top of her arm.

'Elena, here's my mobile number, can I have yours?' Oriana scribbled on an old receipt, they hugged each other and Oriana watched the trio departing down the street deep in conversation. She finished her coffee absorbing the shift in reality, traversing the years to the shoals of friends who chatted loudly, eagerly, over coffee at these tables. *Always someone arriving or leaving, always something to do, somewhere to go.*

Across the city, bells chimed the hour and she came back to the afternoon and knew exactly how she would spend it. She caught a tram and rattled past shops and cafes, metro stations and squares, churches and galleries to Cadorna, Basilica Maria Della Grazie, a humble home for Leonardo's *Last Supper* in a simple stone room fading into the wall. She studied the faces of the disciples, their body language – friends worrying about their leader, talking, consoling, suspecting – one thing on their mind. She studied the faces, traced the subtle hints in the direction of the great betrayer. *A vital moment in history brought to life in all its humanity.*

She returned to the centre and still had time for a quick tour of the Triennale Design Museo with its spacious halls and clean modern design. The imaginative use of old and new materials, integrating function and beauty inspired her. The white walls, light and space gave dignity to all the exhibits. It made her studio seem cramped and cluttered.

Just before six thirty she made her way across the Piazza del Duomo to the Galleria Vittorio Emmanuelle 11. Angelo was leaning against a shop window smoking a cigarette and chatting to a friend who was holding a red motorbike with a girl sitting pillion, her bright blue helmet resting on her lap while she ran her fingers through long brown hair. A car stopped behind them while a van passed on the other side and a taxi beeped. Angelo stamped out his cigarette and shook his friend's hand. They fastened on their helmets, waved 'Ciao' and set off in front of the beeping taxi.

Angelo's face lit up when he saw her, he lifted her off the ground in a bear hug, 'Ciao Mama, come stai?' Oriana laughed, 'Put me down, idiota.' They kissed.

'So where should we eat?' He asked, slipping his hands into the back pockets of his black jeans, 'I'm starving.'

They headed across the square to a restaurant behind the museum in a big enclosed square. Behind his head hugging sunglasses his eyes panned the crowd as they walked and his head pivoted as he picked out pretty girls. Oriana felt the electricity of youth seeing heads turn in his direction with his tight white Tee shirt and unruly black hair. She felt proud to be with him.

They ordered the set menu and settled back with a glass of wine. She looked at his innocent face and dark brown eyes and her irritation evaporated.

'So what have you been up to?' She asked.

'Got a new job, in a night club, it's cool, Emilio put in a good word for me.'

'Andromeda?' He looked surprised. 'Signor Grimaldi told me. I went there.'

'What do you think of it, mama?'

A plate of sliced meats was set before him. Oriana was pleased to see him tuck in. She forked lettuce and anchovy into her mouth. They were both hungry.

'It looks very modern. I don't know much about night clubs.'

He tried to persuade her to go with him one evening. It always surprised and touched her that Angelo wanted to share things with her.

'I don't want to cramp your style.'

'You'd never do that, all my pals love you.'

'One day then, I'd love it, put on my party shoes.'

'And dance the night away.

He put out his hand and they slapped palms.

'There were a couple of calls for you this morning,' she said.

Angelo stopped eating.

'Who's Luisa Peroni?'

He relaxed, 'Luisa ?'

Oriana nodded.

'We went out for a bit, ages ago. She's okay but I'm not ready to settle down.'

'No you're not, you shouldn't lead girls on or leave them dangling.'

'I'll sort it.'

She raised her eyebrows.

'Si, si.'

'That's not the only call, Vincenzo Avitabile wanted to speak to you, said it was urgent. What shall I tell him if he calls again?'

His face closed and he started to turn his cigarette packet over and over on the table. Oriana waited. Eventually the packet stopped its somersaults and he mumbled, 'Nothing.' His arms dropped onto the table and he shook his head slowly, 'No, I don't know.'

'What do you mean you don't know?' Alarm fed her irritation.

'Ravioli alla spinacci?' The patron bent over Oriana.

Distracted she stammered, 'Si, si per favore.'

'E linguine alle vongole?' Angelo nodded and leant back while his bowl was carefully laid down and the patron backed away. Oriana watched anxiously as he turned over his pasta, head down.

After a pause he muttered, 'I owe him money and I can't pay.'

'Parmegiano?' The patron was back with a grater and cheese.

Oriana muttered an automatic, 'Si, grazie.'

Angelo put down his fork while the grater rained cheese over his bowl.

'So, you've been buying things you can't afford?'

'It's not even that, I haven't got anything to show for it. Emilio took me to a couple of his favourite clubs –upmarket places, beautiful girls. I got sucked in; champagne, dinners, presents.' Oriana groaned inwardly, she knew the rest but he carried on. 'I needed clothes, got the new apartment. I hired a car to take one girl out. She was special, used to the best.'

'What was Emilio thinking of?'

'He introduced me to some big names.'

'Rich people, and you're not rich, Angelo you're a waiter with half a degree in accounting. How on earth did you pay for all that?'

'Went from card to card up to the limit, borrowed a bit, used my rent money, then I had a couple of wins at poker, carried on and lost.'

Oriana despaired.

Relieved to unburden himself at last, Angelo continued, 'People started turning nasty, threatening. I couldn't pay, I borrowed and pawned until there was nowhere to go, was offered a loan, took it but I only gained time. I can't pay it back and they are scary.'

Her bag trilled and vibrated, 'Paolo?' Oriana listened. 'Una hora, Paolo, I'll be with you.' She closed the 'phone.

'That was Paolo, Isabella's labour has started, I must go, but not before we sort this out. How much do you owe?'

Angelo looked at his hands and mumbled, 'Twenty thousand euros.'

'Twenty thousand! And interest will double it if you don't pay it off quickly.'

He shook his head, 'I can't. I don't know what to do. I'll go to prison and still it won't be the end of it. I can't manufacture that kind of money. '

'You should have known better. Why don't you look beyond the end of your nose?'

'I know, it's true.' He slumped in his chair. 'I'm sorry. Do you mind if I go out for a minute?'

At a loss, Oriana gestured him on, glad of space to think. Through the window she watched him suck deeply on his cigarette staring intently into the distance, bleak faced, tight-lipped.

He was young, impetuous, but not bad. Angelo always had to learn lessons the hard way. Weariness weighed her down. She knew what she had to do. When he returned she said,

'I have 10,000 euros in savings. I wish I had more but apart from the house your father didn't leave much. You can have that as long as you promise never to let anything like this happen again.'

'I can't take your savings.'

'What use is it to me? There's nothing I need except to see you all secure. Ti servi, Angelo.'

'Veramente?' Anxiously he searched her eyes. She nodded firmly.

'Grazie, mama, grazie. I will pay you back I promise.'

He meant it. She knew he meant it.

The air was heavy with thunder as she walked to the station but she hardly noticed. Avoiding eye contact with other passengers, she settled by a window. Her thoughts ran to the rhythm of the train. *Why can't he settle down like the others? They knew what they wanted and got on with it; Emilio was determined to study law and join his father, Isabella was always adopting stricken creatures or playing with dolls. Farm and family were perfect for her. Lucia, probably the happiest of them all, focused, spiritual, called to devote herself to God. Why can't Angelo find direction? He's not lazy and he's bright. Is it because he misses his father? He didn't see much of Dario, when he arrived Dario spent more time at the office than home – meetings, conferences, flying off to Naples or bent over his phone or iPad. Perhaps that was part of the problem or the modern world's, 'live now pay later' philosophy but Angelo isn't that shallow – gullible but not shallow.*

Big drops of rain were dragging down the window. Oriana was glad she didn't have far to run.

Burrichio purred his welcome and Tancreda rubbed against her legs. There was a dead mouse by the kitchen door, 'Thank you Tancreda,' she said picking it up by the tail and scurrying through the rain to drop it in the bin outside. She peered over the fence looking for her neighbour. He was bending to pull carrots from his garden, revealing a wide expanse of white flesh above his dusty grey trousers spotted black by raindrops.

She stood on an upturned box and called, 'Dino, can you and Rinatta look after the cats please? – The baby's on its way.'

Dino slowly straightened up and came to the fence a little out of breath, 'Buona fortuna, Oriana, hope all goes well. The cats'll be fine, our garden's theirs anyway.' He wiped raindrops from the end of his nose smearing mud across his face.

'There's feed in the garage, grazie, Ciaou.'

Oriana dashed inside, rubbed her hair with a towel and put sweets in her bag for the children and a velvet rabbit for the baby.

Once out of the suburbs her car snaked around a tapestry of rice paddies, fields of wheat or sheep and, in the foothills, ranks of vines and olive trees. Here the big cooperatives gave way to smaller farms where the odd goat stared impassively at the her, hens looked up from damp corn cobs and dogs dashed out, chased the car then stopped and shook the rain off their coats. She headed for a dark green line of poplar trees on the slopes of the opposite hills and the rain abated as she rose out of the valley.

She could hear the rattle and chink of the tractor as she turned into the drive. Isabella must have gone. Paolo stopped the tractor to let a tiny figure in blue dungarees and bright green cap jump down and run up the track to her waving and shouting, 'Nonna, nonna.'

Oriana couldn't get out of the car quickly enough, 'Pietro !' She called.

He flung himself into her open arms and she swung him round and round until they were both dizzy. He wrapped his arms around her neck and clung. She eased him down and bent to peer under the peaked hat into his solemn grey eyes.

'Don't worry, mummy'll be back soon and you'll have a baby brother or sister to play with. Which would you like?'

He considered as if for the first time, 'Brother.'

Paolo, who had been standing back, watching, kissed Oriana, 'thank you for coming. I took her in about an hour ago.' He pulled his cap off and wiped the sweat from his shiny round head.

'How frequent were the pains?'

'Every half hour.'

'It shouldn't be long then.'

'No, please God. I'll leave Pietro with you and finish this field before the rain starts again.'

He whisked Pietro up and shook him above his head making him flail about laughing and giggling then kissed his freckled nose and dropped him at Oriana's feet.

She grabbed Pietro's hand and said, 'Let's go on a bug hunt.'

He did a skip and trotted into the house with her. Oriana left her bag in her home from home, the bedroom she shared with Rosa. They found a plastic box in the kitchen and punched holes in the lid then headed uphill through the stubble field at the back of the farmhouse happy to be together. The short burst of rain had made no impact, the pale coffee coloured earth was baked hard. Shiny spikes of cut wheat scratched their legs. Around the edges of the field dry weeds and grasses vibrated to the drill of crickets.

Head down, Pietro marched on and Oriana followed. He beckoned her over to a clump of grass on the margin. She crouched beside him. A metre down and they were in a different world; cracks looked like canyons, stones seemed like boulders still wet and shiny with the rain amid a jungle of white stalks and green weeds. It even sounded different, what was a dull chorus above became a medley of shrill calls, deep croaks and vibrant strumming. Ants streamed in all directions. Pietro was watching a grasshopper scratching its back. Oriana joined him and was fascinated by the precision of its engineering, the perfect plates of green armour and bright jet bead eyes. Pietro covered it with both hands and Oriana held out the box.

The sound of a cricket vibrated through the undergrowth. They looked at each other, and followed the shrill call. Pietro stopped and Oriana dropped to her knees. Pietro put out a hand and it leapt. He followed, ready to pounce. It leapt and leapt again. Pietro wouldn't give up. Oriana laughed and called 'Ride him, cowboy!' as Pietro leap-frogged through the stubble finally he came back triumphant with the dry rattling creature in his cupped hands.

As they approached the top corner of the field a cream coloured snake with grey arrows down its back slid away toward a pile of stones. They watched, fascinated.

'We must have disturbed it, it's going home to hide,' said Oriana.

'Is it poisonous?' He asked slipping his hand into hers. She held it gently, loving its warm trust.

'Yes, but snakes only bite if they're frightened or for food.'

'What do they eat?'

'Oh that one probably lives on mice and insects, sometimes frogs, or baby birds.'

They stood, hand in hand and watched it ripple around the dry stalks.

'It's strange, how does it move without legs?'

'They contract and expand stretching their way along.'

'It looks smooth.'

He ran up into the woods and Oriana followed. The glare and hum of heat faded. Scorched pine needles muffled her steps. The only sounds were the warbling of wood pigeons and occasional chattering of jays. Pietro returned with something in his hands, Oriana opened the box carefully but he shook his head. 'Look,' he said holding out a large curved shard of deep blue and white pottery. Oriana pushed the dry clay off its surface with her thumbs – there were vine leaves, tendrils and flower patterns of bright ink blue on a white as bright and glossy as the day it was made. She gave it back to Pietro.

'It's pretty isn't it?' He said, 'Pity it's broken. What is it?'

'It was probably a big jar or jug. I think it might be very old. It could be Etruscan or Celtic.'

'What's that?'

'The Etruscans lived here 3,000 years ago. Lots of their things have been found in the ground round here.'

'What kind of things?'

'Pots, stone carvings, bits of bronze...'

'Any toys? Did they have children?'

''Course they had children, they were children once, we all were. We don't often find toys, maybe they don't keep so well or childhood didn't last very long in those days.'

'Were they like us?'

'We're all the same. You think that's pretty, so did they, it probably held wine or oil just like we use today.'

'So we're Etruscans then.'

''Fraid not, they were wiped out by the Romans so we're a different race but people are all the same really.'

Pietro looked troubled, she stroked back his sandy hair and wanted to wrap him in her arms to keep the darkness at bay but she knew he'd have to breast the waves and swim by himself one day.

'Can we look for more?' He asked.

She nodded.

Shuffling among the roots and stones with her feet Oriana found a lump of rounded stone with a line carved across it, she tried to kick it free but it was buried too deep. She took a stick and started scraping away the earth. Pietro returned with a piece of smoky glass and a broken clay tile.

'I don't know if the Etruscans had glass, Pietro, we'll have to ask Uncle Emilio, he'll know. We can use these to dig out the stone.'

They scraped away, piling up dirt like a badger's doorway and more lines emerged spreading out from a circle.

'What do you think it is?' She asked.

Pietro said triumphantly, 'It's the sun.'

'You're right.'

'Can we take it home?'

'Put it in the garden? Okay. Should we let the insects go and put the other pieces in the box?' He nodded.

They carried it together and knelt among the marigolds by the kitchen door to dig out a trench and set the stone upright for Paolo to see when he came in. When they had finished Oriana looked at her dirty hands, Pietro held his up too and she laughed still crouching in the flowerbed. He gave her a sudden hug that knocked her over and they rolled against the stone laughing even more.

'What's going on out there?' called Rosa from the kitchen.

They looked at each other like naughty children.

'Nothing.' Oriana replied.

They brushed themselves down, slipped off their sandals and went into the kitchen. Tommaso was at the sink washing the day's eggs.

'Where have you been?' Tommaso asked his little brother.

'Through the woods, I found this.' He took the pottery from its box.

'Tommaso!' Oriana shouted.

There was a trail of muddy footprints from the door to the sink. Tommaso stepped out of his boots and carried them to the door leaving the tap running. The bowl overflowed. Oriana turned off the tap, shook her head and threw him a damp cloth to wipe up the mess. When he'd finished she said 'Now,' and spread her arms and they hugged.

'Ooh, wet hands!' she wriggled her cold back and kissed his forehead, 'you're as tall as I am.'

'I'll be looking down on you soon Nonna.'

'I'd better watch out then. Helping dad with the hens?'

'The hens are mine, Nonna. It's my business.'

The twins ran through the kitchen in their jeans. They stopped to give Oriana a kiss on their way.

'Don't you want a drink?' She called after them.

She shooed Rosa and Tomaso out of the kitchen and started supper. From the little plot beside the kitchen she pulled a potato plant, shook away the soil, and dropped potatoes into a bucket, cut a lettuce and picked the last of the peppers, some rosemary and thyme then made a frittata with Tommaso's eggs.

Paolo ate mechanically while the children cleared their plates showing off to her, tormenting each other, chatting. Paolo was an island of anxiety.

'Why don't you get off to the hospital?' She suggested.

Visibly relieved he said, 'I'll help clear away.'

'No, we can do it, can't we?' Said Oriana looking at the children who nodded frantically. They carried their plates to the sink where Rosa stacked them in the dishwasher while Tommaso finished clearing the table.

Once Pietro and the twins had had their baths and settled down for the night Oriana left Rosa knitting in her room and Tommaso on his computer and came downstairs to sink into the saggy old sofa in the sitting room but she couldn't rest. She loaded a big log onto the dwindling fire. Waiting pressed on her. She couldn't help thinking about Isabella's pain. It was difficult to accept. She collected a skirt from Rosa for shortening and sewed, glad to have her hands occupied but it wasn't enough of a distraction, as time passed her anxiety grew, anxiety for the baby too. It was gone midnight when Paolo returned looking grey faced and grim.

'Is everything all right?' she asked. Paolo nodded.

'Girl or boy?'

'Boy, he had to have oxygen. He's under observation, but they say he'll be fine.'

'Isabella?'

'It was hard, he was in the wrong position, they had to turn him with forceps. She lost a lot of blood. They're giving her a transfusion. They say she'll be better in the morning.'

He sank down into the chair.

Oriana knew the pain – the world contracted into the battle to give birth then thought of her daughter exposed under clinical light, afraid for her baby, the turning of the forceps, her chest swelled with agony but she saw Paolo, crumpled, defeated, his head in his hands, trying to dispel the images of the last few hours. She stood, touched his shoulder and said, 'a warm drink and bed, Paolo. It's over now and they're both okay. Isabella's in good hands.'

3

Like jetsam on a beach after a storm, Isabella lay propped by stiff white pillows on a high bed, her body scraped out, bones a painful jumble; weak and useless. She was glad it was all over and just beginning, she thought, as she looked down at the bruised and jaundiced scrap of humanity asleep by the bed, his face troubled by little frowns, twitches, fleeting smiles. His eyelids lifted to show indeterminate, puddle grey eyes. Isabella reached down for him and winced at the pressure on swollen stitches. Warm and heavy in her arms, he was real at last.

The door slowly opened and two big hazel brown eyes peered round. 'Mama!' Isabella beamed. Oriana dropped a bunch of blue and white flowers onto the bottom of the bed and kissed Isabella's forehead noticing how tight the pale skin was stretched, her eyes sunk in dark circles. Sadness almost stifled her. She slipped a lock of hair from Isabella's face, looked down at the baby and said, 'Ciao, bambino, how are you? Poor bunny, what a battering you took and what a time you gave your mummy.'

Isabella smiled and offered him to Oriana. 'Thank you,' She settled him into the crook of her arm and sat on a chair, stroked his hand then held a wrinkled foot in the palm of her hand. More in control of her emotions, she asked, 'How are you?'

'Better now, before the transfusion I couldn't do anything I felt like a deep-sea diver. The nurses have been great.'

'I bet you're a model patient, you're certainly a good mother.'

Isabella laughed and caught her breath at a stab of pain. Oriana winced.

'I'm certainly practised.' She replied. She saw a shadow cross her mother's face and said, 'This is the last, no more, six is enough.' Oriana had thought each one was the last, but this really must be the end if Isabella said it.

' Giorgio Enrico, si?' She asked.

Isabella nodded and rested her head on the pillows.

'I mustn't tire you, the children are waiting.'

Isabella brightened. 'Bring them in, we're ready.'

Oriana returned the baby to his cot.

Isabella wanted her children around her. It seemed a long time ago and a different world when she was last with them. She needed their love to bolster her frailty.

Subdued chatter filled the corridor.   They heard Anna's voice above the others, 'I'm taking it.'

'That's not fair,' wailed Maria.

'Be quiet, you two,' hissed Tommaso.

'Sshh,' whispered Rosa as she opened the door and propped it with her back for Anna, triumphantly carrying a long badly wrapped package and Maria, head down with a card. Rosa kissed her mother's forehead and put a tissue paper parcel on the bed.

'What's this?' Isabella pulled an end of satin ribbon and there was a little primrose blanket.

'You knitted it yourself!' She rubbed its softness against her cheek. 'It's lovely, thank you, Rosa. How did you manage it?'

'All those nights I went to bed early to read,' laughed Rosa, relieved and excited.

Tommaso's trainers squeaked on the lino as he squirmed at the foot of the bed, worrying about his mother, thinking that the bunch of flowers he'd picked wasn't much when she looked so ill. Oriana brought Pietro into the room. When he saw his mother in the high chrome bed and the drip, tubes, steel dishes, gauze and scissors, Pietro froze and his face crumpled. Isabella longed to hold him, Oriana bent down and whispered into his ear,

'It's all right, Pietro, mummy's all right. He sobbed.

'No, no, no,' she chanted, 'you don't want to upset mummy.'

Isabella looked at Rosa, helplessly. The twins went to him. Oriana rocked him, 'Mummy wants to see her big boy, she's been missing you.' She lifted his face and he struggled to stop the tears. Oriana dried his face with a tissue, 'Come and say 'Hello' to mummy.' She lifted him gently onto the bed. Isabella stroked his hair and kissed him murmuring, 'Pietro, Pietro, I'll soon be back, don't worry, look at your baby brother.'

Tommaso, at bursting point, went to the other side of the bed and gruffly presented his flowers. His hands were already hardening into farmer's hands. She took the posy and said, 'you brought me a bit of home, thank you. They'll keep me happy thinking of you all. Tell me what you've been up to.'

Awkwardly at first, he told her about feeding the calves and cleaning the olive press then he got carried away telling all that he and Paolo had done together. Pietro slipped off the bed and Oriana took him to the window to look at the cars and ambulances down below. Anna and Maria pushed into his space closer to Isabella.

'Look what we got.' Anna put her parcel on her mother's lap. Isabella looked from Anna to Maria and unwrapped a row of brightly coloured figures on elastic.

'A pram rattle.' She smiled at them both, 'What a good idea, thank you.' Maria gave her their card and forgave Anna.

'You haven't said, 'Hello' to your little brother,' said Isabella. The twins looked into the cot at a dark, bald head and yellow, bruised face. There was an embarrassed silence.

'He's Giorgio Enrico,' prompted Isabella.

'Hello, Giorgio,' whispered Maria self-consciously.

'Will he grow out of it?' Asked Anna.

'Grow out of what?' Demanded Isabella.

'The funny colour. Will he get pink?'

Isabella laughed, ''Course he will.'

Tommaso peered down, serious. 'He's very small.'

'Same size as you were.' Tommaso looked again. Pietro came to the cot and looked in, the baby stirred, moved an arm and he jumped back. It opened its eyes. Rosa asked if she could pick him up. Isabella nodded. His head was turning from side to side, mouth reaching out lopsidedly towards the edge of the blanket.

'He wants a feed. Give him to me,' said Isabella. 'There's a box of chocolates here, pass them round, Rosa. Let's all have a chocolate.'

4

Paolo watched the wind worrying the olive trees, showing silver undersides of leaves and clusters of green olives among gnarled branches, shaking black beads to the ground. 'Buono.' he muttered looking up into the tree.

A short, stocky figure as resilient as his trees, his usually sunny face was clouded by a frown as his thick fingers stubbed the ground in search of fallen olives. At his core was a hard knot of fear – without Isabella's strength it would all fall apart. She had made her dream of a teeming family possible but the land was stretched to its limit, its demands constant. He bit into a hard fruit and nodded, 'Grazie Dio,' then scrambled over a tumbledown stonewall into a sloping field of bleached stubble.

Like everything else in Lombardy farming thrived but that was mainly in the fertile Po valley and depended on big cooperatives. Paolo and his brothers were a cooperative of three on higher ground and he had inherited the rambling house at the top of the hill which suited his large family but came with poorer land. He relied on his olives, sheep's milk and wheat for income. He knew every ditch, spring and rocky outcrop of his patch and loved its idiosyncrasies, changing moods and seasons. Now walking back to the farmhouse buffeted by the wind he felt in tune with the birds massing in trees, twittering on wires, restless with the changing season.

He stopped to watch a scarlet car wind its way between faded green and golden fields, towards him. He quickened his pace to open the gate, saw Emilio grimace as the Ferrari hit the puddle of muck and mud in the middle. The wind took Paolo's hat as he struggled to close the gate. Emilio stood by the car in front of the farmhouse and waited. Paolo joined him smiling, bracing himself for the thump on the back, the congratulations.

'Buongiorno,' they said simultaneously and shook hands all the more vehemently to make up for being trumped. Paolo waited.

'Busy time,' Emilio said looking at the tractor half out of the shed, its loader on the ground in front of a heap of poultry feed spilled over the concrete. 'I was wondering if you've got any buildings you're not using at the moment. I could do with somewhere to store a few things a bit closer to town and I know people who'd be prepared to pay for a place to keep things safe.'

The wind lifted Emilio's hair. Paolo sank his hands in his pockets and pulled his coat around him thinking.

'The olive shed's pretty watertight. I won't be needing it for another month.'

'The olive shed! Perfect, bene, grazie.' Emilio grasped Paolo's shoulders as if to embrace him but Paolo was clenched tight so he slid his hands down his arms. Neither spoke or moved, Paolo studied Emilio's shiny leather shoes and Emilio looked over his head to the barn.

'You'd better say 'hello' to your mother,' said Paolo.

'Mother's here?'

'Isabella's in hospital.'

Emilio stopped, recovered himself then asked after the baby and gave his congratulations.

Oriana hadn't expected to see Emilio so soon. Wet cloth in hand she gave him a big hug as if he were a visiting celebrity. There was always an air of importance, mystery about him even more than Dario. He was a man of the world, set apart, set above. Keen to reward him for thinking of them, she offered coffee and cake, insisted he stay for lunch. He bowed his head to the yoke and sat at the table. Oriana ushered Paolo to join him, keep him company, pin him down, prevent flight. Paolo settled awkwardly at the table. She rummaged for Emilio's favourite biscotti and hurried to the table with fresh coffee.

'So, godfather again,' she said looking into his impenetrable grey eyes, 'time you and Paolo swapped roles.'

His face hardened, 'plenty of time for that.' He pushed back his chair and turned to Paolo who was hunched over his coffee. 'How's Isabella?'

'Recovering.' Paolo didn't look up.

'I saw you in town the other day,' said Oriana, 'with a rather glamorous looking young man.'

'Must have been Ricci, Marco Ricci,' Emilio replied.

Paolo looked up.

'He's owns a hotel and a couple of bars, he's got investments abroad too, quite a head for business.'

Paolo added, 'There was a photo of him in the paper the other day, with another glamorous woman on his arm, all tuxedo and teeth.'

'Gutter press always jealous of the wealthy,' said Emilio. 'I'm defending him.'

'What's the charge?' Asked Oriana.

'Using his legitimate businesses to cover prostitution and drug trafficking.'

Paolo sucked in a breath and said sympathetically, 'Good luck, I can't see any other way he can fund his yacht and all the rest of it.'

'He's a successful business man,' Emilio demurred smoothly, 'there's no evidence against him, it's all here say, circumstantial.'

Paolo raised his eyebrows and Oriana said, 'Well, he's got the best man for his defence.'

Emilio soaked his biscotti in coffee.

'I hear you've been helping Angelo,' said Oriana, 'I'm worried about him, he's got himself into debt.'

Emilio shrugged. 'Don't baby him, mama. There are plenty of ways to earn a bit of extra cash.' He stood up abruptly and looked down at their surprised faces, 'Sorry, I have arrangements to make. I have to go.'

Nothing Oriana offered would tempt him to stay. Paolo followed him out and Oriana watched his back through the window. *He's lost interest in Angelo. He hasn't got time for us anymore.* She pulled herself together. *The practice has fallen on his shoulders and he's got an important case on his mind. And I didn't help, why do I open my mouth? Perhaps Caterina can't have children, that's an awful thought, poor Caterina, she's such a family girl, so good with the twins and Pietro.*

5

The mood in the house lightened over the next few days since the children had seen their mother but Paolo seemed to grow more sombre, more preoccupied as Isabella and the baby improved each day.

'Is there something worrying you, Paolo?' Oriana asked after supper one evening when they had the kitchen to themselves.

'The hospital will be sending them home soon. How can Isabella recover, with five children and a sick baby? And the priest's been asking about the christening.'

'There's plenty of time for that,' replied Oriana .

'Isabella won't see it like that if the priest is worrying, she'll make herself ill trying to do it.'

Oriana knew that Isabella would want to do the right thing and the priest had been concerned when the baby needed oxygen. The Christening had become urgent in spite of common sense.

'Don't worry, Paolo, I can stay as long as I'm needed and I'll ask Mother Carmela if we can have Lucia for a few days.'

Paolo's face lit up. 'That's the answer. Lucia's the only one who can do anything with Isabella.'

'Leave it to me.'

6

The nuns knelt in front of pine benches. Row after row of curved grey backs murmured 'Amen' and rose like an incoming wave. The chapel was cool, bands of coloured light from the stained glass windows played along the floor and columns.

The ridged soles of sandals in front of Lucia were filled with muck and straw.

Sister Veronica's been with the donkeys.

Lucia's mind wandered to Achille, her favourite, pushing his head into her palm while she rubbed his ear.

Discipline, she forced herself back to the words of the Abbess.

The flap and fold of robes and surplices disturbed the air as they rose.

'As we prepare to celebrate the mystery of Christ's love let us acknowledge our failures and ask the Lord for pardon and strength.'

Lucia's habit smelled of tomato plants from clearing the vegetable garden. After one good harvest it was satisfying to prepare the next. She pulled herself back to the words that meant so much;

'... that I have sinned through my own fault,

In my thoughts and in my words,

In what I have done,'

She could see rows of purple, white and brown onions laid out in the sun to dry, the end of her day's work. *Concentrate, this is more important, this is what it's all about.* Lucia watched the Abbess sprinkle holy water saying the words that she loved.

'Renew this living spring of your life within us and protect us in spirit and body that we may be free from sin and come into your presence to receive your gift of salvation. We ask this through Christ our Lord.'

'Amen.'

Eighty voices quietly chanted, 'Amen.'

Lucia was transported beyond the menial everyday to a different harvest and she was filled with joy. The painted figures of Christ and his apostles shone above the altar. Lucia was fond of their simple little chapel.

'Go in peace to love and serve the lord.'

The Abbess progressed down the aisle followed by four older sisters. Around Lucia some knelt in prayer others, missal in hand folded their arms into the sleeves of their habits and waited.

There was always a sense of fulfilment at the completion of this simple evening routine, beginning the process of calming her mind through the adjustment from the day's work to the evening's contemplation. She lingered and focused on the figure of Christ above the altar. There in the window she saw him preaching the Sermon on the Mount. She could hear the words in her head and knelt as if she were part of the crowd at his feet and spoke to him.

'Thank you for the pleasure of work, the comfort of companionship and the peace of your love. I pray for the troubled in spirit, the sad in

heart and the oppressed in mind. For my family, busy in a challenging

world, to keep them safe and happy. Amen.'

She moved to the cloister, a favourite evening walk with its smell of lavender and rosemary and the squawking and squabbling of the rabble of starlings who flocked into the grounds to roost. In summer she liked to see the swallows swinging overhead now she could hear their agitated twittering in the adjacent field as they mustered for departure.

Dusk softened the silent stone fountain in the centre of the garden, its waters would return when rain had refilled the well only to be stopped by frost until Spring set it free to cool the long summer heat. Lucia followed the path around the garden three times while shadows gathered filling the space and blanking the scene. She thought of evening settling over the western hemisphere and the sun rising in the east, the surge and retreat, systole and diastole of existence, the quiet energy of God's creation. She turned into the relative warmth of a dimly lit corridor to go to her cell and read before supper.

Distant ringing called and she joined others progressing to the refectory with its dark wood panelling, solid tables and benches. She picked up a bowl, ladled beans into it, took a piece of bread and sat beside a tall, ungainly girl with a face like a Great Dane and lank brown hair cropped at chin level.

'Va bene, Bernadette? ' Asked Lucia. The girl's face lifted and shone,

'Si, si, it's wonderful, it's so quiet and everyone is so content.'

Lucia smiled, 'You're not privy to any of the quarrels yet.'

'I haven't heard a door slam or a cup or a book thrown and no-one's screamed or shouted.'

'Maybe not but there are other ways of showing anger.'

'Better ways.'

'More hurtful sometimes. How is your family coping without you?'

Bernadette's wide bony shoulders lifted the ill-fitting neck and sleeves of her grey woollen habit.

'They'll hardly notice the gap-one less mouth to feed.'

'How many brothers and sisters do you have?'

'Eleven.'

'Quite a family. Are you the youngest or the oldest?'

'Third. I have two elder brothers.'

'What do they say about you coming here?'

'I'm mad.'

'And the younger ones?' Bernadette's head dropped, she put down her spoon, pushed her bowl aside and mumbled.

'They cried.'

Lucia turned and looked at the sad, heavy profile and said, 'don't worry, they'll get used to it. They'll be proud of you.' Under the table she held Bernadette's big rough hand for a moment. 'Come on eat up it's a long time to breakfast.'

As Lucia mopped up the last few beans and sauce with her bread an elderly nun tapped her on the shoulder.

'Mother Superior would like a word,' she whispered then continued on her way to the refectory door missing Lucia's look of alarm.

'Have a peaceful night.' Lucia squeezed Bernadette's shoulder as she climbed over the bench and approached head table aware that her mouth felt dry and the pleasant satisfaction with her supper had turned to a queasy feeling. She slipped her hands into her sleeves and waited until the Abbess beckoned her forward.

'Your sister has had a little boy, sister Lucia. Your mother asked if you could help prepare for the christening. Would you like that?' Lucia nodded, relieved. She was pleased to hear her nephew had arrived safely then she felt the usual pang at leaving her cloistered haven, its orderly discipline and tranquillity.

'Your brother-in-law offered to collect you in the morning if you are agreeable.'

'Thank you, reverend mother, yes, I am.'

'You will make the necessary arrangements for your offices for the next week won't you?'

'Yes, reverend mother.'

She stepped back, bowed her head and left the great hall her mind teeming. She thought of the wrench away and back. *'It's always hard to adjust, bit like jet lag I suppose.'* She smiled at the incongruity of associating such sophistication with her simple life.

Reverend Mother said 'a week.' Is the christening to be that soon? Why the rush? It'll be fun, everyone will come, I can catch up with Emilio and Caterina, see Angelo. I haven't heard from him for a while. Her pace quickened down the corridor looking forward to seeing Isabella, Paolo and the children, being part of a big family celebration.

In her room she returned to her convent duties. It was the time of silent prayer, in the morning she would ask sister Veronica if she would take over her reading in the refectory and sister Consuela if she would help with cleaning the chapel. *Perhaps Reverend Mother will let Bernadette clear the courgettes and plant the pumpkins and winter salad.* Her heart sank at having to relinquish this annual pleasure.

After the Angelus in the morning Lucia knocked at the Abbess's door carrying a small black suitcase.

'Enter.'

Lucia slipped into the study and stood in front of a desk in weak light filtered through the ancient glass of a high arched window.

'Ah, Lucia, come in, sit down.'

'Thank you mother Carmela.'

'All packed and ready?' Lucia nodded. 'And your obligations here?'

'All arranged, apart from the garden. I was wondering if sister Bernadette could take over the vegetables.'

'Do you trust her? I know you take great pride in the vegetable garden and you have done a good job there.'

'Bernadette is eager to please and strong.'

'But young and only a novice.'

'But she has had to take responsibility for eight growing children.'

The Abbess sighed, 'Yes, poor girl. You have taken her under your wing, that is a kindness. You have helped. I know she feels the burden of responsibility and questions her calling.'

'She has lacked the peace to search her soul. She needs time.'

'And the support you have given her. She may pursue her calling in the vegetable garden for the time being.'

'Thank you, Reverend Mother.'

'Go with our blessing. Remember you are precious to God and to us here.'

7

Paolo was right, in the week since her arrival Lucia had quietly taken command of Isabella, removing distractions, enabling her to focus on the baby and establish a routine. By her own calm she had settled the children's edgy restlessness and brought everyone together to prepare the party.

In the garden she thanked God that she was still in her summer habit as they arranged tables and chairs in the shade of the laurel hedge and cedar tree. The midday sun was still hot. Battered cars and dusty old trucks jogged up the long drive into the courtyard one after another bringing all manner of food and supplies. Fresh anchovies gleamed in the 'fridge and the dark scent of a ham filled the corner of the kitchen. Smooth pearly grey pumpkins sat by the sink in the scullery with boxes of peppers and tomatoes.

Oriana had a constant smile – Lucia at her side, Isabella nursing the baby and children gathering and dispersing around the kitchen table like a shoal of fish. It was time to start cooking.

Lucia looked at the flaccid yellow and purple bodies of a tray of chickens and said, 'Should I make tortelli de zucca?'

Oriana grinned, 'your tortelli are the best.'

She chose a chicken and set it purposefully on the table. A cloud of white dust rose from Lucia's big enamel bowl. Oriana took a cleaver and chopped the chicken expertly into pieces. The sound of the cleaver was accompanied by the sound of eggshells cracking on the side of Lucia's bowl.

A van drew into the courtyard, Lucia looked through the window.

'Uncle Sebastian and Martino,' she said.

They heard Paolo call to his brothers followed by the chink of bottles and banter as they headed toward the barn. Martino barged into the kitchen then stopped at the sight of Lucia, pulled off his cap and stood to attention.

'Buongiorno,' laughed Lucia.

'Coffee?' Called Oriana from the sink.

'Per favore,' he said rolling his cap in his hands, watching Lucia.

Piles of chicken and egg shells littered the kitchen table. Sebastian came in brandishing a newspaper saying 'La Mortadella's days are numbered...'. His words were cut short by the sight of Lucia with a floury apron over her habit.

Lucia said, 'buongiorno' turning the eggs into the flour with her fingers.

Paolo pulled chairs from the table so they could sit by the window. Oriana put a coffee pot on the window ledge, handed out mugs and went back to the cooker. She lowered the first batch of chicken into the pan and watched the pale flesh sizzle, crisp and bronze in the hot oil.

'Have you seen this?' Sebastian passed the paper to Paolo.

'It's not the first time Emilio's been in the papers,' he replied.

Oriana looked up.

'Maybe not, but this is big. Ricci's 'Ndrangheta.'

Paolo's eyes widened. 'I wondered where his money came from.'

'Si, si, ' said Martino, 'and it's more than prostitution-he's into drugs and money laundering too.'

Oriana scooped the chicken onto paper to drain and started a second batch.

'Emilio's backed a loser this time,' said Sebastian settling back in his chair for emphasis.

'Ah no, if he's 'Ndranghetta he'll win, no problem. They'll buy off the prosecution, bribe or threaten the witnesses,' said Martino.

Paolo looked from one to the other ready to defend his brother in law then shrugged, anything was possible, corruption at the top percolates down, why should anyone give a damn about law and order?

'Emilio will never be a party to that.' Oriana's voice rang out firm and final.

They all turned to look at her, Paolo put the paper down, Sebastian shook his head and said with some satisfaction,

'I wouldn't bet on it, 'Ndrangheta turns over forty four billion a year, that's power.'

'But not law,' said Oriana removing her smoking oil from the flame.

'They don't care about law,' said Martino.

'But lawyers do, Emilio is a lawyer like his father before him. No one's above the law.' Oriana pronounced the words like a final absolution.

They shuffled awkwardly in their chairs and turned their attention from scandal to football.

When they had left Oriana picked up the newspaper. There was a photo of the man she had seen with Emilio. He was in a marina wearing a short-sleeved shirt and slacks. She read the caption to Lucia.

'Emilio was here this morning,' said Lucia.

'Impossible, he would have said 'hello.'

'It was very early – matins. '

'So early, it probably wasn't light enough, you were mistaken, it was probably someone else.'

'No, mama, it was Emilio and he was with a young man in jeans and a leather jacket.'

'What on earth would they be doing here that early in the morning?'

'Paolo said they were renting the shed.'

'Well they could do with the money but I don't know what a solicitor has to store.'

'Not Emilio mama, men he knows.'

' He doesn't tell me anything anymore. I don't see much of him and Caterina these days, not since your father died. I miss him, my little professor. Do you remember how serious he was as a teenager?'

Lucia nodded thoughtfully, 'big brother Emilio, always the superior one telling us what to do. His room was immaculate with his own computer desk and all those gadgets. Angelo and I thought it was cool,' she said spooning little piles of filling along sheets of pasta. She looked guiltily at her mother, ' and no one allowed in on pain of death.'

'After Angelo deleted files from his computer and you used his baseball gloves in a snowball fight.'

'And beat him, '

'Cold, wet and angry… ' Oriana wagged a finger at Lucia.

'Look at you two!' Isabella, pale and drawn, her belly still swollen, was standing at the kitchen door, 'and all of this,' she spread her arms towards the mounds of half prepared food all around. 'It's enough to feed an army.'

Lucia replied, 'Or Paolo's family.'

'True.' Isabella smiled.

Oriana asked, 'Are you sure you'll be all right? It'll be a long day, tesora?'

'I'll be fine, mama, honestly. You two have taken care of everything. Oh, Lucia, it's so good to have you here.'

She put her arms around her sister and held on.

8

In the still of early morning Oriana wandered into the garden past bunting, balloons and tables to the trees where the children played. A squirrel was rustling under the hazel bush, suddenly a black bird took flight and a bevy of long tailed tits fluttered away Oriana turned to see what had disturbed them. Lucia was standing behind her.

'You're not still checking are you?' she asked.

'Oh no, enjoying it, savouring the moment. I'm still a bit of a child, I couldn't sleep I was so excited. I love parties, but most of all having the family together. I'm so proud of you all. I only wish your father were here.'

'I'm sure he is.'

'It's going to be perfect – just look.' Oriana pointed across the garden over fields to the woods silhouetted against a wide orange sun climbing through purple, grey and white into clear blue. 'And all of this.' Arms outstretched she turned a circle.

Beyond the vegetable garden to the side of the farmhouse a the field speckled with wheat stalks and on the other side of its stone wall olive trees gripped the hill descending steeply to a few rows of vines.

'It is good to have you here,' said Oriana.

Lucia bowed her head and said, 'It's good to be together for a while.'

Oriana sighed and said, 'I'd better see how Isabella is.'

'She's looking better this morning.'

'Thank God. Let it all begin.'

9

Oriana and Pietro left the church to the cheerful clap, clang and clatter of its tinny bells.

'Mama!' Emilio took her by the shoulders and held her at arm's length to enjoy her emerald green silk dress and coat, dark blue stilettos and bag, 'Splendida,' he said, 'matches your eyes.' He kissed her cheeks. His aftershave smelled of spice and bergamot. Oriana took his hands and spread his arms to appraise him in return.

'Che bella figura! and Caterina,' she drew the slender figure from behind Emilio. Caterina's pale blue silk dress skimmed her waist falling in soft folds around her knees 'Bella, bellissima.'

Caterina waited patiently for the end of the greeting pantomime. Oriana tapped Emilio's expanding tummy and said, 'Ecco, the successful business man- another inch on your waist.' She turned back to Caterina, 'You're feeding him too well,' she said then wrapped her arms around Caterina's frail figure, feeling her flutter, moth like, against her breast. 'It's you who needs feeding up. We'll have to see what we can do.'

Released Caterina smiled down at Pietro, 'Ciao' she said. He smiled up at her and his face shone. Caterina was as beautiful as the fairy on top of the Christmas tree to him and just as unreachable.

Emilio rubbed his hands together then ruffled Pietro's hair brusquely saying, 'Well, Pietro, a new brother, eh, aren't you the lucky one?'

Caterina knelt to give him a hug and a kiss.

'What a smart tie,' she said straightening his blue spotted bow, 'you do look grown up.'

He stroked the soft silk of her skirt. She touched his hand. 'So, you're not the youngest anymore, you're big brother now, look after him, won't you?'

Petro nodded sombrely.

She stood up and held his hand but Emilio put his hand under her elbow and said, 'see you in a minute mama. We've got to take Paolo and Isabella up to the house.'

He led Caterina away and she looked back over her shoulder at the two of them standing in the porch like stones in a stream with people flooding around them.

'Have you seen Uncle Angelo?' Oriana asked Pietro.
He shook his head. As they wove their way to the car she greeted people; shook hands, kissed and accepted congratulations, all the time looking over heads and shoulders for Angelo.

Rosa and Tommaso were waiting by the car. ''Here you are,' she said, 'I can't see Uncle Angelo anywhere. Have you seen him?'

'Yes, Nonna, he was at the back. He came in late with two gentlemen.' Rosa replied.
Her relief was mixed with irritation – late and bringing unexpected guests, why didn't he 'phone?
Pietro sat beside her in the car and asked, 'What were the candles for?'

'Lights to fight the darkness of sin and evil. You had a candle too when you were baptised.'

'Have I still got it?'

'Yes, in the memory box mummy keeps for you. We'll have a look later if you like.'

At the farmhouse Isabella sat on the verandah beside Giorgio asleep in his cot. Paolo, Martino and Sebastian served drinks while their mother, Beatrice, rounder than any of her hefty sons, sat on a wicker sofa wearing a bright blue dress with fuschia pink flowers, fanning herself and acknowledging each arrival. Her school of grandchildren ran around the grass until the twins led them to the barn where there was a swing, ladder and ropes to play on. Pietro tagged along behind.

Down on the grass neighbours chatted volubly. At the top of the steps Emilio skimmed the faces then headed for his sisters-in-law, Davina and Mirella. Their animated conversation stopped at his approach and they stood passive while he kissed their cheeks.

'Mirella, how are the children?' he asked.

'Bene, grazie Emilio. Where is Caterina? It's been a long time.'

'Too long, Caterina's not far, you'll see her,' he replied and turned to Davina, 'Davina, come stai? How did the holiday business fare this summer?'

'The barn was never empty.'

'How many units do you have now?'

'Three.'

Mirella chirped in. 'It doesn't stop at rents, Davina sells them eggs, oil, veg. And she makes cakes.'

'They can have your cakes?' exclaimed Emilio, 'they must think they're in Paradise.'

Davina began to thaw, 'we have a few who come back year after year. Some have favourites.'

'They even put in requests before they arrive,' added Mirella.

'A profitable Paradise,' said Emilio, 'you'll have to think of something for the winter now.'

'Grazie mille, we're glad of the peace and quiet, there's more to life...' replied Davina.

'More to life than profit? Never!' laughed Emilio and turned his attention to their husbands who were bringing drinks down into the garden.

Oriana caught glimpses of Emilio as he circulated. He had presence, a little island around which people eddied.

Now that the party was under way and everyone was relaxing Oriana was happy to retreat and steal a moment of quiet so she took her drink over to the old walnut tree far enough away for loud voices to become a companionable hum. She sat on the grass leaning against the trunk and Caterina joined her sipping Kir and people watching. Oriana was pleased but surprised. It was not like Caterina to cut herself off, she was usually in the middle of things, playing with the children but Oriana sensed a wistful loneliness in the girl.

She didn't know what to say, it had been a while. She felt that they had lost contact. She didn't know how to break through this new reserve. The easy, chatty family girl who used to pour everything out to her over the kitchen table had gone.

Oriana knew very little of their domestic life. Their hopes or disappointments were no longer shared, unlike Paolo and Isabella's explosive rows and passionate adventures which included everyone. They were side by side at last and Oriana felt shy, afraid of alienating Caterina. She didn't know where to begin so she chose what she thought was a neutral subject.

'What's your garden like at the moment?' She asked, ' mine's a mess.'

'Emilio had someone tidy it up for the sale.'

'Sale?'

'Didn't you know?'

'I'm beginning to think no one tells me anything. You're not selling your beautiful house?'

'Emilio wanted to move further out. He's found a bigger place in the hills.'

'Do you need a bigger place?'

Caterina lowered her head.

'So when's the move?'

'We've made a start, we're doing it gradually.'

'You'll be in soon then? I'd better have your address and 'phone number. You will let me know the date won't you?'

Caterina nodded, took paper and pen from her bag and wrote the address leaning on the bag.

Oriana caught sight of Angelo at the top of the verandah steps. He looked stunning in white jeans, turquoise check shirt, silver buckled belt and white shoes. 'Whatever happened to suits for church? She wondered struggling up. She straightened her dress and said, ' 'Scuse me, Caterina, I can see Angelo, I must speak to him.'

Caterina looked up into the sun and shaded her face with her hand as she handed Oriana the piece of paper.

'Thank you, see you at table…'

Angelo was carrying three glasses of wine. Oriana followed him through the crowd to two figures whose dark suites made them look like black rocks in a sea of bright tropical fish.

'Angelo finalmente.' Oriana intercepted him. 'Where have you been?'

'Mama!' Hands full, flustered, he handed a glass to a stocky man in a dark blue striped suit and introduced her, 'Mama, Signor Avitabile.'

Oriana stiffened, she looked sharply at Angelo. He avoided her eyes, delivered the second glass into the hands of a tall, thin, stoop - shouldered man and took a gulp from his own glass before saying, 'Sorry we were a bit late.'

Signor Avitabile bent over her hand, which had been caught up before she could think to hide it.

'My fault, Signora Rossi, I am afraid I delayed your son.'

She recognised the voice, her eyes slid from his round, moustachioed face down his red striped tie and over his paunch to shiny black shoes then back to his cold brown eyes.

'We spoke on the phone,' she said.

'Si, si.' He nodded, took a handkerchief from his top pocket and mopped his forehead saying, 'Che buono tempo,' gesturing around the garden. Oriana's jaw clenched.

'Congratulazioni.' The second figure flapped, crow like into the awkward silence spreading his arms toward her. Oriana turned to fix him in her sights and Angelo stepped in.

'Mama this is Lorenzo Conti.'

A bird like claw was extended and her hand was briefly enclosed in a bony prison, she shuddered, extricating it quickly.

'You have a big family signora?' He enquired in a reedy voice.

'Two sons and two daughters.'

'Che buona fortuna.'

Oriana noticed a slight accent. 'You're not from Tuscany?'

'No, we come from Naples.'

'Ah, you're a long way from home, Milan is bigger isn't it?'

'And wealthy, signora, quite magnificent.'

He waved like a willow in the wind as he sighed out the words. Oriana watched Angelo drain his glass and study the grass between his feet. She looked at the two strange, ill-assorted figures, only their alienation drew them together. She could not understand how her butterfly son could have ended up in these black spiders' web. Only ten or fifteen years difference in age but she sensed a whole world's difference in outlook.

A gong sounded by high table and Lucia beckoned Oriana. Uncertain for a second, she looked at Angelo then at his guests and said firmly, 'The family are being called to table.' She took Angelo by the elbow, saying over her shoulder, ' Scusi signori, buon appetito'.

She hissed at Angelo, 'What do you think you are doing bringing them to your nephew's christening?'

'They won't let me out their sight until I've paid. They said they wanted to meet my family.'

'What business can they have with your family? Nonsense. The sooner we get them off your back the better. My cheque book's here, see me later ten thousand should keep them quiet for the time being.'

Paolo's mother followed him and Isabella down into the garden to their table and Oriana saw her lost look when Paolo settled father Bernadetto on the chair next to him so Oriana rushed over and stood before her arms outstretched, 'Sofia, how are you? What a beautiful dress!' She took Sofia's elbow, 'look there are Martino and Davina and Sebastian and Mirella, come, come and sit with us.' She pulled back what suddenly seemed a rather flimsy chair between Lucia and Angelo and guided Sofia down onto it then rested her hands on Sofia and Lucia's shoulders while she surveyed the scene.

Isabella was back to her old self, eyes wide listening avidly to Davina wiping her plate with bread and eating it automatically. Emilio was regaling his brother's-in-law with city gossip and Caterina was showing Pietro how to make a hat from his napkin. Oriana checked the other tables down the garden, all the chairs were filled and there were no stranded souls in spite of gatecrashers.

Paolo rose, tapped a knife against his glass and, table by table the chatter subsided so Father Benedetto could say grace. When Oriana raised her head Paolo was filling the priest's wine glass and Lucia was serving him bread. She took the platter of tomatoes, served Pietro and added ham and olives. As the clatter of cutlery diminished Oriana and helpers removed empty plates and brought out dishes of Lucia's pumpkin stuffed pasta. At the far end of the table Martino piled his plate high. Oriana scooped some onto Rosa's plate.

'No, no, too much nonna.'

'It's good for you. Eat up.'

She caught drifts of conversations.

Tommaso's voice. 'Foirenta'll be on top this season.'

'Milan'll beat them you'll see,' said Emilio.

'Mai, Jose Castillo transferred from Lecce in August. E brillante.'

'Seen him play?'

Oriana wiped her plate with bread and started to clear away. She and Lucia filled serving dishes with chicken whispering in the shadowy kitchen like conspirators.

'It's going well, isn't it?' asked Oriana.

' Si, va bene, finora .'

Outside Paolo and his brothers were replacing bottles of wine. There were exclamations of delight at the food, an explosion of chatter and crockery followed by contented quiet.

'I brought you some juice, Pietro,' said Oriana filling his glass and passing the jug down to the twins. She put chicken on his plate and passed the serving bowl to Caterina who took a meagre spoonful and filled Emilio's plate while he talked to Sebastian.

'Berlusconi wants to get back into politics,' interjected Martino.

'In love with the glamour,' said Sebastian.

'And the money,' added Martino.

' E celebrita, favoloso,' laughed Emilio, 'We won't come to any harm with Berlusconi asleep at the helm.'

Sebastian shrugged, 'In bed more like.'

'With a prostitute – or two,' added Martino.

'Why not?' Asked Emilio.

Sebstian searched Emilio's face, then muttered dismally, 'Italians are useless at politics.'

'Because we don't care, we only care about what we can control- our own patch and family,' said Martino. 'Leave politics to the politicians.'

'But we're great at football,' laughed Emilio cutting free a chunk of chicken thigh.

Anna and Maria dotted bunches of grapes along the tables while Rosa and Tommaso set out Isabella's goats' cheeses then the twins stood by Isabella's chair. Oriana joined them and said, 'Yes you can go, but quietly and don't spoil your dresses.' They beamed and ran so fast downhill that she saw them roll over at the bottom and scramble toward the barn covered in dry grass. Oriana was glad to leave the table and follow them down. The buzz of conversation had increased in volume with the wine.

Angelo's interlopers were at the end of a table by the laurel hedge, jackets on the backs of their chairs, relaxed, being entertained by the people around them. Their audacity and selfishness irritated her against the warm current of mellowness from the happy purr of the occasion.

When she got back Pietro had run off to play and puddings were arranged on a table for everyone to help themselves. Oriana asked Caterina if she could fetch her a dessert but Caterina said she wasn't hungry so she took a slice of pear and chocolate torte and one for Pietro. Emilio was looking around the three long tables that lined the marquee and Caterina had her head bent carefully folding her napkin. Oriana sat to enjoy her pudding, pastry crumbled crisp and salty in her mouth combined with wine flavoured pear and rich bitter chocolate, heaven.

The sides of the marquee were lifted to include the tables outside and Sebastian and Martino delivered champagne and glasses to the tables. Emilio rose and tapped his glass. Chatter diminished, cutlery clattered to a rest, there was a cough and the clearing of throats.

'As Giorgio's godfather it is my privilege to welcome him into the family and all of you to our celebration.'

Pietro crept back and Oriana pulled his chair close, 'Twins not playing with you?'

'They run too fast.'

'Showing off to the cousins I expect,' she whispered and pushed his cake before him.

'Giorgio is already blessed with his family,' continued Emilio indicating Isabella and Paolo, 'look at them, what a picture. Rosa already being chased by the boys, Tommaso running the farm – you can put your feet up now, Paolo, eh Tommaso?' Tommaso smiled, Paolo put his hands to his temples and shook his head groaning, 'No, no, no.'

'You'll show him won't you Tommaso? Where are the twins?' Emilio looked at their empty chairs. 'Off with their cousins in the barn? Never mind their pretty dresses, full of energy, full of fun, finally our quiet and thoughtful Pietro, there by his Nonna. Congratulations Isabella and Paolo for creating such a happy family and especially today for Giorgio Enrico. I ask you all to stand for a toast to the new arrival.'

Chairs toppled, napkins dropped, everyone was on their feet.

'May he be powerful and strong, may he shape his world to bring him joy, may his horizons stretch wide and far and may he succeed in all he does. Ladies and gentlemen, Giorgio.' Champagne glasses tinkled, 'To Giorgio'.

Satisfied, the assembly sat and Oriana watched Pietro enjoying his cake. Emilio now surveyed the sea of faces beyond the shade of the tree to the table by the hedge. At the sight of Angelo's two intruders his back straightened and his jaw clenched, he took his jacket from the back of his chair and left the table only to return a few minutes later to tap Caterina on the shoulder and nod toward the car. Blank faced she rose and they melted out of sight.

When Oriana noticed their empty chairs she went in search of them.

'Where are Emilio and Caterina ?' She asked Lucia.

Together they went to the side of the house where the Ferrari had been parked. Oriana stood looking at the gap, 'He is the master of ceremonies, he can't leave.'

'Perhaps he's been called away or Caterina isn't feeling well,' Lucia replied.

'But they didn't say 'goodbye.'

'They probably didn't want to break up the party.'

Oriana found Isabella nursing the baby in the peace of the sitting room surrounded by beautifully wrapped packages of all sizes and exotic plants covered in great balloons of cellophane with copious blue ribbons.

'What happened to Emilio and Caterina?' she asked.

'He had a call, had to get back home, said to say 'Ciao'.'

10

Emilio's foot pressed the accelerator. *Fool, stupid, damned fool. Doesn't he know any better? What game does he think he's playing?* He swerved round bends hunched over the steering wheel on his way to Isabella's. *Taking them to the farm, introducing them to family.* His eyes narrowed. *Just when I'd got it all set up, damn ... Stop collection, move the stuff. Where, where can I put it now?* His mind was blank with anger. He forced himself to focus... *Close to town, safe, ... Mother's garage? Possibile, possibile ...* he settled back in his seat and changed to fifth to cruise up the valley. *The papers? What the hell can I do with the papers?* He smiled grimly, *Wouldn't they like to get their hands on those...? I could do without this, damn Angelo.* He wrenched the steering wheel round a sharp bend burning rubber onto the lane that climbed tortuously to the farm, relishing the power and danger as he swung and screeched upwards.

The car gurgled through muck as he entered the courtyard. 'Shit.' He snarled. 'Shit again.' He stamped on the brake and jolted to a stop on the concrete apron in front of the shed. He took a deep breath and braced himself for the family conviviality, resigned himself to time wasting formalities. The sound of stacking chairs and men's voices led him to the garden. The flood of festivity had retreated leaving its detritus behind- tables folded on their sides, a pile of jars and vases with wilting flowers on the grass by the steps and tablecloths and napkins dumped by bulging refuse sacks. Paolo and Sebastian were carrying tables to the barn while Martino stacked chairs. They hadn't heard his arrival. *If only I could creep to the shed, load the car and be off. Not possible*, he shrugged.

'Buongiorno,' he said.

Martino came and shook his hand. Paolo and Sebastian nodded without letting go of the table they were carrying and continued on to the barn. Emilio saw Martino eye up his suit, *No, I haven't come to cart furniture.*

'Need to get some things from the shed,' he explained.

'Ciao,' Martino called as he dropped a chair onto its pile.

He could see his mother at the kitchen window as he walked toward the shed *.Damn!* She had spotted him. He turned towards the house. The shed would have to wait.

The kitchen was like the centre of a beehive. Oriana had her arms in soapy water washing glasses at the sink. In the utility Tommaso was scrubbing pans and Lucia was loading the dish washer while Rosa put away the last load. He was relieved not to be the centre of attention and allowed himself to be coerced onto a chair and given a coffee.

'Three visits in a week, you being godfather is good for us all,' said Oriana.

'Where is the baby?' He asked.

'Upstairs asleep.' Oriana turned and leant against the sink drying her hands on a tea towel looking at his suit, aware of his unease. He sat on the edge of his chair, avoiding her eyes. Her irritation at his desertion rose but she stopped herself from leaping into complaints.

'So what brings you here today big brother?' Lucia slid the rack into the dishwasher and straightened up to set it going. Emilio always felt a little uneasy in Lucia's presence, he preferred to write to her, keep a safe distance, he knew she had a good brain and probably knew more of what was going on in the family than anyone, even his mother. He knew he wasn't the only one to write to her. Over the years since she had taken orders they had all told her what they couldn't tell their mother and more beside.

Isabella came in tying on an apron, 'Emilio, que buona fortuna!' she kissed his smooth spicy cheeks and felt dowdy.

'Coffee,' said Oriana.

Isabella sat down and took a mug. 'It was a good party wasn't it?' She asked, 'pity you couldn't stay to the end.'

'Yes, what happened?' Quizzed Oriana.

Emilio bristled, 'I don't like Angelo's friends.'

'They're not friends, Angelo owes them money and they wouldn't leave him alone, said they wanted to come.'

Emilio's mouth tightened then he spat out, 'He's an idiot. He shouldn't have told them about it.'

Isabella jumped in. 'He probably didn't think they meant it. Anyway it didn't matter, there was enough for everyone.'

'That's not the point.'

'Why not?'

'They're not the sort to mix with family. It was dangerous to bring them here.'

'Dangerous? That's a bit strong. I thought they mingled quite well.'

'They're ruthless.' Frustrated he stared into Isabella's oh so reasonable face and wanted to shake her.

Oriana intervened, 'Well, they got what they wanted, at least half of it. I don't know what he's going to do about the rest.'

'I've told you there are plenty of ways of earning quick cash, it's up to him. I have to get things from the shed.'

At the door he put his hands on Lucia's shoulders and his face softened.

'I suppose it's 'goodbye,'' he said, 'until another christening.'

'Or funeral,' quipped Isabella.

Lucia looked into his inscrutable face and said. 'I've still got a couple of days... You keep the sword of justice bright, big brother, but don't get too sucked in, there's more to life.'

He hugged her and felt the weight of her habit separating them.

'Pray for us sinners, won't you?'

Lucia smiled. 'It's what I do.'

Reluctantly he turned away. 'Mama.' He gave Oriana a kiss.

'Thank you for popping in,' she said.

'Thanks for the coffee. Ciao Isabella,' he kissed her.

Oriana watched through the window as he carefully made his way around the piles of dirt in the direction of the shed realising she hadn't asked what he was keeping there. There was a gulf between them and she didn't know why. The connections of forty years, from basic needs to shared lives had gone – dispersed, evaporated and she didn't know when or why. She leant on the sink and felt suddenly drained. Behind her she heard Isabella ask.

'Have we really only got two more days?'

And Lucia's reply, 'I've had more than a week. You can manage now, can't you, 'Bel?'

Oriana turned to watch them with a sinking feeling in her stomach. She knew the idyll had to end but it didn't make it any easier. It had been so good.

Isabella teased, 'I'd love to say 'no' just to keep you here but I don't suppose Mother Carmela'd like it.'

Lucia opened her mouth to protest and Isabella jumped in with, 'and I know you love your family there and your prayers. Thanks for everything, little sis.'

Oriana made an effort at cheeriness, 'I'll make a farewell dinner, tomorrow night, a meat treat before you go back to all that beans and cabbage,' she said.

'It's not all beans and cabbage,' laughed Lucia.

'I'll ask Rosa to make her torte di melle,' said Isabella.

'I'm not going to say 'no' – sounds good to me,' said Lucia, 'Back to work, we haven't finished here yet.' She swept peelings off the side into the heavy compost bucket, 'I'll take this out.'

After she had closed the door behind her Oriana and Isabella were quiet, both feeling the emptiness in the kitchen, the gap yawning before them. For a small quiet person Lucia had presence. She brought so much with her, not just calm but awareness and understanding.

'You don't have to go yet do you mama?'

'No, we'll have a few quiet days to settle back into routine then you'll be wanting to see the back of me.'

'Never.'

Isabella hugged her mother and Oriana's chest swelled with love.

'This won't do, better get on,' she mumbled turning back to the dishes.

Through the window she saw Emilio talking to Lucia. *That's kind, he must have carried the bucket for her.* Lucia followed him to his car and Emilio put his hand under her chin lifted her head and stroked her cheek with the back of his fingers before getting into his car. Lucia watched the red Ferrari roll quietly out of the courtyard and waved as he turned into the lane.

11

Lucia opened her window wide to encompass all she would be leaving behind on her last full day at the farm. The damp chill of early morning reflected the melancholy of parting. A metal gate clanged shut. Paolo was already out. They loved their farm, Isabella was happy here but for Lucia it was too haphazard, dilapidated, disorganised. She had abandoned herself to the tug and tear of family life, the cross currents of individual wills, distractions and clutter of domestic routine for long enough.

Her head was crowded with noise: water rushing and thumping in pipes, fires crackling and spitting in need of constant feeding, doors banging, shutters swinging, furniture scraping, feet pounding stairs, puttering over kitchen tiles, words clamouring for attention, circling the rooms, echoing on stairs and landing and, at the heart of it all the kitchen bustle – cocoa and cake, bread and fruit shuffling onto the table in the sleep numb mornings then the work of preparing vegetables, pasta or potatoes interrupted by coffees for the farm, eggs to wash, machine parts soaking in the laundry trough while, in the corner, clothes swished and burred behind glass. Isabella thrived on it, Oriana easily became a part of it, Lucia tried to bring order to its chaos.

To breathe the free, clear air of the convent would be a relief, to become one with the serene calm that allowed her spirit to elevate itself and aspire to the joy and unity of the promised love. She was ready to go home and determined to enjoy her last day as she descended the stairs.

Rosa was alone in the kitchen making a cake.

'Is this your famous torte de melle?' She asked wishing that she could get closer to the girl but Rosa was so retiring Lucia couldn't pin her down.

'Si.' Rosa nodded shyly. She hero worshipped Lucia and always regretted not talking more when her brief visits were over.

'Should I peel the apples?'

'Please.'

They set to work together and Lucia chatted, gently prodding. She got a picture of a rather frightened girl on the brink of leaving school without an idea of what she wanted to do.

'You don't want to be a farmer's wife?' Teased Lucia.

'No, thank you,' laughed Rosa.

Lucia asked about boyfriends and Rosa went quiet. 'Who is he?' She pressed.

'Giacomo, he's in the school orchestra.' She scraped cake mixture into a baking tin.

'You still play flute?

Lucia spread apple slices over the rich sweet cake mixture. Rosa sprinkled sugar on top.

'We've been spending time together off and on for eight months but it's going to end,' she said grimly.

'What do you mean it's going to end?'

'He's in the year above me, he's going to University.'

'That doesn't mean that your relationship is over, you can text, phone, email and the holidays are long, you'll have plenty of time together. He won't forget you. What is he going to do?'

'He wants to study Physics at Sapienza-Universita in Rome. It'll all be over then, he'll forget me.' She slid the cake into the oven. 'There'll be lots of pretty girls more exciting than I am.'

'Exciting can be demanding and isn't always reliable. Anyway who says you're not pretty? You're lovely with those big eyes and all your dark wavy hair.'

Rosa shook her head, 'I'm just ordinary.'

'You're thoughtful and kind, you've learnt to share and take responsibility here more than most.'

Rosa didn't look convinced but she relaxed a little. Lucia poured coffee and suggested they take it through to the sitting room.

Once they had sunk into armchairs by the fire Rosa dared to ask what had been on her mind for a long time. 'Did you have a boyfriend?'

'Of course.'

'What was he like?'

'The most unlikely lad you could imagine.' Lucia chuckled at the memory and told Rosa the story of Giovanni, the odd one out in class at school who always sat at the back, head down, shoulders hunched, silent. He couldn't get on with the boys because he had five lively sisters and a friendly, easy going mother but no brothers at home.

Rosa couldn't picture it, 'How did you get together?'

'He started to follow me home, it was creepy, I didn't know what to do. He never said a word, just followed me to the end of my lane. I'd look round and he'd be standing watching me go through the garden gate. Then one day a cyclist came round a corner fast and knocked me over, Giovanni picked up my books and bag, carried them for me and every night after.'

'Didn't he ask you out?' Asked Rosa.

'He asked if I'd go fishing with him, I couldn't say 'no'.'

'On the way back from the river he picked flowers from the roadside and when we got to my gate he gave me the bunch. Angelo teased me something rotten.'

'Did you kiss?'

Lucia slowly put down her mug and looked into the fire. 'We had been foraging for mushrooms, it was late, the sky was dark and he showed me some of the constellations – he could name all the stars you can see. I got muddled so he stood behind, held my arm and pointed my finger up to the sky – touching close was like an electric shock. I think it surprised us both – we turned to face each other and he kissed me. Sometimes you don't know what's inside – it was like a great wave, blotted out the sky and underneath a current so strong it overwhelmed me. I ran away, ran all the way home.'

Rosa sat quietly looking at her aunt leaning over the fire, the fairest of the family with pale skin and grey eyes, trying to imagine her as a wife but it didn't fit.

'Do you miss him?'

Lucia looked up and slapped her hands on her knees. 'Heavens no, I'd rather hone my spirit than tend a man.'

There were voices in the Kitchen, Isabella and Paolo.

'I'd better check the cake,' said Rosa.

12

Lucia rose at dawn, after her wash and prayers she pulled her little black case from under the bed, put in her sandals, folded her summer habit on top followed by her scapula, belt and coif then she gathered soap, face cloth, toothbrush and toothpaste into her toilet bag. Finally she folded a triptych of the last supper with the entry into Jerusalem on one side and the betrayal in the garden on the other and laid it carefully beside her missal, bible and book, 'Our Lady of the Place.' She was ready. There was a tap at the door.

'Come in.'

Rosa's face peered round the door.

'Hello, I thought you'd still be in bed,' said Lucia.

'No, I've been busy. Here you are.'

Rosa gave her a bookmark with a dried flower arrangement.

'Lavendar and marigolds, how cheerful, thank you.'

'They were the first flowers Giacomo gave me.'

'I shall think of you when I use it.' Lucia inserted it between the pages of her book of the virgin and clipped her case closed.

13

 They all stood in the courtyard hugging themselves against the damp chill of the misty morning to wave Lucia off in Paolo's car. Pietro saw Oriana's lost look and said, 'shall we go for a walk?'

Oriana looked at his earnest face and back to the quiet kitchen.

'We'll need our coats,' she said.

'Okay,' he agreed.

As they crossed the courtyard Ulysse came and wagged his tail hopefully.

'Sorry Ulysse, not today,' said Pietro and marched purposefully ahead.

Oriana hurried to catch up.

'Where are we going?'

'To see Uncle Martino's buffalo.'

'That's good idea, I like the buffalo.'

They walked around a ploughed field and into a meadow full of sheep, a few raised their heads to watch them pass and a ram followed them. They had to shoo him off to open the gate. As they descended the hill a view of the valley, farms and hamlets opened up and the mist cleared. Oriana's horizon expanded with it. She felt free and started to run. They ran together down the hill until they could see the sleek black backs of the buffalo standing out against the thick grass. They stopped running, gathered their breath and calmed themselves before climbing the fence to mingle with the animals. The buffalo raised their heads and looked at them breathing mist from their soft black noses then lowered their heads to crop the grass with a snuffling noise.

'Ciao,' Martino called from the farm gate. He signalled to them to go round to the other side of the field.

'Milking time,' said Pietro.

They stationed themselves each in a corner of the field and Martino circled round the side.

'Muoversi, muoversi,' he crooned to the cows.

Oriana and Pietro shooed them on and they started to amble toward the open gate.

'Andiamo,' Martino smiled to Oriana and Pietro as they followed them into the yard.

Pietro closed the metal gate and the animals nudged each other and waited packed tight until they could plod into the milking parlour and relieve their swollen udders. When the last one was in and connected Martino called to them.

'Thanks, go and have a coffee with Davina, 'see you later.'

'Don't hurry, we have to get back, good to see the buffalo, they're looking well.'

He surveyed the parlour swishing and popping quietly filled with the warmth of the cows.

'Not looking bad at the moment,' he said with pride.

'Ciao,' said Oriana.

'Arriverderci Zio,' Pietro called over his shoulder as he followed Oriana. Martino waved fondly to the boy.

'Go back along the road?' asked Oriana.

'Okay.'

Davina waved to them and beckoned them in as they passed the kitchen window so Oriana pointed to her watch and mimed eating. Davina shrugged her shoulders and smiled farewell. When they got to the lane Oriana said, 'that's blown the blues away, thanks Pietro.'

He said, 'race you back home' and started running, Oriana set off behind him determined to win but she only caught up at the kitchen step. He wasn't happy with a draw but she wasn't ready to be written off yet.

After lunch Oriana helped Isabella with some ironing and played draughts with Maria and nursed Giorgio at the end of the day while Isabella put the twins to bed. She liked to feel his weight and warmth in her arms. The bruising and jaundice had gone and he was filling out. Something so small, so real, the seed of a human being, complex, unique, fascinating.

She looked at the unformed face and wondered what kind of person lay inside the cocoon and what went into the making of a person. *There's so much that we can't escape – the looks we inherit from our parents – tall, short, ugly or beautiful – it matters, we adapt to what we're given. Our biochemistry is beyond our control – hormones, health, internal circuitry. What unique mix do you have Giorgio? 'Will he be handsome, will he strong? Che sera, sera.'* She hummed the tune over the sleeping baby. They were all different, something outside genetics and the world's conditioning. *What makes us what we are – Astrology, the moon, country, weather, everything – the permutations of possible combinations are endless, nothing explains the differences between children even in the same family. There aren't enough words to analyse human complexity – character, personality, temperament – not enough. The Eskimos have two hundred words for snow and we only have two for love and the English only have one, a sad thought and a poor comment on national character.* Giorgio stirred and yawned. She smiled at him. *Precious, another portal to the wonders of the world for me.* Each grandchild had shared their wonder at the world around them giving Oriana fresh perspectives on strange things. She loved their openness to her particular joys as well. There was no age prejudice with them, she was interested and gave them time and that was all that mattered.

14

Isabella was stronger, Rosa and Tommaso were helping, Oriana's cats and garden were beckoning. It was time to go home.

When she turned under the railway bridge toward home there was a battered green Fiat in front of her house. *I'm not expecting anyone.* The driver lowered his newspaper as she turned into the drive. *He's not much older than Angelo, must be waiting for someone off the train. They don't usually find their way down here.*

The house seemed eerily calm and chill after the bustle of the farm. Burrichio rubbed her legs and purred a welcome while Baffina stalked haughtily away. Oriana opened all the shutters and fetched wood from the shed. The 11.35 from Modena rattled past, she was home.

Pietro's shard of pottery was at the bottom of her case wrapped in newspaper. She missed him already. He didn't have a playmate at the farm – the twins were an item and Tommaso and Rosa were too old so Oriana filled the gap playing rambling games of alien attacks or pirate adventures, walking on walls even climbing trees. She smiled unwrapping the porcelain. *It was kind of him to give me this.* She washed it carefully marvelling at its freshness and beauty. *That potter was an artist, it's true, some things don't change.* She put it by Dario's photo on her bedside table before starting work for the day.

The studio felt like home again, she lit the heater and switched on her little old radio. Rossini gave brio to her preparation of clay scrolls piling them up by the bust before uncovering it. Dario's sweater looked substantial, inhabited, but the hollow neck begged for a face, a head, the man she was looking for. She turned the board examining proportions, rubbing patches where the surface was too smooth for wool. She started above the collar at the back of the head and built up to the height of his ears then turned the board and slanted strands of clay down at the front for his deep jawline creating a blunt, square chin.

The clay warmed in her hands, soft and responsive as she joined cords absorbed in remembering his jaw with its slight slackening on either side, a hint of jowls and the cleft in his chin. *Only Isabella inherited that, you didn't like it but I loved it.* She stepped back to check proportion – the jaw was the foundation and frame for all that went above – it had to be right. The sweater dwarfed the chin. *No, no not good enough, it needs to be wider, deeper.*

She unpeeled her smudged tails, rolled them up and started again expanding and extending the neck up into the skull, taking it through to the face widening and deepening the jaw checking constantly. *That's better, now I've got you, you're coming back.* The clay rose into cheeks and mouth. She was in control, a bubble of excitement rose in her chest. It was good to be back. *I spent too long in the wasteland of widowhood, too restless to create, filling my days with pointless activity afraid to come in here and confront myself, angry at being deprived of our last chance of closeness.*

She coiled above the mouth toward the nose then stopped and cut a slit with a wooden scalpel, rolled a reed of clay for the lower lip, warmed it in her hand and carefully moulded it into place and did the same above – *your lips, narrow but soft to kiss. Our first kisses – urgent, greedy, never wanting them to end.* She smoothed the surface and drew a fingertip over the cool lips. *We lost that intensity, impossible to keep but – feast to famine, my absentee landlord – why? Was the job that compelling or did I lose my appeal?* His mouth was straight and firm. She added more clay to soften it and lifted the sides into a gentle smile. She laid another snake above it, turned the board and continued round to the back of the head swivelled the board back and laid lines up and out to the top of the cheekbones. *Your face, it has to be perfect, polished like you, a man of the world.* Carefully she laid soft coils one after another up and over the cheekbones, back into sockets for the eyes. *Startled eyes, Dario's eyes: camera flash, photo in the paper – beside an evening dress, bare shoulders, jewels, breast, black gown, smiling – front page on our kitchen table.* The swell of anger returned, she stopped, coil in hand, then remembered the satisfaction of yelling out years of affronts and dismissals, her self-righteous sense of justification. She stared at the clay mask. *How you wriggled and squirmed protesting your innocence but I stood my ground and the silver plated lie wore away to copper. You started to plead love, need, remorse until I gave up my moment of power and surrendered. You bought the studio and I secured the new romance with a baby, family: Angelo.*

She moulded another soft, thin sliver of clay into the forehead, took another, joined it and spun it round to the back rotating the board. The forehead was taking shape, Dario's head. She relaxed into a rhythm of coiling, swinging the board round to keep the flow of clay on clay – *spinning lines of clay on a wooden board, changing one thing into another – fleece to thread, clay to Dario.* The circles were narrowing as she went. The head was closing into a dome. Coil followed coil in quick succession, the hole at the top of the head was getting smaller. She fitted a line of clay to the narrowing circle at the top of head. The gap was getting smaller so that securing the join was becoming more difficult. She inserted a finger under the edge, into the head, gently squeezing it in. Only a tiny hole remained to be filled, Oriana flattened a sliver of clay, cut it to fit then scratched its edges and around the circle at the top of the head, dampened it, laid it over and pressed it in. The fontanelle was closed, the shell of his head was complete. She ran her fingers gently over the entire surface feeling the contours of his skull and face then stood back leaning on the table behind to study it. The depth of the brow was right and his long cheeks. The smile looked eerie without eyes or nose. *You'll just have to wait, it's dinner time.* She dropped her tools into the sink, scraped and wiped the bench around him then ran his hessian shawl under the tap, wrung it out and carefully wrapped him up. When the tools were rinsed she returned them to their honey coloured pot and said 'ciao,' to the droopy dragon and cheery pots.

Outside she stretched and breathed in the cool air. Twilight blurred the garden, a first few stars brightened the darkening sky, too late for commuter trains, all was quiet. She felt at peace, satisfied with her day's work. Silky fur wreathed around her legs, 'Burrichio,' she murmured. Yellow eyes stared from the top of the water butt. 'Yes Baffina, I'll feed you,' she said and fetched the pan of food, filled their bowls and stroked their backs looking down the garden for Tancreda. *She must have fed herself today.*

Oriana collected wood for the fire and went inside to make pesto and linguine then settled down with a glass of wine, her book and Paganini. Enveloped in the armchair and warmed by the fire it wasn't long before she fell asleep, a deep sleep uninterrupted by the settling of the fire or prowling cats until the insistent drilling of the phone dragged her to semi –consciousness; cold, confused, she stumbled over her book and groped her way into the hall.

'Ciao?' She said, her voice throaty with sleep.

'Mama?'

Alarm spiked her palms. 'Lucia?'

'Si, mama.'

'What time is it?' Her mind groped toward reality.

'Early. Emilio called.'

'Emilio?'

'Sorry, mama, it's bad news.'

Oriana bent over the phone. 'What is it, Lucia? What's happened?'

'It's Caterina, mama, she's dead.'

'Dead?'

The word plummeted through her. Lucia's voice at the end of the phone continued. Vaguely she heard, 'pills', realised that Lucia was describing suicide – *gentle, loving, religious Caterina?*

'Mama?' Lucia's voice called her back. 'Are you all right?'

'Sorry, Lucia.' She paused. 'It's hard to take in.'

'Yes.'

'Thank you for phoning Lucia and for being there for Emilio.'

'Always. The bell for matins, I must go. I'll pray for Caterina.'

'She needs your prayers,' Oriana whispered. 'Arrivederci.'

'Arrivederci.

Oriana stood in the middle of the hall shocked then guilty. *Why didn't I realise? Two weeks ago we were sipping Kir under the walnut tree chatting.*

Why didn't you say? What was so terrible? We let you down, you left your family in Puglia to come to us and we let you down. She re -ran the conversation and went over the day searching for clues. Finally she climbed the stairs, heavy and stiff from cold to wash and change her clothes her head full of Caterina, trying to come to terms with the great rupture in their lives, *You were so full of fun, so clever, how could it come to this? You had the measure of all of us – deflating Emilio's pomposity, Maria's timidity, Isabella's great mama excesses, even Lucia's saintliness, no one was exempt – Angelo's gullibility and my 'slap a meal together without a care then obsess about clay or stone – teasing and laughing, your laugh – light and bubbly, sometimes a naughty chuckle –it's been a long time since I heard it. What happened?*

The little piece of paper where Caterina had written their new address was vital now, doubly precious. She found her bag and took it from the pocket. It still smelt faintly of Caterina's perfume. It would lead her to Emilio in his hour of need.

Glad to be behind the wheel she drove hard down the valley into the foothills, followed the map, passing through sprawling suburbs of waking houses finally a couple of villages with bikes and cars jostling to get to school or work and the clatter of doors and shutters opening and veggies being stacked outside shops. She drove out into the countryside passing the occasional farmstead then wound up past vineyards which gave way to olive groves. The road skirted a wood and forked on the far side. She took the offshoot lane between poplar trees leading to a dead end; a high, white wall with tall, dense cypresses behind. There was a big, ornate gate with a control panel beside it. She got out of the car and spoke into the grille. The gates slowly opened inwards, two dogs, tethered on the lawn, launched into a frenzy of barking as she drove past.

Emilio was standing at the top of wide, stone steps.

'Mama.'

'Emilio.'

Briefly his eyes met hers. She hurried up the steps to hug him but he was too high and turned away as she reached the top. She followed him into the cavernous entrance hall. Finally he faced her shaking his head, 'God knows why now...?'

'It's terrible. I know, son.' Oriana took hold of his hand. 'Try not to think too much. Have you had any sleep?'

He withdrew his hand and turned to a door saying, 'the doctor gave me a sleeping pill.'

The drawing room was dark, cold, still. Heavy mirrors reflected steely light onto dark, carved furniture. Emilio crossed to open the shutters and sunlight blinded Oriana.

'Sit down,' he said.

Disorientated, she sat in the middle of the sofa.

'I'm so sorry son,' she said. 'Is there anything I can do?'

He was standing in front of the window so she could only see his silhouette.

'There's nothing anyone can do.'

Oriana was tense, sitting drawn in tight, shrunk by the size of the room and the sofa, watching him.

'Have her family been told?' She asked.

He nodded and sank into an armchair, 'mother and sisters.'

'I thought she had a brother.'

'He's in Canada.'

'What's going to happen?'

'Funeral's on Friday.' He took a cigarette from a silver case and lit it.

'There's a crematorium nearby?'

'The village church.'

He exhaled a line of white smoke. Surprised, embarrassed, Oriana moved to the edge of her seat, leaning conspiratorially towards him.

'Burial?'

'Why not?'

'Consecrated ground, a priest?'

He nodded. 'You're behind the times, mama, there are ways round that sort of thing.'

This was a world she didn't recognise but Caterina in sanctified ground seemed more appropriate, kinder to her family. *If Emilio can move the boundaries of purgatory, so be it.*

'I'm glad, it's a comfort for you – for us all.'

He nodded.

'May I say 'goodbye'? Pay my last respects?' She said standing up.

Emilio looked at her sharply then sat on the edge of his chair to crush his cigarette slowly, deliberately into an ashtray, a nerve pulsed at the side of his eye.

He stood and looked into her face – handsome, faded, heavy with sadness, guileless –of course she would want to see Caterina, why hadn't he thought of that?

'Follow me,' he said then marched across the room and through the hall.

He mounted the stairs so rapidly that Oriana trotted to keep up. The sweeping marble stairs gave way to a wide galleried landing with several doors. He passed two, opened the next and stood aside to let her enter. It was lit by candles, Oriana hesitated, Emilio said, 'I'll leave you to it.'

The door clicked behind her, the flames flickered and settled back to a deep calm. Caterina was dressed in a black dress, stockings and shoes. *She's dressed for a funeral.* Oriana's throat swelled and there was a pain in her chest. Caterina's little black figure was dwarfed by the expanse of white bed. *You look so small, so far away, why couldn't I reach you? Why couldn't I help? I would,*

I would have moved heaven and earth to prevent this. You had your whole life ahead of you. Caterina's eyes were closed, her child's mouth clamped down at the sides. Oriana stroked silky hair from her forehead and longed to kiss away the little frown. 'I am sorry,' she whispered, 'so sorry.'

She turned to the dressing table where there was a photo of the three sisters, arms entwined, Caterina on the left, hair blown by the wind, laughing at the photographer. Beside it in a silver frame was her wedding photo. Her hair was swept off her face in a crown of pearls. Her white lace dress hugged her neck and arms and pinched her tiny waist. Emilio was holding her hands and looking at her full of pride. He looked like a film star in his silver silk suit, yellow tie and matching rose.

Oriana remembered the day, the excitement, the cold; December, running from church to reception down cobbled streets in red stiletto heels. The gilded room with ruby chandeliers and mirrors all around so she could see Emilio wherever he was, the perfect host and Caterina playing with the children laughing, her dress billowing round the tables. The two of them dancing, looking into each other's eyes, a fairy tale romance.

The elation was still on his face when he came to fetch his mother for a dance. Oh the pride! She felt as if her chest would burst as he led her onto the floor in her red silk dress – her boy, her perfect creation, flying high and Dario, immaculate in his evening suit, proudly introducing Emilio to all his wealthy business friends – how happy they were – Caterina too, all smiles and laughter. She turned to the lonely figure on the bed, 'I love you, little one,' she whispered tears running down her cheeks.

Oriana sat on the stool in front of the mirror to look for tissues and opened a drawer. It was full of Caterina's underwear. She crept to the wardrobe and opened the door an inch or two, in the gloom, she made out dresses, skirts and blouses with ranks of shoes beneath, all women's. She turned to the figure isolated on the bed, withdrawn, beyond pain she hoped, beyond loneliness and sorrow.

Emilio tapped on the door. Oriana jumped. 'Have you finished, mama?'

Quickly she brushed the back of Caterina's hand with hers and whispered, 'Goodbye.'

Then she turned guiltily to Emilio as he came round the door. He didn't look at the bed. With head bowed she left the room. Their feet echoed on the marble stairs.

Coffee was waiting in the drawing room, Oriana watched him pour paying careful attention, not saying a word. She moved forward to take her cup longing to touch him, to give him some comfort.

'Thank you,' she murmured.

He sat by the window and watched her over his cup noticing the redness of her eyes, the moisture on her cheeks.

'She looks so tiny,' Oriana said looking up. His face was pale. He was tense. 'You shouldn't be alone,' she said.

'I'm all right, mama, don't worry about me.'

She wondered at his calm then thought it was too soon for it to have sunk in.

'It's not as much of a shock as you think,' he continued, 'We've been battling this for a while.'

'What do you mean?'

'She'd been depressed for a long time.'

'Depressed?' Oriana put her cup down, surprised. Caterina had always been full of fun, close to her mother and sisters, proud to be married to Emilio, quiet of late, but she was always so positive, she wasn't a depressive personality.

Emilio shook his head in despair. 'The doctor prescribed pills but she wouldn't take them.' He took a cigarette from his case and lit it.

'Did she talk about it?' She asked.

He inhaled deeply shaking his head then blew out smoke saying. 'I can't understand it. She had more than most women, a beautiful home, clothes, jewellery, perfume.' He sat forward, animated for the first time, 'She could have anything she wanted. Nothing pleased her.'

'I'm sorry, Emilio.'

He relaxed back into his chair.

'You have no idea?' Oriana asked.

'What man can get into a woman's mind especially Caterina's?' He looked her fiercely in the eyes, clenching his jaw.

She leant towards him, 'It's been hard, I didn't realise... Let me look after you.' Emilio stiffened, 'I'm fine, mama.'

'I can help with the funeral.'

'There's nothing to do, it's all organised.'

A phone burred in his pocket. He pulled it out, 'Signor Rossi.'

He jumped up, anxious, listening, signalled his departure to her and left the room. Dwarfed by its grandeur and ill at ease, Oriana caught snatches of the conversation, 'I thought it was safe,' 'they're on to me...' 'throw the case'...' discredit...'

He returned, closed the double doors behind him and smiled apologetically. He lifted his shoulders and spread his arms.

'Sorry, mama, can't stop the wheels from turning.'

'As if you've not enough to worry about.' She went over to him.

'Sometimes it's better to have things to occupy the mind.'

Oriana put her hand on his arm and looked into his face. 'I suppose that's true,' she said.

'Don't worry, mama. It'll be better once the funeral's over.'

She put her arms around him. He kissed her forehead. The prospect of all the dutiful ceremonies awaiting him in the week ahead was depressing.

'I'm here if you need me,' Oriana said.

She wanted to reassure him, wished she could cross the gulf widening between them but decided it was his defence mechanism.

'I know, thank you, mama.'

He took her to the car and watched her off the premises, past the barking dogs, through the gates, down the lane between the trees thinking that the machine had been set in motion and would continue to its end.

15

On the journey home Oriana vacillated between admiration for Emilio's fortitude and pity for Caterina's suffering. Beneath it all there was a deep unease that seemed to stem from the house itself – its seclusion, the walls, gates, dogs – it was more like a fortress than a home. Inside, in spite of all the furniture and mirrors, it felt empty and Emilio seemed removed, distant. *What can you expect? He's just lost his wife.'* She crouched over the steering wheel. *I thought we'd share our sorrow, even weep together, I wanted to help him pick up the pieces and carry on.* Instead she was on her way home with a head full of contradictions and a heavy heart.

Her own ragged house was as welcome as an old sweater but it couldn't relieve her misery. She wanted to wind back the clock, sit by Caterina's side, watch and listen, uncover the secret sorrow and resolve it. *I could have helped, I could have prevented it. It didn't need to be this way.* Depression? Images of Caterina playing tag with the twins and Pietro came back – laughing as she ran, grabbing and giving no quarter, teasing Maria for coming from behind the hen house to say 'I'm here' in a game of hide and seek because she was afraid of being forgotten, Caterina returning wet and muddy from the river after a day catching fish and water beetles with Pietro.

Grief closed in on her. It was no good thinking, she had to escape her thoughts, tired though she was, she had to move, do something, like an animal that paces to numb the pain of imprisonment. She wandered around the house then stood in the kitchen too sick to eat. Out in the garden the branches of the persimmon tree hung heavy with red and yellow fruit alive with flies and wasps. She couldn't let it go to waste.

She changed into old jeans and jumper, pulled some cardboard boxes and a big cloth bag out of the pantry. Outside she put on her boots, dragged the ladder from beside the shed and propped it against the tree. The image of Caterina marooned on the bed came back. She stopped for a moment and made herself focus on looking for fruit among the sparse yellow leaves and dark knobbly branches. There was a yellow persimmon beside her. It was warm in her hand as she twisted it free and placed it in the bag hanging from her neck and another below it, smaller firmer.

She climbed higher up the ladder pushing her way through branches into the heart of the tree. They swung back around her like the bars of a prison. Emilio's face, jaw clenched in anger, appeared in her head. The ladder wobbled, she held on. Above her head, at the sunny top of the tree, hung several deep red fruits. She reached up. The first was safely lowered into her bag then another and another. She smelt their sweetness. The bag was getting full. She could hear Emilio's voice on the phone, 'safe place?' 'They're on to me.' What was it all about? 'Throw the case?' He wouldn't do that. Gingerly she moved the bag round onto her back, bracing her knees against the rungs, hands free she pushed away a whippy branch, its frail arrow leaves quivering as she backed down to the ground. In her mind's eye she saw the heavy gates slowly closing behind her and heard the shrill barking of the dogs. *That house was too isolated for Caterina, not the sort of place for children. Couldn't she have children? They could have adopted, we would have helped, we'll never know – no goodbyes, no note – you took your secret with you.* Heavy and weary though she was work was her only way through. She forced herself back to the task, sorted the fruit into boxes of varying ripeness; red, orange, and yellowy green then took the ladder to the other side of the tree and gathered the rest, quickly, urgently until she had filled six boxes, half of which she loaded into the wheel barrow and took to the garden shed. Finally she counted what was left, 'One for Dino and Rinatta, one for Isabella and Paolo and one for the convent.'

The cool of the patio was a relief but its sombre shade sent her back to her Caterina alive, in need of help and nobody able to see it and the photo of three girls – arms around each other – innocent, carefree –*how could I have been so ignorant?*

16

There was wind on Friday morning cold, relentless, piercing wind. It flattened the chrysanthemums and swept Emilio's lilies from the top of the coffin. Rosa and Tommaso gathered them up and gave them to Caterina's mother who kept as close to Caterina as she could, weeping quietly, incessantly. When the priest led the coffin down the aisle she followed and tenderly replaced the lilies, then stood by the coffin unable to leave Caterina's side until her other daughters led her into a pew. Emilio followed the coffin and stepped into an empty front pew on the opposite side. He looked so alone Oriana wanted to join him but it was too late, she stayed by Lucia's side and hoped that Angelo would fill the gap but he arrived at the last minute and slipped into a back pew. Behind her she heard Isabella whisper to Pietro, 'We think about Aunt Caterina's time with us', there was a rustle of paper and hymn books opening. The solemnity of the words, their ringing hopefulness was a comfort whether she believed it or not, reaching blindly beyond was better than staring into the grim present. There was no eulogy, no personal words to bring Caterina and all that was special about her back to them. Oriana felt the omission, especially for Caterina's family. *I should have done it, why didn't I think of it? Emilio said it was all organised.*

Finally the bearers turned the coffin to face the porch and the priest led her out followed by Emilio, hands clasped behind his back and Caterina's mother, supported by her daughters who looked stunned themselves, fighting back their grief for the sake of their mother. As the coffin approached their pews Oriana heard little Maria sob and Paolo cough, she bit her lip and joined the procession out into the cruel wind to the far edge of the graveyard where the ground sloped up to a stone wall under trees. The coats of the bearers beat against their legs. Caterina's family huddled in front of the wall. On the opposite side of the grave, behind the coffin, Oriana and family assembled. Oriana didn't like the artificial separation of their two families so she went to Caterina's mother, touched her shoulder and, when she turned surprised, Oriana took her hand and said, 'I am sorry. She was a beautiful person. We all loved her.' The words rang hollow. The distraught woman searched Oriana's face then gasped, 'Thank you' then folded back down into her grief. Oriana turned to the sisters who were watching, pale, distracted, 'I am sorry, we shall miss her.' Unable to speak they nodded. Emilio stood at the top of the grave staring blankly into its depths. She ran her hand down his arm as she passed on her way back to Lucia. He turned listlessly to her then back again.

As the coffin was lowered into the depths ineffable sadness swelled Oriana's chest and tears burned her eyes. Emilio threw dry earth that spread as dust in the wind and the twins and Pietro each threw a rose. The priest pronounced the last 'amen' and the dark still figures were set in motion stiffly, quietly picking their way through the graveyard. Angelo came to Oriana, slipped his arm around her shoulder and gave it a squeeze. She looked gratefully up at him over her handkerchief.

'Let's go mama.' Lucia put her arm through her mother's.

Angelo ran to ward off the cold. Oriana saw the hunched figure of Caterina's mother picking her way between the headstones with their faded plastic flowers and engraved marble plaques followed by her daughters and their husbands. She wished that Emilio would speak to her, offer some shred of comfort but he was walking briskly, hands in pockets, in pursuit of Angelo.

Lucia joined Isabella and the family at the cemetery gate and Oriana walked along the road looking for Angelo. He was standing by Emilio's car talking to him intensely. She caught snatches of their conversation.

'They won't leave me alone.' Angelo protested.

'So...' Emilio spread his arms.

'Can't do it.' Angelo sounded desperate.

'There's no walking away.'

Through clenched teeth Angelo snapped, 'Enough.'
Emilio shrugged, saw Oriana and said urgently, 'I'm out of action for a while, don't tell anyone my new address.'
Angelo nodded. Emilio got into his car and started the engine. Oriana joined Angelo as the car edged into the road. She watched the Ferrari turn the corner and asked, 'You and Emilio weren't quarrelling were you?'
        'No, mama, it's nothing.'
He turned his back to the wind and pulled up his collar. His lips were blue.
        'I hope not.' She put her arm around his hunched shoulders and said brightly, 'we'd better get you warm.'
        'I'm not going back to Emilio's.'
        'I don't think many people are, I'll drop you at the station.'

17

        Oriana closed her book slid it onto the bedside table and massaged her eyes. The Madonna and child made her think of Emilio alone in his empty castle. She hadn't heard from him since the funeral weeks ago. *What a long shadow Caterina's loss has cast.* Guilt and Winter weather had driven them all into their corners, even Angelo, which surprised her, she thought he would be relieved at paying off some of his debt getting the blood suckers off his back but she had only seen him twice and he wasn't the old Angelo. He brought flowers with his washing but he didn't tease her or loll in his chair chatting over coffee. He didn't peer over her shoulder while she was cooking asking, 'what is it mama?' He said nothing about his job or the flat he was so proud of or girls and he didn't look her in the eyes. It wasn't like Angelo to hide anything, he had always told her everything, sometimes surprising her with the extent of intimate detail. The snatches of hurried conversation with Emilio after the funeral haunted her.
        I can ask Isabella tomorrow if she's heard anything, see what she thinks. She'll probably tell me to stop worrying.
        Isabella had only seen him once as well although he was usually forever popping in to see what was going on as he said. She had noticed a difference too, he wasn't his old devil may care self. 'He was thoughtful, asked me if I was happy, what Paolo and I wanted for the future. 'Don't worry, mama, he's probably growing up at last,' she said, perhaps he'll go back to University, he's got too good a brain to be a waiter.'
        'He can't afford University,' Oriana replied grimly, 'and neither can I. I am surprised at how little Dario left but I have the house and that's the main thing but if University is what he wants then I'll have to find a way to help. It's what I always wanted for him.'

'We mustn't jump to conclusions, we don't know what's going on in his head,' said Isabella.

'Lucia didn't mention him in her letter either and they're thick as thieves, he tells her everything.'

'Probably means there's nothing to worry about then. Angelo's not the only one who's become a hermit, we haven't seen anything of Emilio since the funeral.'

'No, he's cut himself off, his way of dealing with grief I suppose. I don't know what's happening with my sons, they seem to have forgotten where they come from.'

'You can't expect too much, mama, they're city slickers and we're quiet country folk.'

'They can have their excitement, it doesn't mean they're not part of the family or that we don't worry about them.'

'They'll turn up when they need us.'

'Will they ever need me again I ask myself. Emilio hasn't been answering the 'phone, he seems to have dropped off the face of the earth.'

'It doesn't stop him being mentioned everyday on the television or radio.'

'The Ricci case?'

Isabella nodded.

'I know he's busy but he must need someone to talk to sometimes, I worry about him. His reaction to Catherina's death wasn't normal,' said Oriana

'What do you mean?'

'He was in denial, it was as if he couldn't take it in. He was so abstracted. We all react to grief in different ways, it must be the shock.'

'I suppose, but he's had time now and it's obviously not interfering with his work. I'm sorry, mama, but I think you're a softie with Emilio, he's selfish, it's all money and power for him.'

'He's ambitious but that doesn't mean he's hard, he cares.'

'About who or what?'

'All of us, he loved his father, he loves his family.'

'There isn't much evidence of that.'

'Emilio would do anything for you.'

'But it always ends up us doing things for Emilio.'

The door scraped over the tiles and Paolo kicked off his boots and left them by the door. He took off his hat and scratched his head.

'Talking about Emilio?' He asked.

'How did you guess?' replied Isabella.

'I must speak to him. We need the shed next week, we start harvesting Monday.'

'Should I invite him to lunch on Sunday?' asked Isabella, 'that'll stop you worrying mama.'

'Thank you, what has he got in there?' Asked Oriana.

'Not much, I think it's just a couple of boxes,' said Isabella.

'Couple of boxes?' Replied Paolo. 'There are three stacks and some are heavy as hell, I don't know what it's all about but it's certainly not just papers.'

'What on earth?' Oriana looked at Paolo, 'What is he up to?'

'It's not him, he says it's a favour for contacts he has, we're getting a decent rent but it's got to be cleared in the next few days,' said Paolo filling the kettle.

'Why don't we see if Angelo can help move it?' Oriana suggested.

Isabella looked at her mother's worried face.

'Is that ok Paolo?'

'Hummm, it'll take more than the three of us but it's a start. If they can come.'

'Leave it to me,' said Oriana.

18

As Emilio descended into the valley he couldn't resist squeezing the accelerator, the Ferrari sucked in the miles to the other side of Milan then turned back into the hills until he was nudging up the drive to the farmhouse. He winced as he splashed through a thick puddle of muck. Old Ulysses waddled stiffly from the barn with a growl then wagged his stump of a tail while Emilio patted his head looking around the buildings and over to the olive shed. He heard banging and voices. Alarmed, he ran in that direction.

'You haven't moved anything have you?' He asked abruptly.

'Emilio, benvenuto, come stai?' Paolo came forward hand outstretched.

'Bene, bene, grazie,' he said quickly checking the stacked boxes over Paolo's shoulder. 'Ciao Tommaso. Leave it to me, Paolo, leave it to me,' he said waving his hand toward the stack.

'No problem, Emilio, we're making room for the bottles, moving things round a bit.'

'I'll do that,' said Emilio, putting his shoulder to a pile that Paolo and Tommaso were about to lift.

'No, no, you're not dressed for it. You go and say 'Hello' to Isabella and your mother. They're waiting for you.'

'Where do you want them?' Said Emilio.

'We're going to stack them in the far corner for now but we'll need that space too soon enough.' Paolo signalled to Tommaso to grab the other end of a long box.

'No!' shouted Emilio. They stopped, surprised by the shrillness of his shout.

'They'll fall, spill out, get spoiled – they've been paid for. I'll move them.'

'No point doing it yourself when there are three of us. Come on.' Paolo bent over the box again and Tommaso braced himself at the other end.

'Put it down, leave it to me,' Emilio tried to control his voice. ' Leave it to me, you've got plenty to do.' He tried to smile.

'I don't know what you've got in there but they weigh a ton, you'll never manage that alone.'

Emilio took off his jacket and flung it onto the bench. 'Little by little, you'd be surprised how strong I am,' he said trying very hard to sound reasonable.

'It'll take forever.' said Paolo, frustrated.

'It's not far to carry them, you carry on.'

'Okay then,' said Paolo signalling to Tommaso to let go his hold, 'you can use the sack truck, it's by the cow shed. I'm going to hitch up the trailer. Come on Tommaso.'

Emilio watched until they disappeared down the alleyway to the machine shed then fetched the sack truck and started. One by one he staggered under the weight of the long, heavy boxes lifting them onto the narrow ledge of the sack truck and wheeling them into the corner. He told himself to bend his knees to lift but after the first half dozen his shoulders and back were hurting. He collapsed a couple of times but determination and desperation gave him strength.

The higher he had to stack them the harder it got until his arms began to shake uncontrollably and a box slid back down the pile hitting the ground and spilling out the butt of a rifle. He rammed it back and closed the top but it wasn't secure, he looked on Paolo's bench for tape, anything to fasten it with but there was nothing. He toured the shed in desperation and found a tangle of baling cord in a pile of hay, scooped it up and wound it round the box from end to end and round the middle in a panic.

Finally he returned it to the top of the pile and faced the last three cartons. Only iron will forced them into place with every muscle in his arms and shoulders quivering. He reminded himself of miracles where women lifted cars to get children clear and kept repeating to himself, 'I can do it, I can do it.'

It was done, the longer boxes stacked high didn't take up much room in the corner, perhaps they could stay there a little longer, give him more time to find a better place. As he left the barn he ran his hand tenderly over the smaller stack of assorted boxes hidden under the window then dusted off his trousers and picked up his jacket before crossing the yard to the kitchen.

'Emilio! About time!'

Isabella threw her arms around him and gave him a hug. He panted into her hair looking at Oriana over her shoulder.

'Mama.'

Oriana kissed his sweaty forehead. ' You're out of breath, what have you been up to?'

'Nothing, nothing much, just moving a few boxes.'

'You need to keep fit.'

'I'm fit enough for what I have to do.'

'It doesn't look like it,' said Isabella looking at his red, sweaty face. How are you?' Oriana asked.

'Busy, mama, always busy. There's a lot happening at the moment.'

'How's the Ricci case going?' Asked Isabella.

'Difficult, too many vested interests, muddies the waters, don't know which way to turn.'

'Tell us about it,' said Oriana sitting at the table with him.

'I can't.'

He saw her disappointment.

'Sorry mama, it's all 'sub-judice.' He turned to his sister.' Angelo not coming?'

Isabella shook her head.

'Have you heard from him?' Oriana asked.

'Not since the funeral.'

'You weren't having words were you?'

'Giving him a bit of advice but Angelo's stubborn, he doesn't know how to get on in the world.'

'Angelo's got a good heart, he'll find his way without our help,' said Isabella.

'Are you sure you won't stay for lunch?' Oriana asked Emilio. 'You have to eat. I bet you're not looking after yourself.'

'Food's not a problem Mama, I get by, don't worry.' He looked at Isabella, 'sorry sis, too much on at the moment, thanks for the invitation – another time maybe.' He spotted Paolo and Tommaso crossing the yard, put down his cup and stood aware of the stiffening in his legs and shoulders.

'I must be off, thanks for the invitation Isabella, another time…'

'Ciao brother.'

'Ciao mama.'

He bent to kiss Oriana's forehead watching their approach through the window.

''Bye son, look after yourself.'

Outside the door they heard him greeting Paolo and Tommaso.

'It's all stacked, there's plenty of room in the shed,' he said.

'For now but it'll have to go before the end of the month.'

'I'll see to it, ciao, ciao Tommaso.'

19

The 'phone burred and burred while Oriana watched the second hand tick around the yellowing dial of her grandfather clock.

Come on Angelo.

The phone cut out, no answer phone message, nothing.

He's probably asleep. Well, it's time I saw his new flat. I could take some work in to Francesco, it's time I put myself back on the scene.

In her studio she carefully selected pieces from the shelves: a pitcher with an elegant handle, a couple of round friendly jugs, a collection of small bowls each with a different pattern and colour and three platters: cream with classic burgundy scrolls one with squares of colour and lines like Mondrian and a textured pot of different coloured glazes melting into each other. *Something for everyone I hope and cash for Angelo.*

Oriana dressed carefully trying to look business like as much to give herself confidence as to make the right impression. She was afraid that she had been forgotten, that her reception would be lukewarm, her work tactfully rejected. She loaded the car and drove straight to Il Monnier, Francesco's gallery, parked, leapt out and ran through the door before she could lose her nerve.

'Oriana!' Francesco's face lit up. He was still the same Francesco; immaculate, just short of flamboyant, in a turquoise jacket, dark blue trousers and shirt with a yellow tie.

'You look wonderful,' she said.

He came from behind the counter to embrace her, 'too long, too long, thought I'd never see you again.'

'I'm sorry I got lost in a mist, am I forgiven?'

'You lost your love we understood but it has been hard, you have a following.'

'In my dreams.'

'You don't know what you're worth, your work has flair, people see the difference, they want to own it so when are we going to get some more?'

'I brought a few bits for you to have a look at.'

He rubbed his hands together, 'what are we waiting for? '

He followed her to the car and they each carried a cardboard box into the gallery. Francesco delved into the paper wrappings and pulled out piece after piece.

'These are perfect,' he said arranging jugs and pitchers on the counter and spreading bowls in a circle on the floor, 'manna from heaven, splendid, they'll walk out.'

Finally he uncovered the platters. 'Oriana where have you been hiding these? They're superb, you keep pushing back the barriers, these are different, we've got you back full time now haven't we?'

Oriana's chest swelled with relief and gratitude, she laughed, 'I need to keep the wolf from the door.'

'These'll fetch more than a few euros, thank you for remembering me.'

'Thank you for understanding.'

'Ah, artists, I'm used to them.'

'Thank goodness. I'm on way to see Angelo.'

'How are the family?'

'Isabella had another boy.'

'Congratulations – six?'

Oriana nodded, 'no more. How's Fabrizio?'

'Still the same pretending to paint but he's a wonderful cook so why should I complain?'

'He's more than that and you know it.'

Francesco smiled, 'you'll have to come for supper, I'll get him to give you a ring.'

'I'd like that I've been out of circulation so long I've almost forgotten what it's like. You two are good company.'

She checked her watch – past eleven, 'I must go, have a good day, ciao.'

She left the gallery heady with excitement and took a tram to Cadorna rumbling past rows of shops, squares surrounded by cars and concrete playgrounds where young mothers sat chatting on benches. Oriana got out at cluttered old Domodosola and changed to a bus. Via Varesina was wide a main road with high old buildings on either side and a strange mix of shops at pavement level – an Asian grocers, computer repair shop, estate agents, baker's, a restaurant with a striped canopy and a bar on the corner with workmen drinking beer. Behind ornate cast iron railings a once noble municipal building succumbed to neglect and abandonment assailed by its own jungle of weeds. There was no planning here, just random development, each building looked of a different era to its neighbour, only their decay drew them together.

A group of men, young and old hung around the entrance of a tobacco shop which sold tickets for the buses and lottery. It was next to a Spar grocer's and just past that there was a big apartment block with patchy stucco walls and a heavy faded wooden door. It had once been imposing with its moulded panels but that was long ago, 80 Via Varesina. She had found Angelo. The names of residents were typed on paper behind plastic in a box beside the entrance, some had curled up others were faded. Angelo's was new, A. P. Rossi, flat 62. She pressed the button and waited looking along the pavement to a pile of rubbish – armchairs and lamps, a television and rugs dumped outside an empty building. She pressed again, no reply. *Perhaps the bell doesn't work.* A couple with a little boy arrived, said 'ciao' and opened the door for her. They crowded into a small metal lift that shook its way up one floor then Oriana climbed stone stairs checking numbers at each exit.

The flats were arranged in a square around a courtyard emitting a loud screeching noise. She looked over the railings to find where it was coming from. There was a tyre workshop at the back. The courtyard held nothing more than a washing line, some gas canisters and a pushchair; no plants, grass, trees or water. It led to a dark alley full of bins. *He was pleased with this? Independence I suppose – the first time he didn't have to share. I know he hasn't got much money but this is awful, couldn't he find anything better?* Number 62 was on the other side of the square. In the corner there was a broken water fountain full of spiders' webs. The ceiling lights were old and one was cracked. *Why doesn't anyone look after this place? How does that family cope here?* Number 62 was at the end of the corridor without any windows that she could see. Oriana knocked on the door, no response, she put her ear to it, not a sound. She dialled his mobile and the answerphone cut in almost straight away, 'Ciao, Angelo here to say sorry I'm not, send greetings and I'll answer'. *Waste of time. I'll just have to catch him at work tonight.* She retraced her steps to the lift. The courtyard wasn't big, the number of doors floor upon floor and workshops below without much view of the sky or greenery made the place claustrophobic. She found his only window. It was tall with long nylon curtains. *Facing south, I hope he's got air conditioning, it'll be an oven in summer. I hope he's not here long.*

The oppressive place filled her with desolation. She stood on the pavement feeling lost. *Where is he? Am I going to see him today? I have to. It's no good I'm not going home until I've seen him.* She noticed a striped canopy further down on the other side of the road, *a restaurant.* She crossed and read the name, *Trattoria Vittoria, I've heard of that, it's good.* She checked her watch, *they'll still be serving lunch.* The place looked full but a bright young woman welcomed her in, showed her to a table and gave her a basket of peanuts. Oriana ordered water and a glass of Pratello and chose risotto Milanese. The atmosphere was warm and friendly, everyone was enjoying their meal and chatting happily. At the end of her meal the waitress put a selection of sweetie jars on the table.

'Thank you.' Oriana beamed at her grateful to be invited to the party but not the least bit tempted by the sugary treat.

In need of a green space she caught a bus to Sforza castle at Lanza. It took a while to park before she could cross the bridge over the deep grassy moat and walk between its great stone towers into the park. The wind was shaking mottled leaves from trees sprinkling the grass all around and the sun was hidden behind a cloud. She pulled her coat collar up round her neck and walked past trees to the lake. Ducks and geese swam desultorily around the reeds at the margin and sparrows darted through bushes. Oriana sat on a bench listening to the sounds of the park – footsteps on paths, mothers calling children, men talking volubly, women in slick suits and noisy boots strutting purposefully alone or in jeans and anoraks in deep conversation. There were more people than she expected. She watched them in circles holding bikes laughing together, with brief cases or mobile phones preoccupied. *Where are they going? What kind of lives do they lead? What do they do? What makes them happy? We don't stop to question what it's all about we just get on with it – wasting time? Are we programmed? Following our destinies like the Greeks believed or should we jib at life's dictates? Action and reaction is that what it amounts to? I can't not worry about my children, I feel compelled to sculpt, we respond to pressures from within, adapt, compromise. At root we all feel the same sadness at life's imperfections, our imperfections – glossy media smiles designed to hide it make it worse – they isolate, make us feel we are losing the competition. We 'd do better to share our humanity, our doubts, then at least we can reassure each other.* The breaks in the clouds grew fewer, the wind did not let up. Her shoulders were clenched against the cold. *I'd better get back to the centre.*

Piazza Duomo was a hive of people criss-crossing, cycling, calling to each other, workers on scaffolding around the cathedral, council workers tidying the streets. *Pity they don't go round via Varesina like that but poor neighbourhoods don't attract tourists and money. They serve them though, without their work this 'beautiful' machine wouldn't turn its tricks. They deserve the same quality of life.*

Oriana avoided the luxury of Victor Emmanuelle shopping arcade and left the main square to find smaller shops looking for things for the children. In search of something for Rosa she criss-crossed the backstreets until she found a boutique for teenagers with lots of big, soft scarves. She chose a fluffy brown and beige one with specks of orange. *That'll match her warm brown eyes.* She headed back to the centre and bought a sketch pad for Pietro and an engineering book for Tommaso on the way. *The twins, they're so different but I can't be seen to discriminate – chocolate.* The shop was suffused with the rich bitter smell of chocolate and cellophane. Oriana was the last customer. There was nowhere warm to shelter now that closing time had come. It was getting dark, lights began to twinkle along the road. She stopped in a doorway and phoned Angelo again only to hear his disembodied voice chant the same cheery message.

What now? The canal and all the bars, that'll cheer me up. Porta Genova was a favourite spot with its markets, book shops and art galleries but she loved it most in the evening when the bars opened for 'happy hour' which included a buffet. She ordered a Margherita and sat at a table near a heater where she could see the boats on the canal. There was no movement on the waterway, the season was over but along its banks every evening was a holiday. The tables filled with carefree groups drinking and chatting helping themselves and relishing the food. The variety of the buffet was a marvel and everything was plentiful, Oriana helped herself to warm vegetable lasagne and sat enjoying the coloured lights along the quay and the sounds of happy voices. Darkness deepened Angelo might be on his way to work it was time to visit Andromeda.

The club looked just the same as her first visit, door closed, no sign of activity. She checked her watch and tried the door. It opened into a room of black walls lined with black leather sofas, she hesitated. A girl with a tea towel stuck in the back of her jeans like a tail was sweeping the floor, she turned.

'Buongiorno,' said Oriana, 'Can I speak to Angelo for a minute please?' The girl put down her broom and disappeared. The ceiling was studded with little lights and the occasional spotlight hanging from chrome scaffolding. *Cool, I suppose, no wonder Angelo preferred it to Contadini.'*

'Angelo Rossi?'

Oriana jumped, the voice cut down from above, echoing icily around her from the top of a spiral staircase in the far corner, she put her hand to her eyes to block a spotlight and peer up.

'Si.'

'Who is looking for Angelo?'

'Is he here?'

'That depends.'

'On what?'

'Who you are.'

'His mother.'

The silhouetted head moved slowly from side to side as the figure descended the stair. 'I'm afraid we haven't seen him for over a week, we were hoping you might tell us his whereabouts.' There was a dangerous smell between ether and almonds about him, her head swam, he stopped on the third step. Oriana was staring into a striped satin waistcoat.

'I, I'm sorry to have troubled you,' she stammered recoiling from his proffered hand. There was an oppressive atmosphere about him. He came to stand before her, too close, seeming to tower over her although he wasn't much taller.

'Tell him his job is waiting,' he said putting his hands in his pockets, staring down into her eyes. *Eyes like a snake.* Oriana was transfixed, submitting helplessly to his scrutiny.

'Arriverderci,' he turned briskly on his heels and exited through a side door.

Released from the spell Oriana felt light, almost giddy with relief, she longed to get out of this subterranean world, to breathe clean air outside.

She stopped on the pavement and dialled Angelo's number again and was cut off. *I'll check his apartment again.*

A young man in jeans and black bomber jacket got off the bus at the same stop in Via Varesina and watched Oriana cross the road. He lit a cigarette and leant against a wall on the opposite side looking at her. She felt uneasy as she rang the bell again and again without answer. *Is he following me? Why doesn't he talk instead of staring? Why isn't Angelo answering?* He crossed the road and walked away. *I'm getting paranoid, who's going to follow me?* But the paranoia returned when she saw him queuing by a ticket machine at the station. *I'm glad I've got my ticket, he won't know where I'm going.* The platform filled with people and she lost sight of him as they entered separate carriages. The people on the train all looked reassuringly ordinary and there was no sign of the leather bomber jacket. *I don't know why I'm so jittery, it's the frustration of not finding Angelo and it's late, I'm tired, that was silly.*

It was a relief to peer through the dark to her scruffy old house from the top of the stairs at her station. She felt its presence rather than seeing it so she missed the nose of the faded green car jutting out of the underpass.

20

The convent was enclosed by a high stonewall. It stood on a plateau of uncultivated land stretching as far as the eye could see. Oriana drove along a stony track flanked by cypresses and parked on the grass by its heavy oak doors. She pulled at a long chain and a bell rang deep and soulful on the other side before fading into silence. Three donkeys in a paddock on the other side of the track briefly raised their heads to stare patiently in her direction then returned to their pile of hay.

The door opened slowly and a tall girl in a novice's habit beckoned Oriana to follow. The wide gap between the girl's hem and her big feet in stiff leather sandals made Oriana smile. She was led to the cloister.

'Please wait here a moment.'

The central garden was split into four triangles by box hedging with a bay tree in each corner and a stone fountain in the middle. Oriana recognised rosemary, sage and thyme, camomile, mint and oregano and inhaled the smell of lavender from around the fountain. It combined with the gentle trickling of the water to calm and sooth Oriana. She felt the distance between this world and Milan and regretted her intrusion, regretted troubling Lucia. A door squeaked and Lucia approached looking concerned. Oriana's chest always swelled with conflicting emotions whenever she saw Lucia – pride, respect, almost awe for her calling and warm, overwhelming love intensified by a sense of loss.

'Mama? Are you all right? Is there something wrong?' They kissed.

'I'm fine, Carissima, It's Angelo, he's left his job, there's no sign of life at his flat and he's not answering his 'phone. No one's heard from him. Isabella thought you might have heard something.' Lucia slowly nodded her head, hesitated, looked at her mother's troubled face and said. 'He was here last week.'

'He came to see you? What has happened?'

'He asked me not to tell you.'

'It must be serious if he came all this way instead of writing. You must tell me, I've got to know. I'm out of my mind with worry.'

'I'm sorry mama, the situation is not good, he got involved with the mafia without realising it.'

'The mafia, mother of god defend us, how did that happen?'

'They lent him money to pay off his debts and when he couldn't pay them back they told him he could work it off as an errand boy. He delivered packets, collected cash and deposited it for them, odd jobs. When he found out and tried to pay them off they wouldn't let him go. He dug his heels in and they got nasty, threatened him and his family. He was frightened and didn't know what to do so he ran.'

'Oh my god, why didn't he come to me?'

'He didn't want to involve you.'

'Do you know where he is?'

'Hiding in the hills above Sienna in a stone barn at the farm of an old girl friend.'

'A barn?' groaned Oriana, 'I've got to see him. We've got to find a way out of this.'

'He begged me not to tell you, he wanted to keep you all out of it, he kept saying, 'you don't know what they're like.' And he was afraid you might lead them to him too.'

'So I was being watched,' Oriana stepped back, hand over her mouth. She looked into Lucia's eyes, 'I was followed near his apartment but I have to see him, find out what he's going to do. I can get things for him. Now I know, I can shake anyone off, I won't let myself be followed, I will be careful I promise. I'm not going to blunder straight in.'

'You must do what you have to, mama, remember they're clever and determined and there are lots of them and few of us.'

'But we're family and that's strength enough.'

21

Oriana waited for Sunday so Isabella could accompany her on the train to Sienna to make it look like a family outing. From Sienna Oriana took a taxi to a village some distance from the farm and walked, stopping and checking again and again.

The farm was quiet, a dog tethered in front of a shed barked a warning but no one came. Hens pecked around the yard, buckets, brushes and shovels were propped against walls as if work was only temporarily interrupted. Oriana rapped on the farmhouse door, no answer. She walked down through the buildings – hay barn, cowshed, feed store, machinery bay – no sound of activity just the snuffling of a few heifers in their stalls. She opened a gate to an exposed field and walked into the biting wind. The ground was dry and hard with cold. She followed a hedge climbing the hillside, came to some trees and skirted around over open ground.

There was a little stone barn in the next field with grass growing on its roof, nibbled planks for a door and boarded windows. She hurried toward it and pushed the door whispering intently, 'Angelo? Angelo?' The door dragged and shuddered over uneven ground.

Angelo rose wide eyed from a pallet of straw in the corner.

'Mama, what are you doing here?'

His face was covered in dark stubble and his hair stuck out like a crown of thorns. He was wearing a baggy grey sweater over a black polo neck jumper but he was shivering.

'I've been worried out of my mind,' she hissed, 'why didn't you answer your phone?'

He looked nervously through the gap of the open door to the white glare outside.

'They can tap a phone and I didn't want to involve you.'

'I'm your mother, I'm involved.'

'Did you come alone?' He asked.

'I left Isabella in Sienna.'

'Were you followed?'

'No I wasn't.'

'How do you know?'

'I detoured and watched, Lucia explained.'

'She shouldn't have told you where I was.'

'She had to, I was worried. I want to help.'

He sank to the floor and put his head in his hands. 'There's nothing you can do. I've been a fool.'

'No one died of that or the world'd be unpopulated. We can sort it out.'

He shook his head. 'I didn't know what I was doing, mama. I didn't know who they were. I didn't know what was in the packages. I thought they were daft paying me so much. I thought I was clever but I was delivering drugs, collecting money from brothels. I could go to jail but it's worse than that, I can identify them, they're hunting me.'

'What will they do?'

He rocked himself and held his head almost crying, 'I don't know, put me out of action, get rid of me. They think I'm a danger to them.'

'Can't you talk to them, promise not to identify them?'

'The only way they will trust me is if I'm in their pay and I don't want any part of it.'

'What about the police?'

'Police? Half of them are in their pay and I'm guilty too.'

'They wouldn't press charges if you gave evidence.'

'I don't want to give evidence. Don't you realise how many there are? They don't forget – favours or betrayal, everyone's called to account or it wouldn't work.'

'We must get you away from here, far away, new clothes, different name, you need the safety of a crowd, to get lost in another city without their connections until they give up, move on and forget.'

'Nowhere is far enough – there's mafia in every city.'

'But they are all different.'

'It's a family, mama, they stick together especially when they are threatened. I'm finished.'

'Oh Angelo it can't be as hopeless as that, you need time to think, you can't stay here or you'll be ill, at least let's get you somewhere civilised.'

'Yes, it's not fair on Veronica and her dad. I've been thinking I might try Florence they're not there. I can find a job there and hide.'

'That's a good idea. I brought what cash I could lay my hands on and some clothes.'

'Veronica will get things for me and help to disguise me. They've been very good to me here and her father.'

'Where are they?'

'It's Sunday market, they'll be back later.'

'I'll have to thank them some other time.'

Oriana pulled him into her arms and held him tight, 'remember the horrors of the night?' She laughed reminding him of his childhood nightmares and her rescue chant.

He smiled wanly and replied, 'in this circle demons don't bite.'

'Good bye jelly babe, take care, and remember it won't last forever. I know it's not easy but please let me know when you're leaving and that you're safe.'

'I promise, Mama, I'll get Veronica to phone you and I'll get a new mobile.'

'Let me have the number won't you?'

He nodded solemnly and she kissed his cold clammy forehead then made her way back over the rough ground not registering the midday change in the weather. The wind had dropped and the sky had cleared to bright blue. The sun was shining.

She felt cruelly alienated from the chattering birds and chirruping crickets as she walked down hill to the village. A woman passed with a large, floury round of crusty bread tucked under her arm and a bulging basket of vegetables draped with silver beet and carrot fronds. She was holding the hand of a toddler pulling at a bright blue clown balloon. Her daughter was carrying a carton of eggs and a white card box tied with pink ribbon. A bike passed with a caged hen tied on the back.

Of course it's Sunday lunchtime, family time, time to make the most of the last summer sun together. Oriana watched them, hailing each other, straddling the road to chat laden with the day's treats, as if she were the audience in a theatre. She knew how they felt, what it would be like but she didn't envy them, didn't feel excluded. It was another world, interesting, familiar but irrelevant. However it reminded her of what Isabella had sacrificed in accompanying her.

Isabella was nursing Giogio in the shade of a tree in the main square. Oriana cupped Isabella's chin in her hand, looked into her eyes and said, 'thank you.'

Paolo collected Isabella from the station in Milan and Oriana caught the train home, tired but satisfied that no matter how serious the situation there was a plan and she had been able to help. Crossing the little bridge across the railway line she recognised the green car bonnet protruding from the under pass and realised it wasn't innocent, her chin rose a little higher as she walked resolutely to her door.

Once inside she couldn't relax, couldn't read, her thoughts drowned music, she was too edgy for the cats to settle, she picked up tapestry but busy hands left her mind free to roam. Finally she sank into a hot bath with lavender oil and her knotted muscles began to unravel. Her bones ached with tension and her head felt heavy. *I'd better see Emilio, we can't carry on like this. He's a solicitor, if he can't help who can?*
***

When Oriana turned her little red fiat into the poplar lane a big silver saloon was approaching on the other side with four smart middle-aged men talking earnestly. Their heads turned as she passed.

At the gates she spoke into the intercom, 'Emilio, open the gates please.'

'Mama? What are you doing here?'

'I've come to see you.'

'Why didn't you 'phone? It's not a good time, mama, now is not a good time.'

'Should I go back?'

'No, no, of course not, it's a long way.'

'Far enough.'

The gates started to open and the dogs began to bark. Emilio came down the steps and guided her into the cold, shadowy drawing room.

'What is it mama?'

'Can't I come to see my son?'

''Course, of course but you didn't 'phone.'

'No, I didn't. I didn't think it would matter, we have a problem.'

'What's that?'

'The mafia are threatening Angelo, he's on the run.'

'What can I do about that?'

'Help, you have contacts in the city, you must be able to straighten it out. He says he can't go to the police.'

'No the police are probably not a good idea, not with the 'Ndrangheta, no one can beat them on their own ground.'

'He's no threat to them, someone has to tell them that. He can't live his life on the run forever looking over his shoulder.'

'They aren't going to take any notice of me or anyone else. He shouldn't have got involved if he didn't want to play their game.'

'Is that all you've got to say? Your father would have left no stone unturned.'

'Father could do no more than I can. I've spoken to Angelo before, he takes no notice, anyway where is he?'

'Do you remember Veronica? He's on her parents' farm in the hills behind Sienna. Why don't you talk to him at least, find out who they are?'

'If he wanted to speak to me he would have 'phoned.'

'He's frightened of calls being traced.'

Emilio smiled and nodded, 'he's right.'

'So you'll throw him to the wolves without a second thought?'

'He knows what to do to save his skin.'

'Get further sucked in to their evil world? Is that all you have to say?'

'There's nothing more I can say or do. I am in court next week, I have work to do.'

'I see. That's how you get all this.' She gestured around the room.

'People depend on me.'

' But your brother can't.' She turned and at the door said a grim, 'Good luck, son.'

22

Emilio had been her only hope now that straw had gone she felt alone in her empty nest. She stood by the Madonna and child in her pyjamas and shivered, the bedroom was cold but she couldn't climb under the covers. She pulled a scarf over her shoulders and picked up Dario's photo.

'You're well out of it. What would you do now? Leave them to their own devices? Mothers don't stop caring. I can't give up. What would you think of Emilio now? Better not to see it. Somewhere along the line we lost him, he's changed, unrecognisable. What can I do?'

She set Dario back and started to pace the room, rapidly, forcefully, her body full of pent up energy. *Never. Stone, stone, heart of stone – no, no, heartless. What happened before my eyes that I didn't see?* She paced and turned, paced and turned, arms wrapped around her body. *I wish I could say that witch Baffina stole my child and substituted another but there is Emilio; same round forehead, snub nose, child's hands but those eyes – cold, impenetrable.* She shuddered and continued pacing and turning faster and faster. *It's a tailor's dummy that speaks to me now not my son, the little professor who shared all his gleanings, the wizard who believed anything was possible.*

Her feet speeded up of their own accord, pacing and turning.

How could he? How could he leave his younger brother to hide in terror without hope? How could he stonewall his mother? What is important enough to have sucked all feeling, all humanity out of him?

Like a clockwork drummer she paced up and down rapping out the words. *Where is love, loyalty, gratitude, protectiveness? I should have recognised the signs, he didn't weep for Caterina, didn't sit by her side in that room to say goodbye – there was no chair by her bed – no regrets, no sign of grief, no mourning, it was a stranger who attended her funeral, my son was no more.* She paced and turned, paced and turned. *Did I create this monster? What did I do wrong?*

She looked at the child in the Madonna's arms. *Can a child be spoiled by love?* Her pace was slowing, *the last time I looked he cared for all and sundry, shared their joys and sorrows, at least I thought he did, what do we know of other people's inner darkness? Even a mother? Especially a mother, we're the easiest to delude, we delude ourselves.*

He was charming once – he had old Donna dancing and giggling at his wedding – quiet, private Donna, so bent and thin we didn't think it possible. In his hands she was a child again. What happened to that Emilio, my son Emilio? Gone, gone. Her head screamed the word, reality hit and exhaustion felled her. She sat on the edge of the bed. *I must let go the reins, the horse I thought I was guiding has long since bolted. I mustn't let it drag me with it. I need rest to think tomorrow.* Helplessness and frustration confounded her compounded by exhaustion. *I need sleep, but how can I surrender to it? I must get warm.* She crept under the duvet and pulled it around her neck. She was too cold to warm the bed. *Angelo, wrap yourself well, I wish I could phone.* In the numbness of darkness she finally slept a leaden slumber.

23

Golden light from the sun lit Pietro's pottery and Dario's confident smile. Consciousness and helplessness returned at the same time. *What can I do? Nothing. I've got to get over my anger, put its energy to work.* Dario stared at her. *Get back to you and our story, trying to lay your ghost.*

The studio, as much a state of mind as a place – cut off from the world – secure, peaceful, creative, exploratory, home of predictable obedient clay. She lifted the damp hessian tenderly and whispered to the half formed moist clay face, 'just you and me.'

No longer invaded by light and air the bust had presence, the proportions were his but the surface was rough, undefined – the shape without character. *Your nose ...* Angelo's frightened face haunted her. *He's still a child but he had the courage to say 'no.' He's out of his depth and so am I. How could Emilio abandon us?* She studied the blank face in front of her trying to remember Dario's face, his nose. *How big in proportion to cheeks, your chin, forehead?* She flattened a lump of clay cut a triangle and modelled a nose – long and thin with a raised bridge. It was a struggle to concentrate. *Some things are beyond your control, accept it – and do nothing? What mother ever accepted that when her child was threatened? There's nothing else to do, I mustn't make things worse, can't phone, but not knowing where he is, how he is...* The thought paralysed her for a moment. *This is no good.* She braced herself and flattened the centre across the bridge. *How wide did it spread at the end? How long were your nostrils? Details are lost with distance, not the distance of death, death freezes some moments in surreal clarity – no the distance of routine, courtesy – the cataracts of familiarity.* She curved either side up to the centre and straightened the sides then held the nose in the centre of the face to check size and proportion. It fitted, with a wooden knife she cross-hatched the edges and its place on the bust, moistened the area, pressed it in and smoothed the join. It felt like coming home. Dario's nose, long and straight – clay becoming flesh, closer and closer to the man she had loved and lost *I thought I'd lost the details but you were there waiting to get out.* She tucked a thick curtain of brindled hair behind her ear and bent to define each nostril, long and tight to the sides then shaped the septum using a tiny sponge on a stick to moisten the clay.

She squeezed the warm pulpy clay in her hand savouring its plasticity, its readiness to obey her command, to shape itself to her will: Dario in her hands. *Making you from scratch examining each part in turn – luxury, to re-discover the territory that was mine, long lost, recaptured, to have you in my power and show the world my prize – handsome, successful, mine again. I can make you the way I wanted you to be, not you but us, your eyes for me alone, the hunger of your lips, the need that made my life a fertile realm before the desert years.* She looked at the deep red earth picturing Dario's face. *I can turn back the clock, let love soften the features, smooth away the frown, mask the impatience. It's coming back, I remember, I can see, feel your eyes, forehead.*

Her hands knew the way and worked automatically leaving her mind free to return to her sons, the tension at the funeral, their angry words. *What did Angelo want Emilio to do? Why did Emilio drive away?*
Dario's character was climbing up the blank mask. She stroked the clay above the jaw smoothing the cheeks, pressed her thumbs into the middle of each to hollow them a little and stood back to check. The bottom half of the face was familiar, in proportion. She focused on the caverns for the eyes. *Blank eyes,*

Tiresias, the blind prophet, she smiled, *you were never that – 'all seeing?' – in court maybe but I'm the magician here, I'll give you back your eyes.* She used a wooden scalpel to emphasise the circle of bone around the eyes then pressed her thumbs into the clay all around to hollow round the eyeballs. *How high the eyebrows?* She stepped back to assess. *Higher, the bone above his eyes jutted out, hiding them, his steep craggy forehead – think, think.* She moulded the thick wall of clay into half domes above each eye then dropped down over the nose. She squeezed and moulded the clay into the folds of a frown. The forehead lowered over his eyes shelving back up to his low straight hairline.

Oriana returned to the blank hollows below. She cut eyelids from the bulges in the clay checking from one to the other for balance, smoothed the surface all around then made a hole in the centre of each eye and surrounded it with a light circle. Fine lines radiating out from the pupil created the irises. Oriana stood back and studied her work – neck and shoulders looking comfortable in their bulky sweater, deep angular chin softened by its dimple. His smile and frank open eyes made him look guileless even with his overhanging brow and steep forehead. It was reassuring but not quite right. *His eyes were smaller, deeper set, dark – eyes revealing nothing.* She started to sculpt the lids again cutting away clay burying them deeper in their hollows, smaller narrower, pupil and iris tighter, closer, impenetrable.

Eyebrows, hardest of all, most telling – heavy along your overhanging brow, not too close together: balanced, perfect – defining not dominating your face. I was surprised to see them raised in appreciation of Sharon. I shouldn't have been. She was stunning and confident about her art. Her daughter was beautiful too. All of a sudden you grew taller, spread, sparkled, chatted and charmed them – the dip and dance of a mating bird, as impressive as it was irritating. I'd forgotten that Dario. The scalpel dug into the clay curling into little worms along the ridge of bone above the eye sockets defining his brows.

Another party came back to her, a summer barbecue, guests lingering on, twilight, shadows lengthening, comfortable chat round the table: time to fetch candles. In the kitchen she had seen the red flag of a sweater draped over shoulders, sleek navy trousers and moccasins –Dario's back bent over flowers, a flowered silk tunic, fair hair falling under his dark head – *Gina, my old school friend, pressed against the 'fridge, her arms under his sweater moving, his arms circling her frame; her eyes over his shoulder, staring into mine, Dario unaware.*

No candles – table full of dirty dishes, empty bottles, black night cooling; alone with him, tired, wanting him to go away and leave me in peace, leave me clean: empty, lost, but clean. I was sick of wallowing in a mess of anxiety, inadequacy and loneliness interspersed with campfire moments – they weren't worth the rest but he wouldn't let go. His determination to hang on gave me value – he was drunk, stupid, it didn't mean anything, he couldn't care less about Gina, he really needed me, his beloved Oriana. The bed is a dark and secret place – Gina was 'il primo piatto'.

She straightened up and sighed, '*bitter sweet, that's life…*' then bent over the bust trying to shake free of the memories, regain control, make the man she wanted,. The line of his eyebrows was furred with caterpillar squiggles, she carefully shaped and tamed them tapering them into the side of the head thinning over the nose. Finished. He was coming to life, almost there.

Ears might make you more human. She took a wedge of clay from the bin, cut two pieces, weighed them in her hands, beat the clay airless softening it with water then started to mould the outer curve of an ear from top to lobe, holding it against the head to get proportion. She worked in toward the centre, struggled for line and curve and depth and appraised the result. *A perfect ear but any old ear won't do, it has to be recognizably Dario. Ears are as individual as fingerprints. I must get it right this time – it has to be perfect, no guessing, I need a photograph to follow, side view is difficult, there's got to be one somewhere.* She was warm so she turned down the heater but left the radio on while she went to the house.

The flowerbeds were a tangle of overgrown stalks and dead flowers the air smelled of mildew. Tancreda was stalking something in the grass at the far end. Oriana's trainers did not disturb the house's calm. She pulled a stack of albums from their sideboard and flicked through the first which was full of family photos, *All these smiling faces, happy children, handsome parents, it's so distant they look like strangers. I don't recognize myself.*

She looked at a picture of her and Dario stretched out on a beach with Isabella in between covered in ice cream. *She must have been one, one and a half? Nearly thirty eight years, where did they go? Another world. I mustn't get distracted.* There were no profiles of Dario nothing but full frontal smiling poses, she turned page after page until finally there he was, hugging his knees looking out to sea, dark hair damp, body all gold, silhouetted against sunset's red, orange and purple. *I was pleased with that photo; it captured the time too when he was leaving the old firm to start out on his own. Mum and dad looked after Emilio and Isabella while we had a week's break in Alassio. It was Spring the bay was peaceful, the air was clear and the sea turquoise. We found a dune surrounded by stunted bushes with a dip in the middle – fine, cool sand and settled down to kiss, hands re-discovering each other's bodies – arms, chest, stomach, nipples, kissing, licking, crouching, climbing, rolling over each other to get closer and closer with the sound of beach vendors and children playing outside and the carping cries of seagulls overhead close but remote from our secret world.* She detached the photograph and took it back.

The lobes of the ears were not long enough and the tops were too wide, not tight enough on the curl, it needed more clay. She stripped them off and took fresh clay from the bin pounded and prepared it, cut it into two and made two long discs then carefully moulded a curve down into the bend of the lobe studying the photograph and from the top looped into the whorl around the hole guarded by its triangular flap of cartilage. *That's better.* She laid it on the bench and copied it then prepared the surfaces on each side of the head. *His left ear was slightly higher should I do that? Idealising art or 'warts and all'? 'Warts and all' is what I'm aiming for, Dario, our Dario – lopsided – but people will probably think it's my bad technique – artistic vanity – I don't want to look a fool, sod it, he's mine.* Each ear was placed as nature dictated. *And you look pretty perfect to me. Now you're still, not quick silver running over surfaces, scattering, joining – ceaseless motion, impossible to gather, dangerous to hold. 'Satisfied?' You used to ask me. Am I satisfied?* The eyes looked inward, at their own private joke, not at her. A sense of unappeased loss still nagged somewhere in the centre of her being. *So many years waving my hand in the air, 'Here sir, here.' What did I want? A place on the raft of your life, comradeship through the stormy seas, but you never felt the wind or the rain – they were your absences, dismissal. Your marriage was happy, you had the attentiveness, the nurture you wanted.* She slowly slid the board full circle examining shape and proportion, checking every detail, feeling a sort of wonder at the art but frustration with the subject, he was perfect, she had made him as perfect as she wanted, but not hers. She could not clasp his spirit, his love, to her and comfort herself with it. He had gone denying her that and nothing could bring it back.

Shadows stalked the studio, it was late. It had been a long journey and she was tired. She wet strips of Hessian, wrapped him up, tidied the bench, rinsed her implements and set them ready for the morning then crept quietly away. The garden was dark after the glare of the studio light and the grass was wet.

She was glad to light the gas for her linguine, it warmed the kitchen while she blitzed basil, garlic and pine nuts with grated Parmesan adding lots of Paolo's best olive oil. She took her bowl of pasta through to the sitting room and switched on the television in time to see Emilio being stopped as he ran down steps in front of the law courts followed by newsmen. Behind them at the top of the stairs, two younger men stopped to watch the interview.

'Not a good day Signor Ricci?'

'One day's battle doesn't decide the war.'

'No but witnesses and evidence make or break a case in law.'

'For every one of their witnesses we have three.'

'But how credible in the face of the evidence?'

'Concocted scraps, uncorroborated, media meddling.'

'Can you prove it?'

'That's my job. Now if you don't mind, I have work to do.'

Emilio hurried down the pavement with the three men snapping at his heels and the two younger men trailing at a distance.

He's rattled, he sounded cross, not his usual confident self. I can't imagine him out of his depth like Angelo, Emilio's a controller. I suppose that's why law suits him. She forked the last bundle of pesto and linguine into her mouth.

I'm still hungry, something sweet. I'll make pasties for Pietro, they'll keep for a couple of days.

Her hands were covered in butter and flour when her mobile rang. She wiped them on a tea towel and pulled it from her back pocket.

' 'Allo?'

'Mama?'

'Angelo!

'Mama.'

'Oh Angelo I'm so glad to hear your voice. Is everything okay?'

'Mama,' he repeated, he sounded terrified.

'Angelo, are you all right?'

'They came, Veronica's father saw them and hid me.'

'Oh my god, how did they find you? I wasn't followed, truly I wasn't followed.'

'I believe you mama. God knows, it doesn't matter now.'

'Where are you?'

'In the woods, I'm leaving tonight. They're smuggling me out in a cattle truck.'

'We'll find a way, caro, we'll make you safe, don't be afraid.'

'Ciao mama.' Silence.

Thank god he's got friends. Who told them where he was? So far out, so unlikely, how could they have traced him? Please God keep him safe.

Rolling the pastry calmed her. She spooned chocolate and hazelnut spread into the centre of each circle folded them over, put them in the oven and immediately felt lost. She couldn't sit, couldn't rest, *There's nothing I can do, nothing anyone can do. I can't be still. I might as well make the soup for Thursday too.*

It was late when she climbed into bed, satisfied with soup and pasties and progress with the bust. As she leant over his photo to put out the lamp she saw Pietro's piece of pottery. *Thank you,* she whispered, *I love you too, only one more day and we'll be together. I'll put sprinkles on the pasties in the morning.*

24

Oriana loved Thursdays, her day on the farm chatting with Isabella waiting for the children to come home from school.

She gave Isabella the pan of soup.

'Thank you, mama.' Isabella's eyes were bloodshot over dark grey circles.

'How much sleep did you get last night?'

'Hardly any or the night before or the night before that.'

'Giorgio isn't sleeping?'

'He's got a cold, he snuffles and struggles to breathe and cries.'

'Have you called the doctor?'

'He came yesterday, Paolo's gone for medicine.'

'You better have a rest today, leave everything to me, concentrate on Giorgio.'

'Can you stay, put the children to bed?'

''Course I can, my things are still in Rosa's room aren't they?'

'Yes, Rosa can move back with the twins for the night. Oh, thank you, mama, I didn't realise how heavy it all seemed 'til you lifted it off me.'

'Go and put your feet up.'

Oriana warmed the soup and the four of them sat around the big table. After lunch

Paolo went back to ploughing while Isabella and Oriana stayed in the kitchen. Oriana put her hand on Giorgio's forehead and said, 'He's not so hot, the medicine is working.'

Isabella settled to feed him and asked, 'Does Emilio know about Angelo?'

Oriana nodded, 'I told him, I thought he would help but he wouldn't.'

'I get the feeling he's got a lot on his mind at the moment.'

'Emilio? The case you mean?'

'He was here on Tuesday.'

'What did he say?'

'I don't know, he wouldn't come in for coffee, Paolo said he was in a hurry.'

'So why was he here?'

'Putting a box of papers in the shed.'

'His house isn't big enough? What's all this leaving things in the shed?'

'We don't ask any questions, the shed's free at the moment, doesn't bother us.'

'Emilio lives in a different world. Why are sons such a problem?'

'They're big boys mama, they'll sort themselves out don't worry.'

On the way home from school Pietro took her down the lane towards the village. They collected chestnuts under a big old tree which had outgrown its little triangle of grass in the middle of the road then they sat on the grass to split the spiky pale green cases to find the mahogany nuts nestled in soft white cocoons. Oriana saw their rich red and black swirls as if for the first time; glossy perfection. They filled her pockets and Pietro's hat. At home she read 'Il Topolino anche Il Gatto' cartoons to him before the house erupted with the grand return of the others and she made supper. At bedtime Oriana supervised the twins' bags and uniforms ready for the morning while Pietro had his bath then listened to them splashing in theirs while she put on his pyjamas.

'Should I read or tell you a story?' she asked once he was safely in bed.

'Tell, please, tell.' He snuggled down in anticipation.

'Once upon a time there was a little Etruscan boy called Fregon who lived on this very hill with his family and friends. He used to watch his father make clay pots for the village. Fregon liked to mould animals or birds from the pieces of clay his father gave him. As he grew older his father showed him how to chip bright streaks of colour from stones to make paint for the clay. Fregon made his family and friends happy giving them necklaces or dishes for food with pictures of trees and flowers on them.

When he grew up his pots were so good that he was asked to make all the dishes for the wedding of the chief's daughter. He made a big bright blue and white wine jug decorated with vine leaves and grapes. Everyone said it was the most beautiful thing they had ever seen. His family was very proud. Little did he know that another boy, just like him, would find a piece of his jug three thousand years later.' Pietro was staring, wide eyed, at her face, she smoothed back his hair, tucked the covers around him and kissed his cheek. He closed his eyes and fell asleep smiling. She crept out and passed Tommaso on the stairs, 'Ssh,' she whispered , 'He's asleep.'

'Don't worry, he never wakes when I go in.'

Oriana sipped hot chocolate by the fire with a very sleepy Isabella and Paolo.

'I hope you two get a good night.'

'He's getting better and the medicine'll knock him out so we're all going to sleep like horses.'

Rosa popped her head round the door, ''night, 'night.'

Oriana settled into her familiar little room. There were still more of her possessions here than Rosa's because Rosa had only just 'grown into it' as Isabella and Paolo put it.

In her sleep she was going down a dark corridor of interview rooms leading to an empty court where crime and sin hung in the air. Then she was running through a wood with chestnuts and acorns beneath her feet hearing her breath in deep pants like a hunted animal. She woke coughing in the dark; confused she lit the lamp. There was smoke coming under the door. She grabbed her wrap yelling, 'Paolo, Isabella, wake up. Fire! Fire!' She ran onto the landing and looked over the banister, in the hallway below she could see smoke pouring across the floor from the kitchen. The door to Tommaso and Pietro's bedroom opened, she yelled, 'Get out! Get downstairs!' and pulled the next door open, Rosa was shepherding the twins out. Finally she ran into the end bedroom. It was full of smoke, Isabella was coughing clutching a screaming Giorgio, Paolo was at the open window, 'It's below here, it's the kitchen.' He shouted, ''phone the fire station, I'm going to get water.' Tommaso followed his father while Oriana followed Isabella carrying Giorgio down the stairs and 'phoned from the hall hearing crackling flames on the other side of the wall.

The end of the farmhouse around the scullery entrance and kitchen was burning violently, flames reached up to Isabella and Paolo's window. It was licking around the end of the house, hotter and hotter, raging ever more furiously as it fed throwing out sparks and spreading. It sprang onto the roof, six months of drought made the house explode in the force of the flames. From the shelter of the barn Rosa and the twins watched, silent and wide eyed with terror, shivering in their pyjamas. Isabella, Giorgio and Oriana joined them, ' I'll get coats.' Oriana said and ran into the hallway there was the hiss of burning wood. She looked up the stairs. The landing was thick with smoke. She pulled coats from the stand and the rug from the floor and ran out. Sirens whined in the distance. Rosa was holding the baby, 'Where's mama gone?' asked Oriana.

'She's looking for Pietro,' said Rosa.

'Pietro? Didn't he come out with Tommaso?'

Rosa shook her head, 'We haven't seen him.' Oriana ran across the yard and up the stairs, she knew what to do, she pulled the sleeve of her dressing gown over her mouth and crawled along the floor calling, 'Pietro, Pietro.' The paint on Isabella's bedroom door was blistering, inside she could hear groaning and creaking, snapping noises, she crawled along the landing, 'Isabella? Pietro?' her eyes were stinging and running, her lungs were bursting, she coughed and choked. She heard voices down below and banging, calling. She crawled into his room, she could hardly see, she reached her hand over the edge of his bed, feeling along its length, 'Pietro, Pietro.' It was empty. She went on to her own room which was furthest from the fire, calling 'Isabella, Pietro'. From the doorway she could just make out Isabella kneeling by the wardrobe door, 'Is he there? She called. Isabella's head was shaking from side to side, there was no sign of Pietro. 'Isabella we must be quick, he must be outside.' Isabella did not move or speak. Oriana crawled across the floor to her and followed her eyes; crouched in a corner of the wardrobe was Pietro holding flimsy flowered material, head back, leaning against the side, chin up, pale, still. Isabella pulled him into her arms and looked at Oriana, 'He's not burned, thank God he's not burned. He needs air.' She pulled him out and laid him full length on the bedroom floor, bent back his head, pinched his nostrils, pulled down his jaw and forced air from her lungs into his.

'Isabella, Isabella.' Paolo called from the stairs. A fireman appeared at the door of the bedroom , 'You've got to get out now the roof's alight.' Isabella breathed and blew again, she said, 'Pietro what do you think you were doing hiding there? You could have been burnt alive.' She breathed and tried again. Paolo appeared at the bedroom door, watched the scene and groaned, a guttural sob, like a wound in the smoke filled room, deep, animal tears. He knelt beside Isabella and took her by the shoulders to get her away but she stooped and breathed, stooped and breathed, pounded his little chest then rubbed her mouth viciously with her fist.

'Argh! The taste of burning, he's burned inside, aach! I can't bear it!' She clutched him close. 'Come back, come back. We'll go to market tomorrow, just the two of us. I'll get you chocolate frogs.' She started to rock his rag doll body.

'Chocolate, you like chocolate and the story of Panoffini. I'll read you Panoffini tonight, clever Panoffini, caught the naughty cat didn't he? We like that story don't we?' Oriana knelt close to her, 'Isabella, there's an ambulance here for him, he needs a doctor, we must go, it's dangerous.' Paolo bent and gently pulled her up still clutching Pietro. Oriana tried to ease him away, Isabella clung.

Paolo took off his coat and wrapped it around her. 'You might slip, carissima, look at your feet.' Isabella looked down, she didn't recognise them. She didn't remember losing her slippers. Paolo nodded to Oriana to take him. She gathered his precious warmth to her pressing him to her stomach and carried him down the stairs. His weight in her arms denied all fears, the figures in the dark were unreal. In the glare of the ambulance she uncurled his little body on to the narrow bed. Clutched in his hand was her flowered summer dress. A deep sob wrenched her chest. *I wasn't there. I let you down, sorry.* Tenderly she smoothed his hair from his brow and kissed his forehead. She sat beside him to unravel the thin silk from his fingers and held his hand stroking the back of it aching to be holding him still. Isabella sat beside her blindly staring in front with a grey faced Giorgio, wheezing and whimpering on her arm.

On arrival Isabella and Giorgio were wheel chaired through the dark rear entrance. Oriana watched as Pietro was transferred to a trolley which, in its turn, was sucked into the same shadowy maw. She followed. Still shivering cloaked in red blankets. Paolo and the children huddled like shipwreck survivors on a sea of chrome and plastic chairs. Oriana sat by Paolo. One by one the children were checked and each returned silent, listless, to sit in line. Paolo and Oriana refused any treatment, resenting any minute away from the children. Oriana wanted to curl up and rock, she hugged herself, whispering intently, 'What was it? What happened? Oh please God it wasn't me, it could be me, I was cooking. Did I leave something on? I'm usually so careful with Pietro around .' She sobbed at his name. 'If it was me, oh my God, if it was me...' Her voice rose then strangled into sobs.

Pietro, staring ahead, hissed with fierce intensity, 'It wasn't you.'

'But it started in the kitchen. I was the last one cooking.'

'It wasn't you.' Paolo said determinedly looking ahead.

'I don't deserve you to be kind to me, Paolo, not after this.'

'It wasn't you; the firemen found petrol, it was started outside the kitchen wall.'

'No!' A gulf opened up, 'Why? Who would want to do that?'

'God knows, I don't.' He leant forward clutching the back of the chair in front.

Bleak, bleak, bleak, Oriana felt exonerated but becalmed on a sea of anguish overwhelmed by the still silence of despair.

The woman at the desk took Paolo over to a junior doctor waiting by a door.

'The baby needs oxygen, nothing to be alarmed about. We'll keep him in for a day or two to keep an eye on him. Your wife has suffered a little from smoke inhalation, physically she'll be fine but she is understandably shocked at the moment. It is probably just as well she'll be here with the baby.' Paolo nodded bowing to fate. A little later a sallow, grey haired woman in spectacles came over to Paolo, 'Signor Giordano?'

'Si.'

'I am sorry but the fire service have reported your home will not be liveable for some time. Do you have alternative accommodation? We can make arrangements for you if necessary. She looked at their pyjamas under their coats. 'I can find some clothes if you like.'

'I'll speak to my mother and brothers, they'll help,' said Paolo.

For Oriana the inevitability of nightmare had taken over, the hospital had swallowed them up, Pietro disappeared, Isabella and Giorgio whisked away now the rest of the family were going to splinter out into the dark world.

25

A clock was ticking but time had no meaning. She had collapsed into an armchair as soon as she got through the door. Her limbs felt so heavy that the slightest movement was an effort. She ached all over. She had seen light creep through the darkness, watched it penetrate the corners of the room, seen all the dead photos present their faces, her wedding photo, Isabella's, Lucia's ordination and five christenings. A cat had curled up on her lap, others came and went. She drifted in and out of consciousness. Greyness and shadows reclaimed the room, darkness descended again.

Ringing, ringing, from afar. She must get to it, must answer. Clumsily she lifted the receiver, 'Ummm?' Her lips were stuck together. Her mouth was dry, tasting of smoke.

'Mama?' Lucia's voice, 'mama, are you there?'

'Si,' she croaked. It sounded alien.

'Are you all right?'

'Si.'

'Are you sure?' Silence.

'Mama, Emilio is here.'

She had to tell her but she couldn't speak it out, to say it was to confirm it, make it real, re-live it; better left hidden in the darkness with her alone.

'Mama, can you hear me?'

'Si.'

'Emilio's in trouble, he needs you to do something for him.'

'Emilio?' Her mind groped. 'Busy, too busy.'

'He's here mama, at the convent. He can't go home.'

'Angelo no home.'

'Emilio, mama.'

'Emilio?'

'He's here, mama, at the convent.'

'Convent?'

'Mama, he left papers in the olive shed at the farm. He wants you to get them for him.'

'Farm? Farm's gone-burned.'

'The farm burned?'

Oriana nodded like a child. 'All burned down.'

In the background Emilio's voice echoed, 'The farm burned!'

Lucia gasped, 'No! No! Isabella? Paolo? The children? Are they all right?'

'Pietro, little Pietro.'

'What ?'

'Lost.'

'Mother of God help us. What do you mean, lost, not dead?'

'Si.'

Suddenly Emilio's voice, 'the house or the buildings? What was burned mama?'

'All ruined.'

'Was the olive shed damaged?' She saw the shed again, lit by the flames, she shook her head and murmured, 'No.'

'Thank God. Mama, there are important papers in that shed, I need them urgently. Will you get them for me?'

'I can't go there, Emilio.'

'I'm sorry about Pietro, mama, about the farm. I'll do all I can to help put it right. People get over these things. It's only a folder of papers, mama, you can put it in your bag.

'I can't go there.'

'You must, mama. It's life or death to me.'

Lucia's voice, ' Emilio's in trouble mama, you can save him, you won't let him down will you?'

Emilio urged, 'It's not a lot to ask, mama. Will you do it?' Oriana nodded.

'Si.'

He continued, 'there's a metal box with a padlock in one of the cardboard boxes, the key is under the press. There's a pale blue folder labelled 'R' will you bring it please mama?'

'Can you do that, mama?'

Oriana groaned, 'Si.'

'You mustn't be followed, don't let anyone tail you.' His voice insisted. 'Do you understand?'

'Si, si. I understand,' she said wearily.

'We'll be waiting, mama.'

Like an automaton she climbed the stairs washed her face and put on warm trousers and a jumper before standing in the kitchen to drink long draughts of water.

When she left the house it wasn't yet light. She drove carefully through silent suburbs with only the occasional tram. No one followed as her car edged slower and slower up towards the farm-black, silent, wet. Not a soul for miles. She shone her torch to the house, a surreal picture; one half a gutted ruin gleaming in moonlight with a network of little black rivulets spidering down away from it, the other still pretending to be a home with ghostly lace curtains at the windows and shutters spread to welcome the sun.

Pity overwhelmed her. *An innocent family, where does the hatred come from to do this? Why? Why?* Transfixed by the gorgon sight it was difficult to turn her back on the pain. She forced herself to turn to the olive shed at the end of the courtyard. It was dry inside, it smelt of last year's oil. Space was cleared around the olive press and at the far end. All was tidy ready for the new crop. *How can they carry on after this?* Weak light filtered through the window onto the press.

Where are the boxes? She peered through the gloom and found a stack of three boxes in the corner. She pulled parcel tape from the top box and opened the flaps – papers, letters, accounts, statements –the grey bureaucracy of law. She dropped it on the floor and opened the next to find old newspapers hiding a grey metal box with a padlock. The key was under the press as Emilio had said. The box was full of different coloured folders labelled alphabetically, she lifted each in turn looking for 'R.' it was a slim pale blue folder, she slid it free and put it on the window ledge then locked the box, hid it under its newspapers and closed the flaps. She picked up the folder and held it in the light from the window. *What is so important?* She rifled through a motley collection of letters and papers. A handwritten letter on thick cream paper caught her attention.

Appartamente Madeleine

Corso Garibaldi,

Brera.

9 Augusto 2009.

Caro Emilio,

Our brother Armando Rizzio has been betrayed by one of his own dealers. The police are investigating. This touches us, you must stop their prying and lighten Rizzio's sentence as only you know how. Rizzio is a valuable member of our family. We remain in your debt as ever.

Ringraziondola anticipatamente,

Enrico Domenico Mancini.

Dealers? Family? Who is Enrico Mancini? Her stomach tightened into a knot. *What is all this about?* A crumpled invoice fell out when she tried to insert the letter back into the folder. She read.

Villa Larian,
Moniga del Garda,
Brescia.
05 Gennaio 2010
Signor Marco Ricci,
Apartamento Madeleine,
Corso Garibaldi,
Brera.

Caro Signor Ricci,
    I have not been paid for delivery of 06 Ottobre:

Danica Levak 18 yrs 12,000 euros

Tanja Curkovic 17 yrs. 12,000 euros

Total   24,000 euros

They were accepted as fit for work, no complaint was made. If I'm not paid before the end of the week there will be no further supplies.
    In attesa di una sua risposta,

Arturo Costa.

    The thin paper shook. Oriana's mouth was dry. *This isn't happening, I can't believe it, it isn't true, what are they doing – girls – a business deal?* She groaned, *it's horrendous. Emilio can't know about this, it's not normal. Does this really happen – like this – cold and clinical? Ricci? Paolo said he was suspect but – girls – people trafficking? Emilio can't defend him, he's guilty, what can he say?*

She put the receipt on the window ledge. Sickened she looked at the folder. *Do I want to know anymore? Leave it alone. What if it's not true? There must be something here that will tell me it's a joke, lies.* She took the first letter in the folder and read avidly in suspension of disbelief, looking for evidence of fiction.

Appartemente Montenapoleone
Via Massarenti,
Milan.

10 Ottobre, 2010

Spettabile Padre Romano,
    Your suspicions are confirmed, the Camorra are trying to undermine our support for Marco Ricci. Signor Rossi's brother has been working for them. This must cast a shadow over Signor Rossi's allegiance. Our family may be threatened from within. I am sorry to voice these doubts but my loyalty demands it.
        Distinti saluti,

Arturo Esposito.

Angelo was a threat to Emilio so long as he worked for the Camorra so why didn't he help him out of it? What were they really quarrelling about? How did Emilio get mixed up in all this? Allegiance? Allegiance to whom – 'our family/' not the Camorra – the 'Nandreghetta? They're ruthless, who would help them, surely not Emilio? As if hit in the solar plexus she dropped onto the last case still clutching the letter and re read it. *It can't mean anything else.* She put the letter back on top of the folder and took the receipt from the window ledge. *Who is Romano? Why did Emilio have a letter addressed to him?* She picked up the folder and put the receipt back. *This is full of poison, a dark evil world on paper. What is Emilio going to do with it?*

Oriana stood but didn't move, her mind was blank, filled with strange silence, an almost preternatural calm. She left with the folder in her hand.

26

Mother Carmela showed no awareness of Oriana's dishevelled appearance, gaunt face or red sunken eyes, she simply took Oriana's hand in the softness of hers, smiled and led her along quiet corridors of timeless serenity to Lucia's cell door. A tap and she was through.

Lucia gasped and hugged her, 'Oh, mama, it's so sad, I'm sorry, sorry.'

Mother Carmela waited outside.

For Oriana nothing was real, nothing was finished, it wasn't over yet.

'Mama, here's Emilio I must go it's time for chapel.'

Lucia passed through the doorway and carefully closed the door.

Emilio saw the blue folder in her hand, put his hands on her shoulders and kissed her cheek.

'I'm sorry, mama, it's terrible. I'll do what I can, I'll help pay for repairs. We'll get through this together.'

Oriana pushed his hands away and looked into his face.

'Money won't bring Pietro back, give him his life and us the joy of it.'

'Accidents happen mama, all we can do is help.'

'This was no accident, it was petrol.'

He reeled back as if struck. 'Torch the farm? Who? Why?'

'The sort of people in this folder.'

'You've been prying.'

'What do you want this for?' Oriana brandished the folder.

Defeated he dropped onto the bed and held his head.

'Well?'

He lifted his head and studied her face but he could not fathom her mood. He sighed wearily resigned.

'The Camorra want me to throw the Ricci case, when I refused they discredited me with my other business associates, I am threatened by both now. Those papers will give me back credibility and the power to stop the Camorra.'

'Who are these 'business associates?'

'Who do you think they are?'

'Tell me it's not the Mafia.'

'Where else am I going to find work?'

'Where any solicitor gets cases – from decent people in need of justice.'

'That's not my talent, I specialise in circumnavigating law and avoiding consequences. Justice is blind you can pinch its backside with impunity.'

'Why did you leave the file at the farm?'

'I can't leave things like that in the office and they knew where I lived. I knew they'd ransack the house. It's my insurance.'

'It wasn't the first time you've used the farm. What have you been leaving there?'

'A few precious consignments that needed to be kept out of harm's way.'

'The farm was burned because of you.'

He got up and stood before her, 'never, never did I think they would do anything like that.'

'No, no, you didn't think, you didn't think about Isabella and Paolo, only about your own skin, your own convenience. You knew full well what you were involving them in. Are you so deep into that evil world that you've lost track of what it's about? How it treats people? Addicting girls to drugs and selling their bodies to abuse? You expected them to be soft on you and yours? I shame to name them as part of you. Shame to own you, oh, I never thought I would ever say that.'

'Playing for high stakes. It's the real world mama.'

'No it's your world and it's made you what you are. Why have I been so blind? Caterina, Angelo, now Isabella, even Lucia, you don't care about anyone and now you're threatened by the people you sacrificed your family for. Who can you count on now? A life without love, a wife driven to suicide and no children? What makes all that worthwhile?'

Emilio stood up, 'the closed little world of family? Who cares? Behind the doors of power and in the courts I can make my mark, alter the big picture – politicians court me – powerful companies stand or fall by my word, I can have anything I want –money, power, prestige, friends, mistresses.'

'If that's what you want but not at anybody else's expense, not on the back of suffering.'

'Suffering? We give people what they want, what they've always wanted, if we didn't someone else would. The 'Ndranghetta are efficient, they see that everyone has a fair share and they police their own empire.'

'Honour among thieves? There's no such thing, their empire is based on slavery; women slaving as prostitutes, addicts slaves to drugs, gamblers slaves to false hope and corrupt businesses enslaved by their own greed, all ruining their lives for illusions. You feed off their weakness and swallow your own hearts and souls in the process. Have you lost all trace of humanity Emilio? Do you have no sense of the suffering you cause? Can you not see another person as a vulnerable, sensitive fellow being? Hasn't life taught you the importance of kindness?'

'I'm no priest, mama but I need some of that humanity now.'

Weariness washed over her and she sank onto a wooden chair by Lucia's desk. 'For once I'm glad your father is dead, not to have to hear this.'

'Father? It's his practice I inherited, who do you think introduced me to all those important clients? To my new family?'

'To the 'Ndranghetta? Not Dario, he would never have anything to do with the mafia. He was respected by the best people in Milan for his honesty and decency.'

'Feared and treated with respect because he was powerful.'

'Never, that's not possible, I would have known, he couldn't keep that from me.'

'It's easy to keep family and work separate.'

'Not between husband and wife.'

'His clients were his business, you didn't have to see them.'

'But I entertained people.'

'And no one has to talk shop at table, especially if it's private.'

'Did Caterina know?

He nodded, 'she found out and hated it, said she wouldn't bring children into a mafia family. She was angry and bitter and foolish.'

'Your father would never do that to me.'

'What was he doing – providing school fees, holidays, luxuries, where did that come from?'

'Not other people's misery I hope.'

'It didn't matter to him why should it to you?'

'Decency.'

'The mafia has its code.'

'And you've run foul of it.'

'I have my insurance there, that's all that matters.' He nodded towards the folder on Lucia's desk.

'Every man for himself, a poisoned jungle.'

'Not if you play the game.'

'It's not a game.'

'No and we're not children.'

'Are you telling me that my life was a charade? Never.'

She laughed shaking her head slowly from side to side.

'Which is the charade, work or family? Let's face it, neither, he was a husband and father as well as a clever solicitor and successful business man, different roles, end of story.'

'But our life together was based on trust, sharing, belief in the good....'

'The good of the family, always looking out for one another, I'm in trouble, mama, real trouble.'

He dropped on his knees.

'I need that folder, please help me mama,'

He peered up as if from the abyss. She looked into his dark eyes, Dario's eyes and said quietly, 'I can't, Emilio, no one can.' She stood, stepped around him and left the room with the folder in her hand.

Outside the convent Oriana leaned against the stone wall and gulped air as if she were drowning, then in rapid pants until she felt dizzy and her fingers tingled, 'Slower, slower, calm, calm.' Gradually the pounding of blood in her head subsided and she moved on wobbly legs to the car. As she opened the door, from the other side of the wall the ethereal notes of 'Pie Jesu' reached her.

27

The local police station was a low, flat, concrete building with fluorescent lights. There were only a couple of officers having a quiet Sunday. When Oriana walked through the door the younger of the two left their conversation and came to the counter.

'What can we do for you?' He asked in a friendly tone.

'It's what I can do for you,' replied Oriana.

'Oh really?' He said with a smile.

'I have evidence of crimes.'

He swept his eyes over her dishevelled appearance, grey hair and wrinkles, saw the dark circles under her eyes and came out to lead her to a chair by a coffee table.

'Tell me all about it,' he said kindly sitting opposite her.

Oriana held out the folder saying, 'there is evidence in here of 'Ndranghetta dealings and corruption among people in top positions.'

He ignored the proffered folder.

'You wish to make a complaint?'

'No, I have no complaint, justice has a complaint, the decent families of Milan have a complaint.'

'You're here to set the world to rights?' He looked her over and said sympathetically, 'someone been giving you trouble?'

She shook her head slowly, sadly, 'No, I'm not mad, not a down and out, not eccentric, my daughter's house was burned down,' she stopped, it seemed a long time ago and just yesterday at the same time. 'I can't remember when.'

'A house burned down?' He asked in a more business like tone.

'No, not that, it's not that, look at the file.'

'How can a few pieces of paper have hurt you? You can talk to me, we're having a quiet night, I've got time, you get it off your chest.'

Oriana stood up, 'I'm no fool, this is full of vital information I need to see it safely into the right hands before I leave. Who's in charge here? Where's your senior officer? I need to speak to your superior.'

'No need to get agitated.' He looked at the folder, 'Important information you say? So how did you come by these 'papers' eh?'

'That's irrelevant it's what's in them that matters. Stop playing games and look.'

'But there might be someone searching high and low for this folder at this very minute.'

'Enough, I'll go elsewhere.' She headed for the door.

'No, no don't you go rushing away before I see what it is you've got.' He reached out his hand. Oriana handed it over. He opened it, flicked through the varied papers scanning headings then craned his neck to one side to read a little of a letter, recognised a name and started to pay attention. His artificial smile vanished, he stiffened and selected another. Silently Oriana watched the second hand of the clock on the wall behind his head turn circles. He looked at her staring stolidly at the wall behind his head.

'Where did you get this?'

'From my son.'

'Who is your son?'

'Emilio Rossi.'

He snapped the folder shut.

'Would you wait a moment please?' She nodded and sat. He disappeared through a door into the back room. The neon light hummed insistently, in the distance a siren sounded. The chair was hard. A grey haired man bulging through the buttons of his uniform emerged holding the folder.

'Signora Rossi?'

She rose. It was accomplished.

Outside grey dawn grappled with mist and darkness.

Her house looked bedraggled in the cold morning light, faded paint barely covered the splintered window frames The silver birch was too big for the little garden and showered its debris over weeds and untamed bushes. Shivering she made her way to the kitchen door. Baffina came between her legs, almost tripping her up but she carried on walking mechanically. In the gloomy kitchen she opened the 'fridge and stood devouring scraps of food straight from the shelves.

The sound of the 'phone was like an electric shock. She ran to it thinking, 'Paolo, Isabella.'

'Signora Rossi?' said a strange voice.

'Rossi? Signora Rossi? No there's no Signora Rossi here.'

She returned the 'phone to its cradle and slowly, painfully climbed the stairs.

28

Oriana's eyes opened onto Dario's grin, she swiped it across the floor and sprang across the room to shred his face. *Lies, lies, lies – my life, founded on a lie, my husband, the man who shared my bed for forty years – a cheat, a common swindler.*

On the wall above her head Botticelli's Madonna and child stared tranquilly into space. 'Damn Botticelli, better Brueghal and Bosch,' Oriana cried tearing it down.

Ignoring the slivers of glass beneath her feet she swept back the curtains, pulled on jeans, jumper and shoes then strode down the landing to Emilio's room where she had stowed all things Dario. The wardrobe opened onto a row of different coloured sleeves and trouser legs releasing the sickly smell of stale clothes. It made her queasy. She slid her fingers between linen shirts and silk trousers, supple cotton and fine mohair, only the best. *They should go to charity* then shook her head. *No. I don't want to, handle them, pack them, I can't face people, expose my shame, it's enough to bundle them into bags to throw, throw? Throw where?* The thought of them lurking somewhere disturbed her. *– no, better to burn them, make a fire, burn everything – yes, a bonfire I can have a bonfire.*

She wrenched jackets from the rail and flung them on the floor, lifted down heavy suits and added them to the pile: trousers pinched between wooden hangers, tossed onto the growing mound then pelted shoes and moccasins on top. *They'll burn.*

One by one she upended drawers from the chest over the heap raining down sweaters, scarves and ties. Last drawer: cards and files, old diaries, programmes, papers, *good to start the blaze.* She looked at the pile of clothes – crumpled, empty, lifeless – *costumes for the daily life of a con man,* then rubbed her hands on her sides. *I'll never be clean, it's in me, my past, who I am. No it's him and everything he stood for – and dragged me into, our history, our lives, all of us – the children too. He' made a mockery of family life, every thing I believed in. It's my fault, I dropped my guard, stopped looking or didn't want to see what was before my eyes. Well I see it now, I was a fool – happy holidays, happy Christmas, happy Easter, happy Families – a sham – lies, lies.*

Clear it away, get rid, She carried load after load down into the dining room and threw them out of the French windows onto the patio, rammed the rest into a suitcase and threw it after shouting *Away, away, get out, finish. I should have done this long ago.*

She paced the house, seeing it as if for the first time – pictures and ornaments – nest building, souvenirs of innocent times, ignorant times. *Domestic trash, barnacles to be careened away.* She went from room to room seeing only the lees of family life. *This house is silted up with the past, full of dead things, time to get rid, burn away the lies. All of it can go, nothing useful, necessary: sweep pretence away.*

Photos, photos everywhere, I didn't realise how many. She stood in front of a photo of Dario's sixtieth birthday full of family and friends. *All those people, did they know?* Beside it there was an old wedding photo in an elaborate silver frame. She picked it up. *We look like a couple of kids, unrecognizable, strangers. When did it change?* She flung it on the table, fetched a laundry basket and swept her arm along the top of the sideboard tumbling Isabella's wedding, Emilio's graduation and Lucia' s dedication into the basket. *Out, out, all of it – false reassurance, mockery.* She surveyed the room, *getting better.*

In the hall she ripped paintings and prints off the wall. *More, more, get rid of it all, there's nothing worth keeping, strip, strip everything away – fire fodder, fuel for the fire.*

She yanked fiercely at the curtains in the sitting room, tore them down laid them out and filled them with vases, carvings, dishes and trinkets. She opened drawers full of mats and fusty smelling tablecloths, children's party toys and colouring pencils, paper puzzles and crayoned drawings of little houses with big grinning people and tipped them out. She banged the corners violently to get rid of crumbs, sweet papers and dust. *Old, dead, stale, gone, no more,* she shuddered and backed out of the gutted room rubbing her hands down her sides, her mouth curling in disgust and ran up the stairs,

She pulled board games and jig saw puzzles from a cupboard on the landing: *outgrown long ago, scrap.* She looked at the neat stack of photograph albums: *The biggest lies of all – smiles, smiles –perfect family, I was lying too, lonely and afraid of you, if only I'd known you weren't worth it.* She loaded the linen basket and breathed deep, the knot of claustrophobia was loosening. The house was gaining space and tranquility. *I can clear the attic, how many times have I promised myself to do that? The fire can sort it, free, clean.*

She ran down to the garage and hauled a ladder up to the landing to set it under a trapdoor. She climbed up and hefted herself onto the edge of the hole, swung her legs round and crawled along the roof space until she could stand. There were old tennis racquets and balls, boxes of children's school work and toys, books on one side, old clocks and vinyls that Dario had collected and things he intended to repair on the other. Oriana pushed each one toward the opening and arranged them around it, climbed onto the ladder and pulled them down one by one.

She was enjoying herself, didn't want it to end – old cleaning stuffs in the laundry room: rags, dusters, aprons, old mops, crumpled packets of fertilizer festering in cupboards, corners, closets; she threw them out, hungry for fuel, fodder for the fire – more, there must be more. Dark cupboard prisons opened to the world: freedom. She emptied armloads of stained cloths and spindly brushes into cardboard boxes along with rusting tins and plastic bottles, the thud and swish as they tumbled beating like a tarantella in her soul.

Outside beyond the stacks of boxes and heaps of jetsam beside the garage, in the garden and on the patio night was pulling down the blind on trees and fences, blurring the particular into the general and the tidal wave of domestic flotsam into anonymous waste.

The chill air checked the riot in her blood as she scanned the garden for a safe place to set light to it all. It had to be in the middle between the cherry and persimmon trees away from the station and Dino and Rinatta's fence. She stood and looked at a watery moon hovering close to the horizon saddened not to share the fire, the exorcism but there was no one she could tell, no one to witness the burning of Dario and their perfect family life. *What would Isabella and Angelo think? Worse than mad this time, he's their father, the children's grandfather, better for them to let the lies live on. Does Lucia know?* She shook her head. *Not even Lucia could suspect that of her father, how much has Emilio told her of his problems? I'm on my own burning a ghost. Burn one name will I find another?*

Oriana fetched matches and firelighters from the sitting room. *Paper, lots of paper – under the bench in the garage – nothing thrown away, sometimes useful.* She dug out a pile of Dario's faded old *Corriere della Sera* and *La Republica. damp, damn, have to get mine from the kitchen.* There was an untidy collection of *Il Fattto Quotidiano* and Art magazines by the armchair. *They'll do.*

There were a couple of pallets in her little shed, she propped them together in the middle of the garden, scrumpled paper and pushed it underneath then poked cherry branches in and around followed by a broken chair. She carefully unloaded a wheelbarrow of prunings, spread old suitcases and wooden framed pictures over the top then crouched to strike match after match, lighting both ends of the little den. She stood back to watch blue flames creep along blackening paper until the twigs caught and wind roared up through the structure. Branches crackled and smoked licked by red and yellow flames flaring into a pyramid. She watched delicate blue flames curl over the baby in the Madonna's arms, springing the canvas free of its frame.

The heat threw her back. *Cremation time.* She hurled a bag of clothes onto the fire, watched shirt collars curl and surrender to the flames, took a suit and slung it into the furnace – *expensive lies, but lies are cheap.* She took another – sober grey: *every bit the professional; decent, reliable – you can't tailor corruption.* She held up the next: blue, hand-stitched, pricey – *to colour over crime, paint out deceit. Fire's not a fussy eater it'll all go down.* She swung it round over the crackling wood. The fire blinked, stifled by the mass then billowed into a puff of flame. *Fire, the great leveller: hats, shoes, skis, golf clubs – the parts you played, the games you tried – the dross you left. Melt, dissolve, disappear, Dario dancing in the flames.*

She loaded the wheelbarrow again and pelted the fire with photos and albums. *Family photos, unreal images, I have all the memories I want in my head.* She slid paintings into the flames. *Dario's 'investments,' neither art nor décor.* She fed the flames glorying in the sparks and flares, flashes and mini explosions of consummation, *'Bonfire of the vanities!'* She yelled, raucous laughter rattled from her throat. Never leaving its side, she forked and lifted feeding it oxygen to work its magic. *I don't need any of this, all a load of rubbish in the end. Why do we fill our lives with clutter? There's freedom in letting go. All I need now is white walls and space to think. The Japanese have it right, shogi screens and pebbles.*

Everything surrendered to the fire's alchemy Oriana watched yellow flames turning wood and paper from scorched brown to glowing red then black charcoal, grey ash and finally white powdered perfection converting her agony into light, she gloried in, warming her face and body, cleansing her soul.As its jagged profile crumbled into soft furry mounds her anger melted and she relaxed and opened to the peace, the soothing quiet of its decline. *All gone, all I have to do is let you finish the work.* She watched the fire crackle and puff little balls of flame as it shifted. She was hungry, very hungry. She ran to the garage and chose a big, silky potato from the sack, wrapped it in foil and took butter and salt back to the warm glow. She poked her parcel into the embers at its edge. There was a rickety wooden chair lying on its side by the barn, she upended it and sat watching the flames mesmerised. The fire devoured on until its centre was an incandescent ball of red, pink and yellow. Above its aureola the bright black of the sky was filled with stars reaching on and on forever. She dropped her head back to stare at the vastness. *Puts all this in perspective, how tiny we all are, Dario, Emilio, me – what does it all matter?*

Nothing left of Signora Rossi – eviscerated – gone, goodbye. What's left?

29

When she woke Oriana wandered round the gutted house; tidemarks on walls, bare floorboards, dust and cobwebs, it sapped her energy. *Oh for a day in the studio, lost in creating, carried away by an idea, something I care about and what have I got? My tribute to the cheat who made a mockery of my life. What gave me the idea to go down that road? Did I sense the hollowness, blame myself?* She stood looking out of the windows. *We sat out there reading newspapers together, normal, ordinary people. I was the one jumping up, never still, off into the house, to see the children, town or the studio. Running away?* She looked at the mysterious studio door. *He didn't follow me in there, my retreat, my secret sanctuary. There's unfinished business there now, now I've seen the light. It wasn't my fault I was lonely, he knew the gap between us could never be bridged. Honeymoon?* She laughed raucous, harsh laughter. *That bust is a lie, I'll show the world what you really are, finish you off and rid myself of physical connection. Now his bust will finally show the man.*

The studio felt warm and comfortable, his bust lurking on the side hadn't contaminated it. She lifted Dario's stiff old shirt from the peg behind the door without the disgust she expected. *The fire purging his malign influence?* She smiled at her own dramatizing. *More likely familiarity and layers of clay.* She buttoned it up, lit the heater and switched on the radio. The bust was wrapped in lengths of damp hessian. Oriana started to peel them off one by one. *Like unwinding a mummy, Secrets of the Pharaohs, what will I find?* A perfect head in raw, red clay, face radiating a smile – nostrils slightly lifted by it, eyes reflecting it in lines like ripples, her anger welled up as if Dario were there before her and was compounded by anger that he was not.

I can wipe the smile off your face for a start. Feverishly she beat a small piece of clay and flattened it into a bandage. She sprinkled water over the drying bust and sponged the surface rubbing away at the mouth. She scratched the surface of the lips and did the same for the clay plaster to attach it. She smoothed the edges and took a wooden knife to cut a slit straight along the middle rising slightly at the sides. She rolled twin pipes and laid them over and under the line, then lifted the thin lips into a sardonic grin. She stood back and checked his mouth for accuracy. *Yes, I've seen that too many times, you always knew better than anybody else. That's more like it. Those laughing eyes are only half the story, let's see what was underneath.* She spread a ribbon of clay over his eyes and lowered the lids so that they half hid them then lowered the lines at the sides making them droop which gave the eyes   a sinister weary look. She dug away an eyebrow, applied another sliver of clay and lifted it in a quizzical, sarcastic arch then dug furrows in his brow– another Dario – in control, superior, dismissive, a Dario she knew and had denied.

Hair, what am I going to do with your hair? When she went to take more clay from the bin Prokofiev's Romeo and Juliet was on the radio, *I love that,* she turned up the volume and let it swell inside her as she threw the clay at the bench to burst any dangerous air bubbles. She rolled a pile of narrow strands then proceeded to attach them from the temples to the forehead and across in a low line. His hair continued on up over the top of the head, gathering toward the crown in concentric circles. *You were proud of your hair, proud you didn't lose it like everyone else. It was hard to tame but you found someone to trim it sleek and professional, all part of the great con. Let's see what I can do with that.* Her fingers worked rapidly in tune with the powerful music, hair piled onto the clay skull until the crown was filed. She stepped back to see the effect and burst out laughing. Thin snakes of clay hung untrimmed over his forehead, cheeks, down the sides of his neck. *Dread locks! Medusa! No, nothing so threatening.* She hugged herself laughing at the caricature – *a clown with a red wool wig. I'd better give you a bit more credibility than that. What you did was far more nasty, out there as well as here with me. I'd better cut you into shape.*

The music of the court ball drowned the roar of Emilio's car and she was bent over the bust as he passed the window. The door burst open and he was yelling before he was through, 'What the hell have you done?'

'Emilio, I didn't hear you…'

'No, I bet you didn't.'

He strode to the radio and switched it off.

The sudden silence was a shock.

'You took my papers to the police?'

Oriana calmly put down her knife.

'What was I supposed to do?'

'You don't know what you've done, you fool, what made you meddle in things you don't understand?'

'I understand justice and equality, responsibility and care; the important things.'

'You've signed my death warrant.'

'Don't be ridiculous.'

'It's not the police, Madre mia, it's the Camorra, those papers were my insurance.'

'Insurance – horror stories of human trafficking, drug running?'

'The Ricci case, the 'Ndrangheta want a cover up, want him off the hook, the Camorra want him to go down because he wouldn't cut them in. The Camorra threatened me and promised me big returns if I played their game. They are the most powerful but the 'Ndrangheta are my family and they don't take kindly to betrayal. So long as I had those papers they daren't touch me. Now both families are gunning for me, I'm done.'

'The mafia need clearing from the face of the earth, you knew what you were getting into.'

'No one will ever do that, you might as well live with it.'

'Without selling out to it.'

'You can't survive without them, they have the power, they can eliminate me like treading on a snail.'

'The police will protect you and Milan will be the better without Ricci and his backers.'

'You're up in the skies, the police can't protect me, half of them are with the mafia. Do you really think prison will keep me safe? Do you want me in prison?'

'I didn't want you working for the mafia, I don't want people exploited or the suffering that drugs and prostitution cause, you're my son, no, I don't want you in prison but you're part of Italy, Milan, the people. I thought you and your father were making everyday life better not worse. It's too late for your father but you could change, make amends, live a decent life.'

'With a prison record?'

'There's such a thing as a second chance.'

'Prison for me is going to change nothing, Mama it will not keep me safe, they will kill me sooner or later. I'm you're son, you are the only person I can depend on. Help me mama, retract it, call it back, tell them they're forgeries, lies, you were taking revenge for a family quarrel, you were put up to it, anything but get it back before the 'Ndranghetta find out, get me out of it, please.'

'And let it carry on the same? I can't.'

'Family first, father worked hard for you, so did I, you never went short.'

'Do you think I cared about your money?'

'Of course you did, don't be stubborn Mama, we're part of you, what's to be gained from carrying this on?'

'Less exploitation, less pain, justice.'

'What's justice but revenge? An eye for an eye, that's how the mafia keeps order, what's the difference?

'A whole world of difference, people like your sister don't have their houses burned, children aren't killed where there's justice.'

'You're a stubborn old fool, no wonder father kept a mistress.'

'Mistress?'

'Didn't you know?'

'How was I to know?'

'Tell tale signs, lip stick, perfume, long hours, surely you knew?'

'You know I didn't.'

'He must have been very careful, you had plenty of time.'

'What do you mean?'

'Twenty years, she had a flat near the office.'

'But he was always home for dinner.'

'Often late and not every night.'

'Weekends – he was here at weekends.'

'Apart from golf, fishing, meetings...'

'No, no, I would have known.'

'But you didn't.'

Oriana leant against the bench, 'No, I didn't. I didn't look, I didn't want to see.' She stared at Emilio's pale tight - lipped face, chin defiantly high. 'You knew all that time. Why didn't you tell me? Why didn't you try to stop it?'

'What does it the matter? Bit on the side, no big deal, you're not the first.'

'Twenty years?'

'Became a habit I suppose, something he couldn't get out of – you and her the same in the end – old shoes too comfy to throw away.'

'You met her?'

"Course.'

'What was she like?'

'No children, divorced, happy with the flat, didn't need much.'

'Just my husband.'

'Well she didn't say 'no'.'

'What did she look like?'

'Not bad if you like that kind of thing.'

'She wasn't at the funeral.'

'She was.'

'I didn't see her.'

'You weren't meant to.'

'Do the others know?'

'Isabella and Angelo? God no.'

'Not Lucia.'

''Course not.'

'What's she called?'

'Leonora Moretti. Mama it's no big deal, it's not as if he left you.'

'Ah, I'm supposed to be grateful am I?'

'It could be worse.'

'I can't see that at the moment.'

'The real world, mama, the past is dead and over. You've put me in danger mama, only you can undo it, please for God's sake take it back, help me.'

'There's nothing I can do for you, you and your father, traitors, go away, leave me alone.'

'You can't abandon me.'

'You're in a pit of your own making, family isn't important to you, only money and power, you got it wrong, Emilio, you have to find out who your real friends are and what that means.'

'Mama.'

'Go away.'

'I've nowhere to go.'

'Go beg a bed from Isabella, tell her what you did.'

'I didn't do it mama.'

'You did and more, get out.'

His mouth opened a little, 'Get out!' She yelled and picked up the heavy bust.

He swung round and strode swiftly out slamming the door behind him. Dario hit the door and crashed to the floor shattering into pieces skidding along the floor all the way back to Oriana. She sank slowly down the side of the bench to the floor and crouched, head on her knees wrapped in a tight ball.

Why does it matter? It shouldn't matter, not now, not with everything else. A whine rose from her throat to her nose. *But it does, it does. The last piece of you I thought was mine, what little we had, the tenderness of bodies caressing – desire, possession – lies, lies, exclusive rights denied, why is it so important? What's wrong with sharing?*

'Forsaking all others...' *My creamy smooth Adonis – warm, wanting me – me full of me from your want, your need, your love. It is, it is important,* 'and *forsaking all others, keep thee only to me. 'Why wasn't I enough? What did she offer that I couldn't? Were my limbs too short, too long, my hair, eyes, breasts, lips, were they dulled by comparison with her?* Oriana wiped a hand across her mouth, *the humiliation of your hands* and rocked from side to side.

'Free', 'fun,' without children to fret over, house to repair – a fellow traveller in the workaday world, someone with anecdotes to tell – full of cynicism, sophistication – making my rustic simplicity a bore? What did she take? What did she have of you that was mine – did you 'love her, comfort her, honour and protect her?

Where does that leave me? Reduced to a puppet, a wooden puppet — Mrs. Punch, tawdry, dry, splintered – the droll, the butt of jokes. Did you laugh or cry at me? Was I just the can on another bitch's tail? Talk, you talked together, the two of you. What did you share of me, how far the betrayal? Your twenty years in league while I wandered in the wilderness.

Left overs – neither of us could have the man, the whole man. I had nothing but lies; truth was left for her – loneliness for me when I was with you, for her when you were away. You had it all without a qualm, you betrayed your children too, they believed in you.

They're all that's left, my children, I need my children, my grandchildren. Where are they? What have you done both of you? Isabella, Paolo, Giorgio and the twins, Tommaso, Rosa how are they coping? That's where I should be. She shook her head. *I can't face it, my precious little family with a great big hole. There's nothing I can do. I can't see them and I can't be like a satellite circling apart, I have to be with them but Pietro will haunt every space. How are they coping? The unit shattered. Thank God They're in Davina's cottage, I couldn't bear the farmhouse, that's full of us, Pietro and me.*

30

Much to Oriana's relief Martino's farm was in a dip so the burned shell of the farmhouse could not be seen. The holiday cottage was a recent conversion – clean, modern, fully equipped but not home, for Oriana that was a blessing although it added a sense of unreality. The farm was quiet when she arrived and so was the little cottage. She opened the door slowly, tentatively, feeling awkward, afraid of intruding on their grief, as if guilty for their pain.

Rosa and the twins were playing cards at the table and Isabella was changing Giorgio's nappy on the breakfast bar. The girls stared at her and mumbled subdued 'hellos' without getting up. Isabella looked up from the baby without a word. Oriana wrapped her arms round Isabella and gently held her. She went to the twins and kissed the tops of their heads. Rosa stood and they embraced.

Where's Tommaso?' asked Oriana.

'Up on the farm with daddy and Uncle Martino,' replied Rosa.

'How are things there?' Oriana.

'The olives are ready, the animals have to be fed,' said Isabella.

'Of course, one forgets.'

'Farmers can't and we need the money more than ever.'

'Of course, I'm glad Paolo's got his brothers.'

'And they let us have the cottage, they've been good to us.'

' I suppose it means the children can still go to school.'

'After the funeral.'

Oriana froze, her stomach lurched and pulse quickened. *I'm not ready for that, I can't say 'goodbye, I don't want him to go.*

'Where is Pietro?' To speak his name hurt.

'The undertakers collected him from the hospital this morning. Would you like to see him?'

Oriana sank onto the arm of the sofa, 'I don't think I could cope with that, I'm sorry.'

'No, we went together this morning, took him his 'Il Topolino'.'

Tears leaked onto Oriana's cheeks, 'sorry, I didn't want to do this, it's so much worse for you.'

Isabella strapped Giorgio into a carrier and put her arm round her mother's shoulders.

'It's all right mama, we all have to cry. I know how close you two were.'

'I read him Topolino.'

Isabella put her arms round Oriana, 'It was your thing, you and Pietro, he loved anything with you.'

'When will the funeral be?' said Oriana wiping her nose.

'Friday.'

'That's quick. Is there anything I can do?

'Davina and Mariella have taken it on.'

'I'm glad. It seems like we are filling the cemetery. I should have been next.'

'Don't say that Mama.'

Isabella looked at her mother, Oriana's cheeks were hollow and there were dark circles under her eyes. She looked tense perched on the arm of the sofa.

'You've lost weight, are you all right?'

'Yes and no, like all of us.' *Tell her? Tell her the whole sordid story – her father and brother? No, leave it be, she's got enough to deal with.* 'Have you heard anything about the fire?' she asked.

'Nothing more after they said about the smell of petrol outside – nothing about where it came from, there was no can, no sign of intruders.'

'Between the fire and the firemen's hosepipes I don't suppose there'd be much left for them to go on.'

'They did a good job, saved one side of the house and most of the roof.'

'Will insurance cover the damage?'

'More than, Paolo used part of the money his father left him for insurance thank goodness.'

'No idea who did it?'

'It's a mystery Paolo and his brothers keep worrying at. You know Paolo, he hasn't got an enemy in the world. We pay our debts, our suppliers know us and our main neighbours are Martino and Sebastian, there are no grudges there.'

'Have you heard from Angelo? He was shocked when he heard. He wanted to come back.'

'I know I told him there's nothing he can do, nothing anyone can do. I'm glad he found a job.'

'Chef in a pizza place, typical Angelo, he fell on his feet there.'

Isabella smiled, 'And he's charming the pants off his landlady.'

'She gives him dinner.'

'Angelo doesn't know his own power.'

'Unlike some, seen anything of Emilio?'

Isabella shook her head, 'I thought he might come and see us.'

'He can't.'

'Why not?'

'He's in trouble with the police.'

'The police?'

'He's been working for the Mafia.'

Isabella's eyes widened. 'No, he wouldn't.'

'He's been covering up for them, defending them.'

'Never.'

'You've got to believe it, how do you think he got his luxury house, Ferrari, his sense of importance?'

Isabella looked stunned. 'Poor Caterina, no wonder she was unhappy,' she murmured.

'The Mafia came first.'

'Power, wealth, cruelty, how could Emilio let himself be sucked into all that?'

'Too much temptation, too easy for him, they needed him.'

'And now?'

'I don't know what will happen to him now, he got himself into trouble between rival families and they've turned against him, he's on his own.'

'The Mafia won't stand by him?'

'He got too big for his boots and double crossed them over the Ricci case.'

'I wouldn't like to be in his shoes.'

'No.'

'What will happen now?'

'He'll be convicted of perverting the course of justice I suppose.'

'Well he's the best lawyer in town so he'll wing it somehow.'

'It's a bit more serious than that – they've got damning evidence and a witness.'

'Who?'

'Me.'

'You? You would stand witness against Emilio? Never.'

'Someone has to put an end to it.'

'The Mafia, never, it's like digging a hole in sand.'

'I want Emilio out of it.'

'Not like this though surely? In prison?'

'It was his treachery that caused the fire.'

'What?'

'He was trying to play one family off against another and they set fire to the farm as a warning that went wrong.'

Isabella gasped and covered her mouth with her hand.

'The Mafia – us? What are we to the Mafia?'

'A way of getting at Emilio.'

'Do the police know it was them who set fire to the house?'

'Not yet but it'll all come out now.'

'Was that why you did it mama?'

'Partly but what they do is evil, it has to stop.'

'You can't stop it, mama.'

'I can strike a blow, if more people tried they would be weakened, who knows it might end, it won't without trying.'

'It's a dangerous game mama, be careful.'

'I don't care for me, it's about here, family, future generations, Milan.'

Isabella studied her mother's face for doubt but her mouth was set hard.

'You need a break Mama, why don't you take a day off and get away from it all? Have a day with Sofia, one of your lunches, you haven't seen her for a long time have you?

Oriana shook her head, Sofia, her closest friend and soul mate, their intense enlivening lunches, it all seemed part of a different world, a different self.

'No I haven't.' Her voice was thick and low.

'It would do you good.'

'Maybe.' The seed had been sown; the healing balm of confession, of sharing her troubles without compromising another.

'Promise?'

Oriana nodded not trusting her voice.

A van pulled up in front of the cottage.

'That'll be Paolo,' said Isabella.

The girls had finished their game. Giorgio was slumped asleep in his carrier.

'Should I start lunch?' suggested Rosa.

'I'm sorry, I should have brought something,' said Oriana.

'It's Tuesday Mama, not Thursday, we've plenty of pasta and Davina made us a cake. Set the table girls.'

'Let me do that,' said Oriana taking peppers from Isabella.

It was Sebastian in his overalls knocking at the door.

'Come in, come in,' called Isabella.

'Where's Martino?' he asked.

'Up on the farm with Paolo, they should be back any minute. Would you like lunch?'

'No thank you, just wanted to borrow the chain harrow this afternoon.'

'Sit yourself down.'

He looked at the clean sofa and sat on a dining chair.

The water was boiling for the pasta. Isabella held a thick bundle of spaghetti until it softened down into the pan.

'Will you have a glass of wine, Sebastian?' Asked Oriana.

'Okay.'

Oriana poured glasses for the three of them. Isabella shook her head, 'Not while I'm feeding Giorgio.'

'Of course, sorry.'

They heard Martino's truck rattling along the path.

'Daddy's here,' said Maria looking through the window.

Paolo, Martino and Tomaso burst into the sitting room.

'Sebastian.'

They hit each other's shoulders and shook hands.

'Just the person we want,' said Martino

'There's a whole load of rifles in the shed,' announced Tommaso.

Sebastian looked at Paolo, 'where did they come from?'

'Emilio has been using the empty buildings for storage. I didn't ask what, it changed from time to time but those cartons have been there a while. He stacked them by the window all by himself when I needed more space.'

'That broke his back no doubt, city slicker. No wonder he didn't want anyone else to see,' Sebastian whistled, fanned his fingers and shook them, 'ooh la la – guns!'

'It's worrying with the police around investigating the fire, if they're found I'll be in trouble.'

'How could he do that to us?' Asked Isabella then looked at Oriana and her shoulders dropped wearily.

'What should I do?' asked Paolo.

'He doesn't want anything to do with that does he Martino? Get rid quick is what I say,' said Sebastian.

'How and where? It's not possible.'

'It's an expensive lot of gear,' said Martino.

'And dangerous,' added Paolo.

'Who does it belong to?' asked Sebastian, 'did Emilio say?'

'No, just that he wanted to rent the space for a contact. He gave me fifty euros a month.'

'And you asked no questions,' said Martino.

'He's my brother-in-law, I had other things to think about,' replied Paolo

'It's Emilio who's got to get rid and right now, get him over there right away,' said Martino.

'He's right,' said Sebastian, 'better speak to him.'

'We tried, he's not answering.'

'Mobile and home?'

'Have you tried the office? They'll know where he is.'

'Lunch time, I'll try later.'

'You'll not find Emilio, he's been arrested,' announced Oriana.

The three brothers turned to face her.

'What the hell for?'

'Mafia cover ups for a start.'

'He's been working for them?' Paolo asked Oriana, she nodded.

'That'll stir a hornet's nest,' said Martino.

'And we're left with his arsenal,' said Paolo

'It doesn't belong to him,' Martino reminded him.

'What the hell are we going to do with it?'

'There's only one thing we can do,' said Sebastian, 'tell the police.'

'I'm implicated for having them in my shed and the owners will come gunning for us,' said Paolo sinking onto a chair.

'The police have got to be glad to get their hands on them, tell them what happened,' said Martino.

'I don't want to get Emilio into any more trouble.'

'Will Uncle Emilio go to prison? Tomaso asked Oriana.

'I don't know Tomaso but if he's done wrong then he must pay the penalty.'

31

Life in Porta Genova is centred round its canals; markets straddle them, bars jostle along them and cobbled alleyways lead into courtyards from their quays. Art, craft, books and eco fashion feature in its shops with food and wine being left to its sprawling markets. It has an atmosphere all of its own and friendly is top of the list of its charms. Oriana and Sofia's favourite restaurant was on the quayside.

Oriana didn't have far to walk from the station. There wasn't much activity on the water boats moored along the quays were mainly shut up for winter but the bars and restaurants were buzzing with as many people sitting outside as in enjoying a respite from the rain, smoking with their friends. Oriana walked the length of the canal to the main road and back down the quay on the opposite side. A waiter was standing on the waterfront outside their bar touting for trade. He recognised Oriana and waved her inside. Sofia was at a table by the window, she leapt up put her arms round Oriana and gave her a warm loving hug. Oriana clung to her overwhelmed by her own need.

Sofia returned to her chair and asked, 'How are you? What have you been up to?

Oriana steadied herself, 'no, no, tell me about Francesco's inamorata,' she said.

'You were right Carmela is lovely and perfect for Francesco – sporty, organized, nothing like me.'

'But you got on well with her.'

'Like you said, our love for Francesco drew us together, not apart.'

'No one could fail to get on with you.'

'I don't know why anyone puts up with me.'

'You're a free spirit, Sofia, you love life and people.'

'Buongiorno Signorigne.'

The waiter smiled down at them pen poised over his pad.

'What are you going to have?' asked Sofia, 'my turn.'

'I bet it's not, let me.'

'We'll fight later, what do you fancy?'

'Scusi,' Oriana said to the waiter.

They studied the blackboard.

'Gnocchi and cheese, per favore,' said Oriana, 'I need comfort food.'

'I'll have the spinach and tomato penne and two glasses of red wine per favore.'

'Bene, bene,' said the waiter closing his pad.

'So tell me about you – the baby doing well?'

Oriana's mouth tightened, she could only nod. Sofia sat up concerned.

'Is everything all right?'

'No, no it's not. There was a fire…'

'At the house?'

Oriana nodded holding back tears.

'Anybody hurt?'

The dam burst, Oriana started to cry. Sofia ran and held her, rocking slightly. The waiter with the tray of drinks turned back.

Sofia waited.

'Pietro's dead.'

'Oh no,' Sofia groaned, held her tighter and kissed her forehead. 'Oh Oriana I am so sorry.' She crouched to look into Oriana's face. Oriana kept her head down unable to deal with sympathy and fumbled in her bag for a handkerchief.

'There's been so much going on' she mumbled, 'I haven't had time for it to sink in.'

'Dear oh dear, there's nothing I can say, and there's more?' She peered earnestly into Oriana's face. Oriana nodded lips tightly compressed then tried to sound more positive continuing the saga.

'Angelo's in Modena please God, running from the mafia.'

'Mafia, how did he get mixed up with them?'

'Debt, he couldn't pay so he worked for them without realizing what he was doing.'

'And when he found out he couldn't get out?'

'You've got it.' Oriana blew her nose.

'You have been having a rough time.' Sofia returned to her chair.

'That's not the end of it, our law firm is in the pay of the Mafia, cheating the system to get them off.'

'Never, I don't believe it – Emilio?'

Oriana nodded, 'Dario too, from the beginning.'

'No, the odd case maybe but dependent on the Mafia, not possible.'

'My world has been turned upside down.'

'You had no idea?'

Oriana shook her head. The tray of wine was finally delivered.

Sofia picked up her glass, 'You need this.'

'If only it could wipe it away, ' Oriana sipped not tasting the wine for the turmoil in her head, all of a sudden she had an understanding ear, someone who knew her and she didn't know where to start, what she wanted to say.

'It'll dull the pain,' said Sofia and chinked Oriana's glass.

'How could they keep that secret all this time?' Sofia asked.

'Don't bring work home, that was the rule, especially with them working together, I respected it, they had to relax.'

'You never suspected?'

'None so blind as those who don't want to see…'

'Oh Oriana,' she reached across the table for Oriana's hand. 'This is so far from you.'

'From everything we believe in, you and me. I feel like a light bulb shattered into a thousand pieces.'

'We'll just have to put you together again. You're strong my friend, you'll get over it, we do, women are survivors.'

'I don't know who I am anymore. I'm not what I thought I was, I hate everything that my life was founded on. I was a fool thinking that I could hold my head up high in the world supporting men who brought justice to the poor. People must have despised me.'

'No one who knew you, not your friends Oriana or the people who bought your art, they know the kind of person you are or your family, they depend on your kindness, they share your values.'

'Emilio?'

'Like father...? You had nothing to do with that.'

'I betrayed him to the police.'

'You did what?'

'He sent me to collect his papers, Mafia papers, their dealings – sickening – people trafficking, drugs, gambling, he was supporting all of that and the farm fire – the farmhouse was burned because of him, Emilio's double dealing, they did it as a warning.'

'Oh my God.'

'They played a dangerous game and my boy died.'

'You told the police, that took courage.'

'No just outrage and Pietro in my arms...'

'You have been through the mill.'

'One person in a family gets involved and it drags all of them down. What did I do wrong to make him so hard?'

'You are not responsible for Emilio, for any of them now, they've long since grown and flown.'

'But we make them what they are.'

'They share our lives for a brief spell Oriana and they're buffeted by others from the start. They have their own chemistry too you know, we're not Gods. They take on the world in their own ways adapting as they see fit.'

'And all we can do it watch and worry.'

Two plates of pasta arrived.

'More wine please,' said Sofia.

'Buon appetito,' said the waiter and left.

'This is good,' Oriana had forgotten the pleasure of a shared meal. 'How is Bruno?' She asked.

'Busy with his book.'

'His health is better?'

'The medication keeps him well but he can't do much these days. The book keeps him going.'

'Philosophy?'

'Umm, he's in good company.'

'He's impressive and so are you, any more poetry for me?'

'Should I send you some?'

'A comfort that stays, I go back to your poems every now and again. I keep them in a drawer in the studio, my territory.'

'Thank you.'

They ate in silence enjoying the comfort of warm pasta mulling things over in their heads.

'How bad is the damage to the farmhouse?'

'One end is gutted, they're staying in one of Martino's cottages.'

'Were they insured?'

Oriana nodded mouth full of warm cheese and potato, 'they are, thank God.'

'Some comfort then.'

'Yes.'

'What about you, are you going to stay where you are?'

Oriana put down her spoon. 'I don't know what to do. Everything in the house seemed a sham, I couldn't live with my pathetic pretense of 'Happy Families' so I burned it all.'

'Everything?'

Oriana nodded, 'the lot.'

'That was some bonfire.'

'Satisfying, years of pain melting away, warming me.'

'Was it that bad?'

'He had a mistress, I thought it was work that kept him away long hours and preoccupied when he was home.'

'How did you find out?'

'Emilio, angry at me going to the police.'

'Spite, how do you know it's true?'

'It all fell into place, why not? The shock is how long it lasted.'

'How long was it?'

'Twenty years.'

'I didn't know you were unhappy with him.'

'I wasn't in the beginning, it's difficult to let go. I always felt ashamed of my unhappiness so I could never share it with anyone. I was devastated when I heard about her – Leonora Moretti – she's been sharing my life for all that time without me knowing it.'

'That's awful, you were too god for him, he didn't deserve you – what kind of a man was he – a liar and a cheat, he's not worth crying over.'

'I don't know what happened to him or when but that wasn't the man I married.'

'I'm sorry.'

'Sort of pulled the rug from under me, I despise myself for being such a fool.'

'It's not you, you are loyal, you tried your best. He wasn't up to you.'

'It all seems such a waste of time and energy – the agony of loneliness, the desperate attempts to make him happy, keep the peace.'

'You needed to be loved, you were eager to please. He should have treasured the gold mine he had instead of digging for tin.'

'Who knows she may be platinum.'

'Bet you she's nothing to write home about.'

'I don't know what she's like.'

'Someone happy to carry on an adulterous affair, do you want to find out?'

'I am curious, how much does she know? How involved was she? What attracted him enough to lead a double life?'

'Some men enjoy the subterfuge as much as the cause like children.'

'In some ways I'm still in denial, the reversal of everything I believed about him, the person I had in my mind as we shared a meal, a bed, the father of my children I am still groping to get to know this different Dario.'

'It'll take time.'

'I want to close the lid on the Pandora's box, file him away. There's only one Dario who is a complete mystery now and that's Leonora's. I've been part of her life too, she's had time to get to know me and my family, I'd like to know how much privacy I have left, what impression he's given her of us.'

'Do you want to meet her?'

'I don't see any reason why not, it's the final piece in the jig saw that was my husband.'

'Don't get hurt.'

'Nothing can hurt me more than the shocks of the past two weeks, I'm bomb proof.'

'I hope so, be careful.'

'The thought of that little adventure has given me an appetite, this gnocchi's good.'

'I don't suppose you've had much time in the studio with all this.'

'I had just got back in there when it all erupted. I took some of my old work to Francesco the other day and he didn't send me packing so I'm getting back in harness.'

'I bet he welcomed you with open arms, you underestimate yourself, you're a serious artist. I'm glad you're getting back to it, you've got more to offer the world than a hot dinner.'

'Battista phoned as well, someone was leafing through his print stand and liked the photos of my reclining loop, he's talking of a commission.'

'That's brilliant Oriana, quite a challenge.'

Yes, getting back into stone won't be easy, at least not until I've found my subject.'

'Then it'll roll. What got you back to work?'

'A bust of Dario.'

They both erupted into laughter and the waiter kept two full glasses of wine above their heads until they had finished then set them carefully down. They chinked glasses,

'To friendship!'

32

The church was as full of children as adults, people stood at the back and down the sides, young families holding hands. As they filed out after the service a tall boy in a dark blue anorak slipped into step beside Rosa, she lifted her head and put her hand over her mouth to stifle a cry, 'Giacomo!' He took her hand and walked beside her. Isabella rose from her torpor for a moment and Lucia squeezed her sister's hand smiled and nodded in their direction. Oriana was surprised. *Rosa's a quiet one and deep, whoever he is, it's good of him to come. She wasn't expecting him.* They all crowded round the little grave ignoring the steady drizzle holding hands or hugging themselves in grief. Rosa and Giacomo stood looking solemnly at the edge holding hands. Oriana felt ashamed that Emilio was not there and she missed Angelo. When Pietro's little white coffin was lowered into the ground the twins wept uncontrollably, Oriana pulled them into her and held them without a word while they buried their heads in her coat. Isabella held Giorgio's sleeping body tight, her breathing shallow and rapid in an attempt to stave off tears. Lucia had her arm around her sister's shoulder. Paolo succumbed and sobbed with Tomaso looking lost by his side.

After the covering of soil and the final blessing Oriana felt rooted to the spot, she didn't want to leave him.

'Can I walk with you?' Lucia took Oriana's arm.

'Oh, yes, yes we must go.'

'Back to the farmhouse. He had a lot of friends.'

'He did, quiet though he was, he didn't forget people.'

'How are you mama?'

'Numb.'

'It'll take time, God will help you find a way.'

Oriana almost laughed feeling overwhelmed, 'he'll have a hard job to unscramble here.' She pointed to her head.

'Only you can do that but he'll help.'

Davina's sitting room was warm and comfortable after the drizzle. Isabella and Paolo stood by the door accepting condolences and Rosa introduced her 'friend from school,' Giacomo.'

He shook their hands. 'I am deeply sorry for your loss,' he said.

'Thank you,' said Paolo.

'Thank you for coming, Giacomo.' Isabella looked at Rosa, 'I'm glad you have a friend with you.'

'Thank you mama'

Rosa fetched Giacomo a hot chocolate.

'How did you know?' She asked.

'Your friend Silvia told me.'

'It was good of you to come.'

'I had to be with you, I know how close you are to your family. I heard the house was burned, how bad is it?'

'Bad enough, we can't live there, we're in one of Davina's holiday cottages.'

'How long for?'

'We don't know, people have been very good, the builders are making us priority.'

'You can't farm long distance eh?'

They smiled weakly at each other.

'Aren't you going to introduce me?' asked Lucia.

Rosa blushed and bowed her head, Giacomo was looking into Lucia's eyes, 'I'm Giacomo,' he said.

Rosa said, 'this is my aunt Lucia.'

'Pleased to meet you sister Lucia.'

'And I you, I've heard a lot about you.'

'Oh really?' Giacomo looked at Rosa.

'My favourite Aunty, she helped with Giorgio's christening,' Rosa explained.

'And Rosa made me her famous apple cake.'

'We did it together.'

'How is university, Physics wasn't it?' asked Lucia.

'That's right,' he said surprised. 'It's a lot of work but I don't mind that, it's interesting.'

'You have some good tutors?'

Giacomo nodded, 'very good.'

'Have you made many friends?'

'One or two in the hall of residence but some can be show offs.'

'No one on your course?'

'They're a bit intense and some are from the same school so they stick together.'

'I wouldn't worry about that, University will sort them out and you'll all find your own way round.'

'I'm happy to keep my head down at the moment,' said Giacomo looking at Rosa.

'I'll leave you to it, I'd better circulate, I'm glad we've met.' Lucia extended a hand and they shook.

'She's nice,' said Giacomo, 'why didn't you tell me about her?'

Rosa shrugged, 'don't know, she's always there even though it's in the background.'

'Some people are like that, they make themselves indispensible.'

'Mmm, that's it, I'd better help serve people' said Rosa.

'I'll join you.'

The dining room table was laden with casseroles, salads, bread, cakes and biscuits brought to them throughout the week by Pietro's visitors. Rosa and Giacomo took plates and circulated.

Oriana left her wet coat in the bedroom. As she came downstairs Elena was being welcomed by Paolo and Isabella.

'It's been a long time but I remember playing with Clara and Guiseppe in your garden,' Isabella said to Elena.

'The wilderness?'

'It was much more fun that way, how are they?'

'Neither of them is married, I'm longing for grandchildren.'

'Give it time.'

'Elena!' Oriana touched Elena's arm.

They embraced.

'Oriana, I am sorry, the fire, it's awful.' She looked up at Oriana's face, 'Everyone sends their love – Francesco and Battista. Francesco said you're making a comeback, I'm glad. Your stone sculpture made ripples in the art circle, Battista says he has a commission for you.'

'It's all a bit vague at the moment. I haven't worked stone for a while.'

'I hope it goes well, I'm sure it will.'

'Thanks Elena.'

Sofia and Bruno were shaking rain off their umbrella at the door.

'Do you know Sofia and Bruno?'

Elena looked over to the couple and shook her head, 'can't say I do.'

Oriana brought them over. 'I'd like you to meet Elena,' she said, 'I must see if there's anything I can do, I'll see you later.'

'It's sad isn't it?' said Elena.

'Yes,' said Sofia watching Oriana's back disappear into the sitting room. 'Oriana doesn't look well.'

'Not so bright as when I last saw her,' agreed Elena.

'Not surprising really,' said Bruno, 'how do you know her?'

Oriana picked up a bowl of olives to pass around. Paolo's mother was holding court in a corner of the sitting room surrounded by friends and family. When she saw Oriana she waved her over.

'Who would have thought,' she said and pressed a handkerchief to her face.

'We're in the same boat,' said Oriana, 'he was a very special little boy.'

'He was, he was kind,' Beatrice sighed.

'Nothing we can do but be brave for Paolo and Isabella and the children.'

'Yes, we must.'

'Can I fill your glass?'

'Oh no thank you, that's enough, I brought some pastries, if you could pass me one of those.'

'Of course.'

Oriana took the plate to Beatrice and went back to the table to meet Rosa's young man.

'You're still at school?' Said Oriana, 'You're far too tall and grown up.'

Giacomo laughed, 'It's my last year.'

'So what are you going to do?'

'Physics at University then a job as a data scientist if I'm lucky.'

'Sounds good, what about you Rosa?'

'Fashion design if I can get a place at college.'

'I'm sure you will, you've made lots of fun outfits in the past few years.' She turned to Giacomo. 'I'm sorry we have to meet in such sad circumstances.'

Giacomo nodded, 'I had tickets for 'Amice per Abruzzo' this weekend, the concert for the victims of the earthquake, I'll have to sell them.'

'No, Giacomo, it would do Rosa good to get away, there's nothing we can do for Pietro, grieving is not a day, a week, a year, our loved ones never leave us it's a re-location, an adjustment that takes a while to settle in. We're all sunk in our own sorrow Rosa is a sensitive caring soul, your support and the break will help. It's for a good cause too, you mustn't cancel.'

'What do you think, Rosa?'

Rosa looked at Oriana, 'if Nonna thinks it's all right…'

'That's settled then, what are your favourite songs?'

''Vita' Gigi D'Alesso,' said Giacomo quick as a flash.

''Alle Porte Del Sogno' Irene Grandi,' said Rosa.

'It's Laura Pausini organizing the concert,' said Giacomo.

'I liked her 'Donna D'Onna.' Said Oriana.

Rosa and Giacomo looked at her, 'you've heard it?' Said Giacomo.

'I like all kinds of music and I like dancing too, so 'course I've heard 'Donna D'Onna.''

'Giacomo plays in the school orchestra.'

'That's how we met,' said Giacomo.

'So music brought you together, we'll have to dance to that in happier days.'

'We'll keep you to it, Nonna.'

'Cool,' said Giacomo. Oriana laughed in relief.

Feeling guilty they separated to circulate and Oriana looked for Sofia.

'How are you?' asked Sofia.

'Nothing seems real, in suspended animation…? I don't know.'

'If there's anything I can do…'

Oriana nodded, 'si, si I know, I can depend on you, thank you Sofia.'

'Si, si Bella, we're here, it's a tragedy, sorry, sorry,' growled Bruno in a voice thick with emotion.

'Thank you, thank you for coming.'

'Meet again soon?' Sofia held on to Oriana's hand.   Oriana nodded squeezed her hand and turned back into the crowd saying, "bye Bruno.' She took a plate of biscuits for the twins and found them drinking orange juice in the kitchen with Sebastian's son and daughter.

'Here are some biscuits for you all.'

'Thank you Aunty,' said Rinaldo who was about the same age as Tommaso.

'Have you seen Tommaso?' She asked.

'He went home.'

Tommaso the dark horse, lost to the farm, the one who shared his room with Pietro, who always wanted to be a big strong man. Do I track him down or leave him in peace?

Leave him to deal with it alone at the moment. It must have been awful pressure to be with Paolo all the time. He has had to be strong for his father, now he has a bit of space to come to terms with it himself.

Isabella brought a stack of empty plates into the kitchen and shooed the children out to socialize.

'How are you mama?'

'Numb at the moment, how are you?'

'Distracted right now, it's tomorrow and tomorrow that is the problem.'

'I know.'

'Yes, you've just had eighteen months of tomorrows, I forget.'

'A husband later in life is different from a child.'

'It's the unexpectedness that is difficult, I can't believe it or don't want to, I'm confused.'

'All you can do is hang on to what you've got.'

'Paolo and the children and you mama, you've always been a rock for us.'

'Crumbling with time I'm afraid.'

'Never, you've a will of iron.'

'And fists of steel?' Oriana raised her eyebrow that she used to do to quiz her children when they were naughty. They both smiled.

'You didn't need them,' said Isabella.

Oriana felt at ease with Paolo's friends and relatives, all the people who had turned up to say 'goodbye' to Pietro. Dario's funeral was a colder fuller affair, more formal, distant somehow. She felt no connection with the smart suits, diamond studded tie pins and shiny shoed guests there. She had been grateful to leave it to Emilio to shake their hands and accept their tributes. Now she knew why – she wasn't the alien, they were.

People left in quiet groups until only family remained to clear everything away. Davina and Mirielle tried to send Isabella and Oriana away but Isabella was glad to be out of their temporary cocoon into the wider, more familiar space of a farmhouse with things to do. Oriana wanted a quiet moment with Pietro so she took her leave and returned to the deserted cemetery with it's little mound of raw earth covered in wet flowers.

'Thank you,' she whispered, 'thank you for giving me so much...'

She felt dispirited when she got home but at least the house itself wasn't a challenge, it was no longer the family museum, it didn't mock or oppress her anymore. Aimlessly she passed through the empty kitchen to the hallway and heard a low, growling miaow coming from the sitting room. Baffina was prowling from room to room. She passed Oriana, went into the kitchen and settled back on her haunches, eyes focused on her empty shelf. She leapt from the floor where she usually had a chair to leap from so she could only reach the edge. Her claws scratched the wood as the weight of her body pulled her down.

'Sorry, sorry, ' Oriana bent to stroke her. Baffina's throat rumbled. 'I know, it's your home too.'

She brought a chair from the back door and stood it in the middle of the floor but Baffina ran out through the cat flap. Oriana went in search of the others. Tancreda had installed herself on a couple of sacks in the corner of the garage and Burrichio was outside on top of a pile of old grass clippings behind the garden shed. *What have I done?* She filled their bowls and took them into the house.

'I'll get proper beds for you, you can stay in the kitchen.'

The next morning she took a brush and swept floors, walls and windows gaining energy as she tipped away the dust and mess. She filled a bucket with hot water and detergent to scrub the floors and left them overnight to dry before she washed the walls, cleaned the windows, frames and doors, everything until her body could do no more and exhaustion let her sleep.

33

Their secretary answered the office phone quickly, Oriana gathered her courage and tried to sound casual, confident.

'Good morning Tessa, how are you?'

'Signora Rossi, good thank you, how about you?' Deferential, curious Tessa waited.

'Well thank you, life moves on...'

'Yes, yes...'

'It's better that way.'

'I'm glad, can I help?'

'I've been clearing out some of Signor Rossi's belongings and I thought his friend in the city, Leonora I believe might like one or two things. Do you have an address for her?'

'Oh.'

'Are you still there?'

'Yes, yes, I'm here.'

'Do you have Leonora's address?'

'To give her some of Signor Rossi's belongings?'

'Well they're not much use to him now are they? Don't worry Tessa, it's all right.'

'Really?'

'I wouldn't be asking if not.'

'I'll look, should I call you back?'

'No, I'll wait.'

It wasn't long before she returned, 'La Farina, 108 – 123 Campo Di Marte, in the centre.'

Oriana wrote it carefully on the notebook she had ready and said, 'Thank you, good day.'

'Thank you, Signora, good luck.'

Oriana googled a street view, the block was relatively recent, brick, not too high. Her determination to follow this through only foundered once and that was when she opened her wardrobe to choose an outfit, black seemed hypocritical. She had had enough of it anyway, trousers? Even her best looked dowdy but she was too tall and gangly for skirts and blouses, it had to be a dress but she didn't have many. She found a dark green fitted dress of fine wool that she thought was plain enough and jade earrings to match. Shoes defeated her. She had given up stilettos long ago. Her boots were all too clumsy so that left her with moccasins.

The car park was almost empty, she checked her watch; six o clock, everyone was probably still at work. She hid her little fiat in a far corner and looked up at the red brick front with its wrought iron balconies. There were lawns with Japanese cloud trees and neatly trimmed box hedging at the front and shallow steps that ran the length of the wide glass entrance. Its doors separated smoothly as she reached the top of the steps and a man looked up from a counter.

'Can I help?' He asked.

'Leonora Moretti per favore.'

'Is she expecting you?'

'No but we're old friends.'

He looked at Oriana's frank face, her hazel green eyes, scanned her lean figure in the sober green dress and coat then said, 'apartment 67, third floor.'

'Thank you, have a good day.'

The lift surrounded her with mirrors. *My hands are too big, sculptor's hands, not fit for anything else.* She swapped her bag from one shoulder to another. *I don't know why I chose this shiny little thing, backpacks are much better.* There were little lines above her nose and her donkey brown hair was speckled with grey and gold. *God I look old, I wonder how old she is?* She inspected the little lines that cut her upper lip *–disappointment? Bitterness? Life. I hope she doesn't think I'm here to make a scene. She must be as curious as I am but she's been able to follow my comings and goings and I don't know a thing about her.'*

Her footsteps sounded military as she counted door numbers along the tiled corridor down to 67. She was glad there wasn't a spy hole in the door, it gave her the slight advantage of surprise. When the door opened she looked down at a neat figure in a fitted black suit with coarse black hair tailored close to her head, deep red lips, plucked eyebrows and a look of surprise that was quickly replaced by a triumphant smile.

'Signora Rossi, welcome.'

Instant recognition, no need for introductions then. Leonora stepped aside and held the door open for Oriana.

'Thank you,' said Oriana wiping her feet looking at a white tiled floor with a narrow grey border. There was a white wrought iron table with glass top and mirror above it and empty pegs on either side.

'Follow me.'Leonara's feet were bare. She was wearing glossy black tights.

Her sitting room was spacious with a long low grey sofa and two woven metal chairs with blue and green cushions. An artificial palm tree stood in a corner by sliding windows onto a balcony that overlooked rooftops across the river to the hills. Beside a stone fireplace at the far end of the room there was a low oak cupboard with photographs, the only sign of life in the room. They looked familiar, Oriana recognized them – Dario and Emilio on the day of their partnership, Dario with a rose in his button hole and Isabella on his arm in her wedding dress *home from home,* except that in between there was one of a younger Dario in sunglasses and swim suit with his arm round Leonora, nut brown in a white bikini sporting a dense halo of hair grinning into the camera. Leonora followed Oriana's gaze.

'It's been a long time,' she laughed.

Leonora's voice startled Oriana, made her realize her vulnerability, she murmured, 'I suppose it has.'

'On the edge, the margin of his life.'

'Why did you put up with it?'

Leonora swept her arm around the apartment. *No expense spared so, was it worth it?* 'And I was the only one at work who got champagne and roses while they moaned about bills and kids and cooking. You miss him too?'

'I thought I did.'

'Well it's all over now and I wouldn't change it. I haven't been home long I was about to get myself a drink would you like one?' A pair of stilettoes lay by the sofa and an open magazine lay on the glass coffee table. 'Prosecco?'

'Yes I will thank you.'

'Have a seat.'

Leonora padded briskly into the kitchen past a doorstop shaped like a black cat.

There were two long narrow canvases one above the other over the mantelpiece – thick dull grey paint with pink and white at the top of one and deep purple under red and turquoise in the one below.

Leonora handed her a large glass of fizzing wine, for an awkward moment Oriana thought she might try to chink glasses but she stood at her side looking at the paintings.

'Sunrise and Sunset, good aren't't they?'

'The titles make sense. '

'Sergio Spata, have you heard of him?'

Oriana looked at Leonora's eager face lit by the windows, make up clogged the pores over her nose, her skin was heavy subsiding a little down her cheeks.

'I can't say I have,' Oriana replied.

'He was being interviewed by the magazine, quite the name, so we had to do it didn't we?'

'Which magazine?'

''Amica' of course, you didn't know I worked there?'

'No. It must be interesting working for a magazine.'

'Not really, I'm in the office mainly on the computer, there are lots of us.'

'It must be nice to work with people.'

'Pough, they're more boring than the job, nothing to talk about but their children and grandchildren some of them, what they're cooking and eating, fat pigs. Not many Italian women look after themselves when they're married. Sit yourself down, ' said Leonora settling down on the sofa with her drink.

Oriana put her glass on the table and perched at the other end.

'Why now?' Her dark eyes challenged Oriana.

'I've only just found out.'

'You didn't know all this time?'

'You know Dario he was always Signor Plausible.'

'He was that all right but easy if you learned how to handle him.'

A lesson I didn't want to learn, not my idea of a relationship.

Oriana looked round the immaculate apartment and said, 'I suppose you did. You didn't have children before you met?' asked Oriana

'A son, he must be thirty now.'

'You don't see him?'

'Heavens no, he's in America I think, leastways that's where his father took him.'

'His father took him away?'

'When he was five, never so much as a 'bye your leave' just upped and went before I knew it.'

'But you traced them?'

Leonora laughed, 'He didn't leave a forwarding address.'

'So how do you know he's in America?'

'He had the cheek to ask me to send things on when they were settled.'

'So you had an address.'

'I wasn't going all that way, couldn't afford the ticket anyway, better off without him.'

'What about your son?'

'Boys need their dad don't they? He was okay with the way things were, I couldn't work and look after him.'

'I'm sorry.'

'Long time ago, better off the way it turned out.'

'Do you travel a lot?'

'Not really, got everything I want here. We went to Lanzarote once, a perfect week, not too hot, went to the top of the volcano – bit like the moon really. Did a bit of sunbathing, pity the sand's all grey. Didn't like the food much, bony fish.'

'Not very interesting then?'

'Don't need much on holiday do you – sun and restaurants.'

'For me it was sea and sand for the children then later if I went away it was usually something to do with art'

'Yes Dario got you a studio to play around in didn't he so what do you do?'

'Ceramics and stone.'

'You're a potter then?'

'You haven't seen any of my work?'

'Can't say I have, Dario didn't talk about it much.'

'Have you never been to Artignano, Studio Iguarnieri or the Lucca Center?'

Leonora shook her head, 'never heard of them.'

'You might have seen my work if you had.'

'You have stuff in galleries?'

'For a long time.'

'I don't know why he didn't mention it.'

'The studio wasn't his territory, my work didn't involve him apart from the occasional opening.'

'I must see some of it,' Leonora drained her glass, 'Would you like another glass of bubbly?'

Oriana looked at her full glass on the table and said, 'No thanks I'm driving.'

'I'll get some nibbles.'

Leonora hoisted herself up, adjusted her tight skirt and headed for the kitchen leaving the door propped open. Oriana watched her tip nuts and olives into bowls and slice salami onto a plate. The kitchen looked new with black granite tops and white cupboards and shiny pans hanging from a bar over a stainless steel range but no sign of food. On the wall opposite the door there was a cat calendar. Oriana stood at the door, 'is there anything I can do?

'You can carry these,' she handed Oriana a plate of ham and bowl of crisps then followed her back to the sofa carrying another glass of Prosecco, olives and nuts.

'Help yourself,' she said rolling up a piece of salami.

Oriana sipped her wine wishing she felt hungry.

'Do you have a cat?' She asked looking at the doorstop.

'Good lord no, they shed fur and get fleas.'

'Not if you look after them.'

'Too much bother, what do I need a cat for?'

'Company?'

'I've got all the company I want on the tele.'

'Will you move when you retire?'

'Heavens no, where would I go?'

'Cottage by the sea.'

'Sounds cold and draughty and no decent shops, let alone hairdressers and manicurists.'

The fingers holding her glass had perfectly lacquered long nails. Oriana finished her drink.

'May I use the toilet?'

Leonora nodded, 'through the bedroom first on the right in the hall.'

The curtains were closed, the room was hushed, the bed, covered in a satin quilt, was reflected in the triple mirrors of the dressing table which had a jewellery box in the middle and photos on either side – her sunset portrait of Dario and an older looking Dario with a pregnant Leonora sitting on a bench. Her heart skipped a beat and her eyes widened. *A baby, they had a baby? Where is it now? Why didn't I know? She's been lying, covering up. I thought I was coping well, why does this make so much difference?* She gripped the edge of the dressing table to steady herself. *It all seems such a mess all of a sudden.*

In the clinical shower room she noticed her hand was shaking as she combed her hair and compared her face to Leonora's dark olive complexion and short wiry hair, her neat body in designer clothes. *I can't go back in there, how can I get out? I want to run.*

Leonora had tucked her feet under her and was settled back in the corner of the sofa facing Oriana's place with her arm along the back sipping her drink. Oriana couldn't sit down, Leonora looked up surprised.

'Everything all right in there?'

'The photos, I couldn't help…'

'Photos?'

'You had a baby, the two of you?'

'Ah,' Leonora's confusion cleared, she became serious.' That's the only evidence of the baby, I had a termination a week later.'

Oriana sank back into her seat, 'why?'

'The baby had down's syndrome.'

'I'm sorry.'

'I suppose it was a blessing in disguise although once I'd got my head round it, it seemed exciting for a while.'

'Yes, baby's are.'

'But demanding.'

'And rewarding but yes, it would have complicated life for both of you. Did you ask him to leave me?'

'At first I thought I wanted him all to myself then with the apartment and the excitement of his visits, our outings and the treats I decided it was better the way it was. I'm a bit of a stick in the mud, like things neat and tidy, didn't really want a man messing thigs up and all those dinners to think of. I'm better by myself when I get up, don't want to see anyone else's morning face.'

'You make it seem quite attractive.'

'It suited me.'

'And Dario, well I'm glad we've met I'd better get back, must'nt over stay my welcome.'

'Oh you won't do that, the number of times I've wanted to get together…'

'We shared a lot without knowing it.'

'One man.'

'A different man to each of us.'

'I thought we could compare notes.'

Oriana was shocked, *Gossip about Dario like friendly rivals? He is of absolutely no interest to me anymore now I've got the full picture.* She looked down into Leonora's cheerful face. *Untroubled waters, she's in control but not of my kind of world.* 'Probably not a good idea,' she said.

'You think not? No hard feelings?'

'No, no hard feelings, it was Dario's decision.'

Leonora led her to the door, 'arriverdeci.'

'Ciao.'

Oriana needed space and green fields so she drove on into the hills, parked the car and walked away the tension, walked through the kaleidoscope of impressions in her head surprised at her own calm. *I'm not jealous I envy her nothing, not the time with him that she stole from me. She doesn't love people she's above them just like Dario. Art's an investment not an insight into human experience. There wasn't a book in the place, she's not curious about the world or people, a closed mind satisfied with itself. Was Dario like that? I suppose he was. He didn't like to be challenged. She's not a rival for anything I want or want to be a part of. They are kindred spirits not soul mates they weren't capable of that.* Once she had walked her way through it and back to herself she felt better, freer. He really wasn't worth regret or jealousy, Leonora was welcome to what she had of him.

34

Her bitterness at being deprived of an illusory honeymoon on his retirement and at the years of loneliness in their marriage, her guilt at her sense of failure from the emptiness of it had gone all that was left was regret that the children suffered from not having a happy mother rather than one who was constantly trying to minimise their impact on their father, trying to keep him happy. Relieved of all that she could go into the studio with a mind free to create, it was no longer a place to escape to or beat out tensions. At last she could create from the depths of her own being not in futile search of something that wasn't there.

She pushed the door sweeping away shards of clay and stood surveying the remains of Dario's bust. *Bits of clay, broken images – good Dario, bad Dario, nothing so simple, the truth was out there not in my head, pity it had to hammer at my door before I went to look. The real Dario? Not worth commemorating.* She swept him onto a shovel.. She emptied the shovel into the bin, *Dust and rubbish, nothing left now* and closed the lid.

Peace seeped through her and with it emptiness, the emptiness of waiting for inspiration. She selected pots and dishes from shelves, *Francesco will be glad of these, tourist fodder if nothing else,* then swept and cleaned the studio preparing for an unknown project before returning to the house. Its bare floors and walls looked old fashioned and neglected. *White, it needs to be white, bright and clear, empty and clean, a coat of white paint, that's what I'll do, I'll paint the place white – fresh canvas for a new life.*

She drove to a commercial centre and bought paint, tray, roller and brushes. On her way out she passed a tobacco kiosk with a billboard outside *Il Giornale.*

'Mafia trial, new evidence.'

She loaded her car and went back. Magazines, newspapers and plastic toys were stacked high along a narrow stand down the middle of the shop. The dirty floor was uneven. Cigarettes were crammed high on shelves behind the shopkeeper, a big man with a paunch and dark stubble.

'Buongiorno,' he said.

'Buogiorno.'

The gloomy interior smelled of tobacco and stale paper. Oriana took a copy of *Il Giornale* from a wire stand and folded it under her arm while she sorted coins from her purse. The narrow glass counter was full of sweets and chocolate and had a lottery ticket stand on top. As soon as she got to the car she started to read.

Ricci Case Last Days

Shock reversal. Solicitor quits, called as witness.

In a dramatic turn of events yesterday Emilio Rossi resigned as solicitor for the defence of Marco Ricci saying that he has been summoned by the police to act as witness for the prosecution.

Thirty-six year old Marco Ricci accused of drug dealing, money laundering and trafficking owns several hotels and apartment blocks in and around Florence. He is known for his celebrity life style with his yacht and succession of glamorous girlfriends. It is alleged that he built his considerable fortune on illegal gambling and prostitution and has recently been associated with Mafia groups. Our reporter has been informed of a conflict between two Mafia families about the outcome of Ricci's trial.

The police are in possession of startling new evidence as to the extent of his criminal activities. It seems that Signor Rossi is implicated in covering up the illegal activities of the 'Ndranghetta over a period of time. The police have offered leniency in exchange for information.

This will now be played out in court under full public scrutiny. What will be revealed in court next week? Follow *Il Giornale's* daily coverage.

Oriana's pulse raced, she threw the paper onto the seat beside her, *What did you expect? This is how it's going to be, you knew things would change. But I didn't know how. How will people react? Will the Mafia target him like he said? That folder was enough to send a whole network down. They won't take his betrayal without hitting back but he's too much in the public eye to 'disappear' surely they wouldn't risk that.*

She picked up the paper and scanned it. *It's all so complicated. Who is going to defend Emilio? Is anyone above threats and bribes, beyond the influence of the Mafia? There has to be. Will Emilio learn from seeing justice at work or hate being exposed to it?*

What should I do? I have to be there even if he hates me for it. Will he think that I've come to gloat? I hope not. I have to be with him, watch over him, my life is on hold until I've seen this through, I don't know how he'll react. Will he ever forgive me? Does it depend on the extent of the damage? Can he see a world apart from theirs? I wish it were all over instead of just beginning. How long will it take?

35

Through the window every blade of grass, plant and tree was wrapped in a coat of crystal hiding the fire's scar and unifying everything in sparkling whiteness. Tancreda's black and brown fur looked darker, warmer as she stalked hidden prey at the end of the garden.

It was early very early Oriana suspected there would be crowds at the trial. She shivered standing looking out of the window in her pyjamas, *I'd better wear something warm.* She chose grey wool trousers, cable knit jumper and matching hat to go with her grey coat, an outfit anonymous enough to blend into the background.

There was already a line of silent people huddled under a covered a corridor with arches around a courtyard. When they finally began to shuffle through the doors the queue behind her went round the courtyard and out on to the street.

It must be more than curiosity that drove them out so early to stand in the cold but there can't be that many actually involved can there? I suppose people like Ricci affect more lives than we think and mention of the Mafia always draws a crowd, thank you F.F. but this is no film, it's nasty and it's big – so many different names and places and my son is at the centre – my fault, I put him in the spotlight, I lobbed a hand grenade. If he follows through he'll be free of the Mafia and so will Angelo. I just hope it doesn't turn out to be a bomb that destroys us. Ricci is guilty. The Mafia is guilty. Public though it is this is the only way to stop it.

She followed shrouded backs into a room with windows on each side – bright morning sun opposite the door and gloomy shadows from the courtyard on the corridor side. The Judge's bench was at the far end with a witness box on one side and the dock on the other. Oriana hid herself at the back close to the door hoping Emilio wouldn't see her. She watched people choosing their seats, *like a theatre waiting for the play to begin.*

A side door at the end of the room opened to reveal a young solicitor followed by Marco Ricci. They sat opposite the witness box. Ricci nodded stiffly to one or two well dressed men in the front row and raised a weak smile for a smartly dressed woman with an older companion behind them then he studied the faces of the people filing in. Oriana was glad they had never been introduced. She kept looking for Emilio as if the show couldn't begin without him. The judge appeared and everybody stood. She scrutinized the people in her row and the backs in front of her. Emilio had not arrived.

A policeman was called to the witness box and sworn in. Emilio's papers were submitted to the judge. The prosecution, a genial middle-aged man, relished uncovering the exact nature and purport of each document with the help of the policeman finally, with a flourish he said, 'evidence of Mafia connections, material proof of drug dealing – your witness' and sat tapping his copies together on the bench. Emilio's replacement bustled forward and attempted to discredit them one by one – forgeries, unknown provenance, not addressed to Ricci.

The cat and mouse continued after lunch and still no sign of Emilio. It was not until she was driving home that Oriana realized. *Of course, he's a witness, he has to wait to be called. Does that mean he can't watch what's going on? It must. I have to wait for him to be called. There isn't much time, all the other witnesses have already testified. For Ricci the letters were no more than the final nail.*

Emilio was the first and only witness the following day. He took the oath looking like anyone's favourite uncle in a brown suit, cream shirt and tie patterned with autumn leaves. The court was even more crowded than the day before. Oriana surveyed them from her back seat – people from all walks of life, not all wealthy or young, mainly ordinary middle- aged men and poor younger women. *Here for the verdict? Baying for blood? Emilio will be destroyed. This is going to be awful. I don't even know which side I'm on anymore. He's not in the dock for heaven's sake. He's a witness on the right side for once.*

The prosecution rose as if to welcome an old friend and asked about the origin of a letter. Emilio dodged, wove around how it came into his possession, pretended ignorance of its existence, swore he had absolutely no idea of its contents. He played the innocent with accompanying outrage and exasperation. Oriana overcame her surprise. *You didn't expect him to go like a lamb to the slaughter did you? I suppose not but there's a difference between that and outright denial, no more victims that's why I did it.* Emilio withdrew into arrogance and sarcasm until he was passed to the defense lawyer and then it was teamwork on the great cover up denigrating every scrap of evidence – lies, set up, every thing 'another place, another time, different people.'
How can signed and dated letters, bills and statements not be credible? She shrugged. *When Emilio is in court. Mr. Plausible, like father like son.*

Her feelings of guilt for his betrayal, her anxiety over his vulnerability slid away and she slumped back in her seat to watch like a charmed snake. The men in the front followed every word stony faced, rigid as letters and receipts were read in court. She could sense their outrage at their dealings being laid out for public scrutiny. Reporters sat forward taking notes, typing onto their phones. Other people were more relaxed, moving, nodding,whispering in horror or satisfaction.

It was not long before the judge called the solicitors to make their cases. The defense tried to dismiss witnesses as biased and evidence as suspect but the prosecution called on the judge to decide whether so many witnesses could be corrupt, Ricci's own extravagant life style at his age coming from a poor background and finally, the 'coup de grace' police verification of the physical evidence.

The judge, who had remained impassive throughout excoriated Ricci and condemned him to fifteen years in prison. Ricci was escorted out followed by his counsel. Emilio ignored the prosecution and avoided looking toward the public seating and the dark suited men in the front two rows. He left through a side door and Oriana did not know if he had seen her.

Outside she saw some of the men from the front row light cigarettes and huddle together talking intensely. She slipped past and out of the courtyard feeling guilty. They knew this was only the beginning, they were mustering their defenses.

The people named in the papers and more gleaned from the file in the shed and Emilio's office would all be indicted. The police had been working on it since Oriana visited the station.

It was only a matter of weeks before they informed her of a trial date thanking her for information that would lead to a significant shake down of Mafia activities. Oriana had to go, keep attending. She was chained to a treadmill. She had to see it through to the end.

The court was as packed as it was for the last day of Ricci's trial with reporters standing at the back. The front rows were filled with men in expensive clothes, older, confident, with 'presence.' Eight accused filed in and sat behind the dock. Their three solicitors sat in front of them while on the other side of the room two prosecution solicitors conferred quietly by an empty witness box. The judge was a woman. *That's good, she'll be unassailable, truth will win if the solicitors reveal it.* Oriana leant forward waiting for the curtain to go up. *Let battle commence.*

Emilio was called to authenticate the papers and was as stubborn in denial as before but this time the prosecution had the measure of him, he knew he was a hostile witness. He bore down on the details and trapped Emilio into demonstrating his knowledge of the letters, his familiarity with the people mentioned. The evidence was substantiated and Emilio's long standing complicity evident. At the end of a crushing humiliation in the witness box which the defense could not reverse Emilio stepped down and looked straight into his mother's eyes – a look of hatred and contempt. Oriana could only brazen it out. She wasn't going to drop her eyes in shame or regret. For his defiant 'I told you so' came her 'if you play with fire…'

Day after day the accused stood in the dock and their crimes – petty or vicious were set out with victims and receivers called to detail the horror. Emilio sat behind the counsel for the prosecution and avoided her eyes. Oriana stayed the course, she couldn't leave, she knew Emilio didn't care whether she was there or not but she couldn't desert him and it would have been unbearable to stay at home wondering about his fate and whether the threat to Angelo was going to lose its sting or Pietro's killers could carry on with impunity. After the first few days the crowd dwindled to a core of reporters, the changing faces of the curious and the men on the front rows who reacted to evidence by sitting back in contempt or leaning forward threateningly.

Winter blossomed into Spring and Summer burned its way to autumn before the miserable soap opera of the court proceedings came to an end. Oriana was overwhelmed with the extent of the tentacles of greed and the calculating coldness with which people were exploited, made dependent on things that destroyed them. The poverty, desperation and loneliness that poured from the witness box enraged her even more because the court setting made it clinical. It detached it from the blood, sweat and fear, the pain and isolation, the destruction of confidence, ability to lead normal lives that people had been robbed of. She wondered if their families were sitting around her watching and hoping for justice. She hoped they were. Oriana felt their impotence and frustration. She could hardly eat or sleep. Her life dwindled to a twilight world of creeping home eviscerated to feed the cats and go to bed. Thursdays at the farm were changed for Sunday when Isabella could make sure she had a meal and the normality of family. Her own stark house was no comfort and her mind was far too oppressed to work in the studio.

Oriana watched her son shrivel, lose his gloss and become detached. She wanted to take him away, look after him and at the same time anger seethed for the accounts of misery he had concealed, the life of lies and greed that he had lived.

After taking its toll on them both the battle ended and sentences were laid down, one after another from Enrico down prison sentences were pronounced. Emilio who was disbarred and fined a hundred thousand euros. Oriana hoped the police would keep him safe from the people his papers had incriminated.

She was exhausted and she had lost Emilio. Now it was over she wanted to console him, excuse herself, explain but she knew he would not listen. She wanted to know how he was affected by the awful testimonies of suffering that he and his father were responsible for protecting. Who could he turn to now? She wanted him to know that his family would stand by him but he didn't answer calls, her letters were returned and his email address had changed. Emilio was drifting away leaving her in an ocean of featureless grey.

36

The house suited Oriana more at night when it echoed with emptiness, cold and secret, full of ghostly shadows. She didn't want to see anyone or be seen. Mornings were cruel – cold winter sun on bare white rooms made her wince – too bright, too exposing, nowhere to hide, nothing to distract the mind and the challenge of another day she didn't want drained her. The sound of the phone drilling through silence called her out of bed to fumble into her robe and go down to shut it up.

'Mama,' Isabella's voice sounded urgent kindling a spark of life in Oriana.
'Isabella?'
'Si, si, I've been trying to get you.'
'The court, I was away…' Oriana groped through fog.
'I know you've been at court Mama, it's over now, I haven't heard from you, you've not been answering my calls, it's two weeks Mama, we're worried about you.'
'Me?'
'Yes, you, how are you?'
'Fine, I'm fine.'
'No you're not, have you been eating?'
''Course I have.'
'What are you doing today?'
Oriana looked round the empty kitchen and said, 'I don't know.'
'Will you come for lunch?'
Oriana stared at Baffina, 'I don't know…'
'What's keeping you?'
'What day is it?'
'It's Thursday mama.'
'Thursday, farm day, Isabella… '
'You'll come?'
Oriana shook her head, 'it's a long way…'
'I'll fetch you.'
'You're too busy.'
'I'm coming.'
Oriana panicked, 'no, no you mustn't come here.'
'Why not?'
'The cats.'
'The cats? What are you talking about mama?'
'I can't leave the cats.'
'They survived your days at court, they'll be all right.'
'No, no I'll come, I'll come.'
'You'll come to us?'
'Si, si.'
'Are you okay to drive?'
'The car's fine.'
'It's not the car I'm worried about Mama.'
'I'm fine, good.'
'Come straight away, I need you here.'
'Need me… All right.'
'We're good mama, missing you.'
'Va bene.'
Oriana put the phone down as Isabella was saying 'arrivederci.'

The yard was tidy and quiet, Pietro did not run out to claim her but Isabella came as soon as she heard the car creep into the yard and opened her car door.

'Mama! How are you?'

Oriana nodded still seated behind the wheel, 'I'm all right, how about you?'

She sat behind the wheel staring through the windscreen.

'Well, come on then,' Isabella tried to sound cheerful.

It was an effort to swing her legs out of the car. Oriana struggled upright and blinked at the sun.

'Where have you been?' asked Isabella.

'Nowhere.'

'I called last week, you didn't answer.'

'Don't remember.'

'What's been happening? You look terrible.'

Oriana looked down at her green cord trousers and cable knit jumper.

'What's wrong with it?'

'They're crumpled and dusty as if they've been on the floor.'

'Floor's fine,' Oriana said slapping dust from a trouser leg. *Did Emilio see me like this?*

'That's not what you used to tell us.'

'Long time ago.'

Oriana made her way to the kitchen.

'You've lost more weight, you haven't been eating.'

'Yes I have.'

'What?'

'Bread, olives.'

'Oh mama you can't carry on like this. What's happening to you?'

'Everything and nothing, where's Paolo?'

'Out on his new tractor.

'Is that a new roof on the barn?'

'Yes, we decided it was worth doing now Tommaso wants to carry on the farm.'

The new kitchen was spacious with everything tidied into fitted cupboards but Oriana missed the mess of the dresser – children's games and phones, fruit and ornaments. The only pictures were a board of photos of the children and beside it an enlargement of one of Pietro sitting on a tree stump looking thoughtful.

Giorgio ran to Oriana.

'Nanna!'

She picked him up and kissed his forehead and cheeks.

'Piccolo criceto!'

She sat with him on her lap.

'What have you been doing mama?' asked Isabella.

Giorgio wriggled down and ran to his blocks.

'Doing?'

Her mind was a blank.

'Yes, mama 'doing', what have you been doing?'

'This and that.'

'That doesn't tell me much.'

'Nothing to tell.'

'The trial is over mama, it's all over, there's nothing anyone can do.'

'Emilio's disbarred, he'll have to sell the house to pay the fine.'

'He's the one to blame mama, not you. Why are you punishing yourself?'

'I'm not punishing myself. It's a dark world.'

'Not here mama, not with Lucia or Angelo, not where there's love, we're worried about you, Lucia hasn't heard from you. There's only Angelo who's heard your voice in the past two weeks.'

The children networking over me?

She replied, 'Angelo's got a new job.'

'I know, in the showroom at Ferrari, that'll suit him. They'd sell out if all their customers were women.'

'What woman wants a Ferrari?'

'What woman can afford one?'

Isabella put a plate of ham, salami and cheese in front of her mother and cut fresh bread. She poured olive oil and balsamic vinegar into a little dish.

'Eat,' she said.

Oriana broke a fragment of bread and dipped it in the oil.

Isabella handed her a glass of wine, 'Drink,' she said.

'Where's yours?'

'Here.' Isabella tapped her glass against Oriana's. 'Here's to a new life for all of us. '

Oriana sipped out of courtesy rather than conviction. Isabella watched her mother surreptitiously as she sipped her wine watching Giorgio. She looked gaunt, her hair was lank and her skin dull.

'Nonna!' Anna threw herself at Oriana.

'Take your boots off!' Shouted Isabella.

Anna and Maria went back to the door and sloughed off their boots.

'No marks mama,' said Maria.

The smooth pale Amtico floor looked clean and bright with its decorative border and central motif in bright blue, Isabella's pride and joy. Maria ran to hug her Nonna and nuzzled her nose in Oriana's cheek.

'How are you Nonna?' She asked.

Oriana smiled, 'all the better for seeing you, what have you been up to?'

'Maria got a prize for Art Mama, show Nonna your certificate.'

Maria went upstairs.

'I'm on the football team Nonna,' said Anna.

'Do you like football?'

'It's great, fast and clever. I scored a goal in the last match.'

'That's brilliant, it's about time girls got a look in.'

Maria gave Oriana the certificate.

'You were top of the year, well done.'

'She's following in her Nonna's footsteps,' said Isabella.

'You'll never be rich but you'll always be happy to lose yourself in your art.'

'What are you making at the moment Mama?' asked Isabella.

'I haven't been in the studio for ages,' she replied shocked at her own confession.

'It's time you got back to it, weren't Francesco and Battista after your work?'

'Francesco took what I gave him but I lost contact.'

'He'd be glad to have more, you know it.'

'True, I could clear some more old stock.'

'Make room for something new.'

'True.' *If only I didn't feel exhausted at the thought of it.*

Rosa poked her head round the sitting room door, 'Ciao Nonna, how are you?' Oriana smelled flowers as she bent to kiss her.

'I like your perfume,' said Oriana.

'A present from Giacomo,' she said.

'He's a nice lad, when's the wedding?' Oriana joked.

'Next July,' said Isabella.

'He finishes University in June and he's got a job in Geneva. He wants me to go with him.'

'What will you do?'

'I'll carry on with design.'

'That's a wide area,' said Oriana,

'Lunch time, the boys'll be starving,' declared Isabella.

'Can I help?' asked Rosa.

'Give me a job,' said Oriana.

'You just sit and enjoy the nibbles. Have you got your phone handy? I'll give Paolo a call tell him lunch is on the way.'

Oriana pulled it from her pocket, 'here you are.'

Isabella called Paolo and left the phone on the side.

'Anna and Maria provided lunch,' she said brightly distracting Oriana while she copied a number from the phone.

Oriana looked at the twins.

'Mushrooms, Nonna, the field was full of them.'

'They're beauties too,' Isabella shook a dark umbrella in the air.

Isabella stuffed ravioli with minced chicken and added thyme and cream to the chopped mushrooms in time for Paolo and Tommaso to stamp into the kitchen pulling off coats and boots.

'It's cold out there,' said Paolo, 'you're better off here.' He headed straight for Oriana and gave her a hug. 'Good to see you.'

'And you,' said Oriana smiling.

Tommaso gave her a kiss on the cheek.

Isabella put a big bowl of hot pasta on the table and served her mother carefully.

'Not too much,' said Oriana.

Isabella handed her a bowl full.

'I'll never eat all that.'

'It'll do you good Nonna,' said Rosa.

It tasted of rich earth, forests and moss and the fresh ravioli slipped down easily filling Oriana's empty stomach. She sliced a piece of pasta for Giorgio and he opened his mouth like a bird to be fed again and again.

'I'm not the only one loving this,' said Oriana helping herself to a spoonful between feeding Giorgio.

'I had a lesson on the new tractor Mama,' said Tommaso.

'How's he doing?' Isabella asked Paolo.

Tommaso looked at his father.

'He's good, no problem.'

'It's great Mama, it's got satellite guidance.'

'I thought you knew where your fields were,' said Oriana loading her fork, the wine had given her an appetite.

'Boy's toys,' laughed Isabella.

Maria said, 'we've got an art project, Nonna. We have to choose our favourite artist and give a talk on him.'

'Or her,' said Anna.

'Alive or dead?' asked Oriana.

The twins looked at each other. Anna shrugged, 'doesn't matter.'

'Does to them.'

Everyone laughed.

'Suggestions anyone?' Isabella asked looking at her mother.

'Can I do you, Nonna?' asked Maria.

'I'm not famous.'

'It didn't say 'famous' it said favourite. My log cabin and woodland animals was my favourite toy.'

Anna beamed at Maria, 'And my theatre with Pierrot and Columbine, I love it.'

They looked at each other delighted with the idea.

'Can we take photos in your studio?'

'Nobody'll have that,' said Anna triumphantly.

'Don't you be too sure,' said Oriana, 'you'd better come for the day, all of you, right Mama?'Oriana looked at Isabella.

'If you'd like that, it's been a long time since we've been round.'

'I know I cut myself off, just wasn't up to it.'

'We understood after daddy's death.'

'And the trial – it's been a long grey tunnel.'

'Can you see the light now?'

'It's beginning, you and Angelo, he calls every week, sometimes more.'

'He's mama's boy, we speak every now and again. He was sorry to miss Pietro's funeral.'

'He liked to play with the children.'

'He's still a child himself.'

'He's growing up fast this last two years, he's got a girlfriend.'

'What's new?'

'This one sounds serious, he's met the family and her Uncle wants to take him into the family firm.'

'What do they do?'

'Parmegiano.'

'Dairy farm – Angelo?'

'No, no, no – they have shops, he's doing the marketing, running the shops and he's loving it – got lots of ideas – not all of them crazy.'

'There's a turn around,' laughed Isabella, 'I'm glad.'

'He's bringing Bianca for Christmas.'

'Bianca eh? Do they want to stay here?'

'No, I've got plenty of room and beds, I just have to make the place a bit more comfortable.'

'You will still come to us for Christmas Eve won't you?'

'Of course and you can come to us on Christmas day.'

'It won't be long, I'd better start thinking about La Befana.'

'What do the girls want?'

'Paints for Maria, clothes for Anna and something for her trousseau for Rosa, Tommaso probably wants a motor bike but I'm keeping quiet about that.'

'They grow up so quickly.'

'Why don't you go and sit in a comfy chair while we clear. Coffee?'

Oriana and Paolo sat at the end of the room facing a couple of low bookshelves under the photos. Oriana remembered the day of Pietro's photograph. It was a picnic at Sebastian's farm. Paolo and Tommaso had played football with Pietro but the ball kept rolling downhill and Pietro got cross and stomped off down the field. She had followed trying to calm him and couldn't stop running until she crashed at the bottom and it frightened him. He ran over and hugged her in silent horror. They walked back up the hill holding hands and she dropped to the ground and leant her back against the tree stump while he climbed on top and sat looking out over the farm.

'That's a good picture of Pietro isn't it?' She asked Paolo.

He looked up at it, 'yes it's got his troubled thoughtful look, that was Pietro.'

'Have you got a copy?'

'Somewhere probably, we were photo mad then.'

'I know a good portrait artist, she could make something of that.'

Isabella stopped with two coffees in hand and studied the photograph.

'That would be wonderful, do you think she would do it?'

'No reason why not.'

'How much will it cost?' asked Isabella.

'My gift to you.'

'Thank you,' said Paolo.

37

The house was no longer her animal den, the place to lick her wounds at the end of each day's battle, she was free but what had tied her to the court would not let go. Emilio had a heavy fine, no job and powerful enemies. *They can't do much from prison, he's got to be all right.* But his words in the studio came back, 'you've signed my death warrant.' *He was angry, exaggerating. Things like that don't happen today, he's too high profile anyway. They can't touch him.* But Angelo's frightened face tormented her,' nowhere is safe enough, there's Mafia in every city. They don't forget – favours or betrayal, everyone's called to account...' *I need to see Emilio, see how he's taken it, see that he's the same determined survivor I depended on. So, he hates me but he's had a lifetime of love from me, he can't have forgotten that and he's got no one else. The court showed him the other side of what he's been doing. Emilio redeemed? Not possible.* Baffina was watching her from the shelf with Burrichio fast asleep in his bed beneath. *He's alone in that empty house. He has to know that I'm with him, he can do better things, still earn a decent living – doing what?* She could not see Emilio stooping to anything menial. *He must know people who'd be glad to use his knowledge.* She drained her coffee cup and took her car keys from the window ledge. 'Arrivederci' she said to the cats.

The car nuzzled its way through mist past overgrown hedges, tangled gardens and finally the Lombardy poplars before his house. The number of cars dwindled to nothing as she approached. Finally she turned into a weedy entrance to be confronted by 'Per Vendita,' a big board strapped to the gates and a heavy chain holding them together. She got out of the car and peered between the bars. It was eerily silent, no dogs straining at their chains barking a warning, no movement, no sound. Weeds pushed up through the gravel, what had been lawn was jungle and a mass of overgrown plants climbed the walls. The windows were dirty, it had been abandoned long ago and with it all hope of even a confrontation. He had disappeared from her radar and she knew he would never return, not to her, Isabella, Angelo or even Lucia. He had turned his back on the life they shared.

After the surprise there was relief as well as sadness. She realized how much she had had to screw up her courage to make this last attempt at contact. She wished him well wherever he was. She could fantasise a redemption, dream of reconciliation but she knew that could never happen with the man she had seen in court.

She turned her back on the house and looked across the road to the fields of grass bent with dew. A blackbird was scratching away leaves under a bush for rose hips or worms. The mist was clearing, bright sunlight illuminated a cloud, it was Friday, the day was hers and the weekend lay ahead. *It's the market on Vialo Papiniano, I can stop on my way home.*

Each of the market stalls had a red and white striped umbrella. boxes of produce were piled all around and the stalls overflowed with pumpkins, onions, garlic, mushrooms, cauliflowers and spinach. Orchards had emptied apples, pears and plums into crates and baskets. The great square was bustling with people. Customers with big bags were bantering with producers, sharing recipes, relishing each item as they chose it.

It was strange to return to a favourite scene after so long, Oriana felt fragile as if she'd been in hospital. She asked a stall holder to cut her a piece of pumpkin then, having taken that first step back into contact with the real world she took a basket and helped herself to handfuls of spinach, a big bunch of watercress, carrots and potatoes, emptied them into her bag and moved on to buy apples, pears and plums. A little van with fresh pasta tempted her to buy linguine. She remembered her empty 'fridge and added Parmesan, Roquefort and Mozzarella – a big loaf and she was back in the land of the living.

The car purred all the way home happy to be stocked with treats and the fridge looked friendlier with shelves full of goodies. She emptied her bag of plums into a colander watched by Burrichio. Tancreda wreathed around her ankles. *It's all right I haven't forgotten you babies.* She unwrapped fish and put it on to poach. Baffina jumped down from her eyrie. There was a knocking at the door.

'Sofia!'

'Oriana!'

Sofia was over the threshold hugging Oriana before she could say another word.

'What brought you this way?'

'You.'

'Me?'

'I've been worried about you.'

'I emailed.'

'I know, less and less about you and how you were feeling more and more about the trial, the terrible things you were hearing and court room game of ping pong. How are you?'

'Sorry, getting better I think, come through to the kitchen. Aperitif?'

'Si per favore.'

Sofia took off her coat and looked for the stand but only Oriana's father's clock was left in the hall. The place was bare and the walls were stark white. She hung her coat on the end of the banister

'What's going on?' she asked in the empty kitchen.

'Autumn clean last year, didn't I mention it?'

'The fire? I didn't think it was that thorough.'

Oriana handed Sofia an Aperol and leant against the worktop, 'sit down.' She nodded to the only wooden chair.

'I'll keep you company.' Sofia stood beside Oriana watching Burrichio twitching in his sleep. 'He's catching a mouse,' Oriana said.

'The cats have got new beds,' said Sofia.

'To make up for the changes, they didn't approve. I was going to make soup, will you join me?'

Sofia nodded, 'Bruno's out for the night. Can I help?'

Oriana gave her the pumpkin and emptied spinach into the sink and turned on the tap.

'Can you chop that while I do the onions?'

Sofia took a knife from the stand and they chopped together.

'Like old times,' said Oriana smiling.

'Truanting from school to cook in each other's houses.'

'Thought we were so sophisticated with our curries.'

'And crepes!'

'Pinching mother's Cointreau for Crepes Suzettes.' Oriana grinned at Sofia.

'I still love those. Should I put this on?' Sofia held up her chopping board of rich orange pumpkin.

'I'll fry the onions first, you can drain the spinach.'

'On to it,' said Sofia lifting handfuls into a colander.

Oriana poured olive oil into a big pan followed by chopped onions and stirred. When the onions were translucent and golden she added the pumpkin and dark green spinach then stirred in a big red chopped tomato and put the lid on to let them sweat.

'Put the kettle on for the stock, vegetable cubes are...'

'In this cupboard,' said Sofia taking the packet, 'some things haven't changed thank goodness.'

'You're like the cats, don't like change.'

'We'll see when I've seen the rest of this 'autumn clean.''

Oriana put olives in a bowl, found some nuts and opened a bottle of Bonardo.

'We can take our drinks through while this cooks,' she said pouring the jug of stock into the pan.

The sitting room was cold. Logs were stacked by the fire but it didn't look as if a fire had been lit for a long time.

'I'll get some sticks and light the fire.'

The bare windows made Sofia feel exposed and the brilliant white paint made it worse. The floorboards echoed eerily. *It feels like an operating theatre*, Sofia thought then shuddered, *after the corpse has been removed.*

Oriana saw the shiver, 'you're cold.'

She arranged sticks on top of a lighter. 'It'll soon warm up.' She sat back on her heels to watch the flames take hold.

'This is good,' she said standing up and picking up her glass, 'come and sit by the fire.'

Sofia sat in Oriana's armchair and put her glass on a pile of books. Oriana pushed the sofa closer to the fire and joined her.

'It's been a year, you haven't wanted to replace anything?'

Oriana shook her head thoughtfully, 'not a priority, doesn't bother me, surprising how little we need.'

'Are you going into a mystic religious phase?'

Oriana laughed, 'heavens no, I leave that to Lucia, she knows what devotion is.'

'So why punish yourself?'

'I'm not punishing myself.'

'Look around Oriana, where's the comfort? Where are you? It's all so impersonal, it's not home.'

'No, I did 'home' I'm not doing that anymore.'

'That was for your family, to make them happy and secure and it did, it's full of happy memories for them, you gave them that, you need to make it your own now, let it reflect you and all that you stand for.'

'What's that? What do I stand for? I don't know anymore.'

'On yes you do, that's why the trial revelations shocked you – you are the polar opposite of the firm and all it stood for – you're alive with creativity and compassion, you relate to people, you don't see them as tokens in a game of profit.'

'What good does that do?'

'It helps every one who ever knew you, your friends, family, it inspires your art and every person who takes a piece home.'

'That's been relegated. The studio is another world, another me, I haven't the energy any more.'

'You passed that over for your hair shirt courtroom hell. Those emails, you absorbed every detail of every crime as if it were your own, you let their dark cruel world put out your light. You weren't responsible.'

'My Husband, my son I was helping them to carry on.'

'They're not you and your being in court wasn't going to help Emilio. You made the right decision for your family, for all of us.'

'What good is it going to do?'

'Eight people less corrupting youngsters, trafficking girls, undermining justice. You made a stand Oriana, an example others can follow.'

'And lost my son.'

'He was lost already.'

'You're right – mother's denial.'

'You've lost yourself in all of this and you're precious.'

'There's nothing precious about me – a duped fool.'

'You believed in the men you loved and they let you down, that's their fault not yours.'

'But I lived with it.'

'No you didn't, you didn't bring up your children to that and your life was at its most vital out there in the studio. The work you created was acclaimed – it was pure, it was good, you would not settle for second best in your ideas with clay or stone.'

'There are thousands like me.'

'True but they're not all as good as you or as good as you can be now you're not hobbled. You used to say the clay or the stone led you, let it lead you now. You're mistress of all you do now, no one to answer to.'

'Apart from you…'

They smiled and Sofia said, 'and Francesco and Battista and all your clients.'

'I've let them down.'

'You've been through a difficult time, people who work with artists understand their intensity – joy or suffering – it is what inspires them, takes them beyond the reach of normal mortals.'

'I feel as if I've been dragged to hell and back.'

'It's the back that's important.'

'Thanks to you and Isabella.'

'You have family who appreciate you, remember that.'

'You're right, soup should be ready, I'm hungry.'

'You have to get back into it, Elena and Celia were saying the galleries were expecting work, they have people in line.'

Oriana opened the dining room door as they passed and hesitated.

'We'd better eat in here if it's not too cold.'

Twelve mahogany chairs and a long table stood in the middle of the dining room with a heavy carved sideboard. The white walls made them look darker, heavier and out of place. The naked windows let in the cold.

'You don't eat in here do you?' Sofia asked.

'I haven't been in here for over a year, I hate the furniture, heavy and dark, reminds me of stilted dinner parties impressing clients.' Oriana looked at the furniture with disgust, 'I don't want it and neither did Isabella when they moved back into the farm house, she had new.'

'Get rid of it, you've got to make this place your nest – build it how you want, surround yourself with things that give you pleasure. Can't we have the soup into the sitting room?'

Oriana smiled, 'good idea.'

'Where have you been eating?'

'In the kitchen with one of the burners on the stove to keep warm.'

'And sitting?'

Oriana pulled a wry face, 'In the court room.'

'Humph, that's got to stop, life begins here and out there.' Sofia indicated the studio in the garden. 'Do you have heating in there?'

Oriana laughed, ''Course I do.'

Sofia was like a great warm wave carrying her on to adventures unknown. In the kitchen Sofia whizzed the soup while Oriana put bowls on a tray and cut chunks of crusty bread. In the sitting room she put on a Pavorotti CD.

'Do you remember that concert?' She asked Sofia.

'It was wonderful,' said Sofia.

'You cried.'

'It was too much, I loved it.'

They dipped their bread into their soup and mopped up the drips with big napkins.

'This is so good I must make it at home.'

'Spinach and pumpkin, my favourite things this time of year, mind you watercresss soup is good too,' she laughed, 'we loved our food didn't we?'

'Still do, and the children.'

'We passed that on, thank goodness.'

Sofia put her empty bowl on the pile of books.

'We had a clear out of books the other day, I've got a bookcase you can have, you know the pine one with the glass doors. Would you like it?'

Oriana beamed, 'I love that bookcase, are you sure you don't need it?'

'The children have long gone de-cluttering is priority for us too but not quite so drastically as you.'

'Your furnishings are wrapped up in a shared family story, your moving on is together.'

'Remaking your home in your own name is the therapy you need. You just have to love yourself enough to feel it's worth doing.'

'You understand as always.'

'Well I hope I've helped to move you on to where you should be.'

'Out there for a start, you have. I'll give Battista a call and see if there's any chance that commission is still in the offing but it's been almost two years.'

'Too long, you're mad abandoning yourself for what?'

'Not a lot of use but inspiration isn't easy with a troubled mind.'

'Some artists draw inspiration from their torture or escape into it.'

'I suppose everyone has to learn to live with their own particular pain in their own way. The thought of work is a relief, a bit of a tonic.'

'There aren't that many people sculpting in stone round here you never know, I bet that commission is still there.'

'It would be good, I feel like a change of medium, I'm sick of clay sculpture.'

'What happened to the bust?'

Oriana confessed, 'I threw it after Emilio.'
'Serves him right.'
Would you like some plums?'
'I would thank you and a coffee to set me on my way.'

38

Summer's growth had once again taken over the path to the studio blocking the door. Instead of relief like the last time she pushed her way in this time she felt guilty for leaving it so long, angry at letting herself get sucked in to a lost cause. The long stone room was cold, the paraffin heater gurgled when she tipped it, *maybe a day's fuel.* She crouched to light the wick and warmed her hands. The studio was less cluttered without the ceramics Francesco had taken and her stone sculpture. She walked to the end where it had stood. Battista said the client loved it. *It was hard hollowing out that stone, getting the sweep of the curves.* But the joy of abandoning herself to the rhythm of the mallet, the intoxicating energy of it and the elation as she broke through came back.

The commission was still there, only she could do it, the client was vague – possibly a figure, representational or abstract, it was up to her. Oriana looked forward to the challenge of stone, she needed something bigger, grander, harder – but what? Subject eluded her, where did she want to go? What did she want to pursue, delve into?

A tall block of limestone was propped in the corner behind her wheel. She pulled a dusty cardboard box away to see it better and ran her hands over its surface feeling the texture – patches of hardness where fossils were buried, softness where carbon decay left a spongy texture. The dusty surface was warm, it's blank surfaces and brutal angles challenged her to soften it, bring it to life, infuse it with spirit and vitality – but what? She lifted herself onto the surface of the workbench and sat, hands gripping the edge of the bench, staring at the stone pillar. *I need to change you into something enduring, worthwhile – stone to man, woman – change. I've changed – sadder, wiser I hope, less trusting. Dario loved success more than family, Emilio power. They didn't change, just became more themselves. That makes them smaller not bigger, men to be forgotten. They were indifferent to other people's suffering and I almost drowned in the misery of it. Thank God for Isabella and Sofia.*

She smiled thoughtfully and looked through the window at the old persimmon tree with an occasional leaf sputtering in the wind. *At least I'm bomb proof and clear eyed now, never again, it's over. To change is strong, metamorphosis the miracle. How much of the caterpillar remains in the butterfly? Ovid's Metamorphoses, all those poor creatures running from reality tragically changed. Denial brought me no happiness, there's more satisfaction in surviving the truth, adapting and triumphing over it. I could bring them back, restore those tortured souls to blissful lives – rebirths – I'll reverse the myths. Syrinx can emerge from the reeds triumphant to shame Pan.* Oriana jumped down and took a sketchbook from a drawer by the door and a pencil and rubber. Propped on a stool she sketched the outline of a willowy figure with reeds clinging to legs and thighs, head and shoulders emerging from tendrils of feathery flowers, chin slightly uplifted. On the next page she started to sketch the back – the supporting reeds, seeds and tiny flower clusters defining thighs and waist – she stopped. *Hair? No hair – no hair means no flowers or seeds – too realistic, no, the reeds will be a prison, a prison of bars and she'll rend them asunder, stronger more modern, that's what I want. How? Not grappling with them like a monkey or a wrestler, not Hercules with the lion or snakes, this is not about physical strength.* She tore out the pages and threw them on the floor.

Stone, stone, remember the stone, prisons of stone... Feverishly she drew, rubbed out and corrected. Page after page landed on the floor in tight balls. Finally she leant back. *That's it. I need a bigger block of stone, Pietra Serena, blue grey sandstone not brown limestone, Fiesole quarry is closest for that.* She changed her shoes for walking boots and grabbed an old leather coat and scarf. Driving out into the countryside did not diminish her excitement. Her head teemed with the project. Detail depended on the stone. She would explore and use the different textures and colours of the quartz, carbon and volcanic sediment in the sandstone. It would become her friend over the weeks and months they would work together.

The hole in the hillside was huge and giant blocks of stone were dotted around the bottom. Oriana parked in front of a shed and jumped out to look for someone to speak to. The inside was filled with the whine of buzzing saws and clouds of dust rose from stations around the far end. There was a little office by the entrance but it was difficult to make herself understood over the noise. Finally the manager smiled and took her outside to a varied selection of tall cut stone pieces. Their breath billowed in little clouds as they spoke. He waited beside her with his shoulders hunched against the cold, rubbing his hands together then left her to it. She examined them one after another. Each one was full of promise but not for her. She stood back to appraise the bigger blocks at the back. The dimensions her subject required were becoming clearer, none of these fitted. She returned to the office and ordered a block two metres by one to be cut and delivered. All she had to do was wait until Monday.

Oriana felt energized. *Project number one Sofia's list underway. Now for the house – that dining room furniture has to go. We bought it from Matteo perhaps he'll buy it back, he may have something else I like. It's years since I went there rummaging around, finding things I didn't know I needed until I saw them – collecting rubbish, but Sofia's right, a bit of home comfort wouldn't go amiss. I can look.* She turned her car in the direction of his little shop.

There were chairs on the pavement and bits of iron bedstead leaning against the wall. Matteo was outside putting a wooden lamp on a table. He watched the car pull up and recognized her as she got out.

'Oriana, how are you?'

'Well thanks and you?'

He shook his head from side to side and shrugged. His fleshy features drooped a little lower and his stomach was a little rounder. He gave his usual lugubrious smile.

'Okay, okay I suppose. What brings you here?'

'I'm having a re-vamp.'

'Ah,' his face converted instantly from the pleasure of seeing her to sadness, 'after the loss…I'm sorry,' he said wringing his hands.

'It's been a long time' she said.

'Two years…?' He faltered.

'Four, I want to get rid of my dining suite.'

'Fruit wood wasn't it?'

'Mahogany.'

His smile vanished.

'Dark furniture, the bottom's dropped out of the market.'

'It doesn't matter, I want to get rid of it.'

'I can't even give you what you paid.'

Oriana shrugged, 'that's life, it served its purpose.'

'Is there anything you like here? I could give you a good deal.'

Oriana wandered round the dark interior – gilt mirrors, dark paintings of cypresses on hills, of rivers or cliffs, stack after stack of china and ranks of wine glasses, chests of drawers and tables of every size and in the middle a little scrubbed pine table with rush seated chairs.

'How much is this?'

'One hundred and fifty?' He tried.

'One hundred and twenty.'

'Done.'

There was a stack of carpets. They pulled them out one by one and she stopped at a big circular cream carpet with an orange, gold and red border.

'I like that,' she said.

'You've got good taste, that's Indian.'

'Not as expensive as Persian.'

'No but this is top quality.'

'How much is it?'

'For you, a thousand.'

'And my furniture?'

'Five hundred.'

'You can take my dining table and chairs and I'll give you five hundred for this including the little table and chairs.'

He took a breath and considered, shook his head but said, 'Okay.'

Oriana took out her cheque book.
'I'll bring them when I collect,' he said.
'When will that be?'
'Mondays are quiet, that's when I deliver. Will you be there?'
'Yes, I will.'

She could hardly contain her delight as she drove away. *Back to life with a vengeance, I can feel the blood circulating in my veins.* She stopped at a favourite little take away for a rectangle of pizza loaded with tomato, olives, cheese and Proscuitto and while she queued she saw a big bunch of bronze and gold chrysanthemums outside a shop on the other side of the road. She crossed and bought them and another bunch of bright yellow for Isabella. The car was filled with the musty aromatic smell of chrysanthemums and savoury richness of her pizza as she drove home longing to make a coffee and eat. She arranged the bronze chrysanthemums in a jug and put it on the hearth in the sitting room then sat eating her pizza visualizing the carpet. *The curve will go into the bay. Gold curtains would look good with that. I'd better measure.* With the measurements of sitting and bedroom in her bag she headed for the nearest department store.

Oriana loved any raw ingredient begging to be made into something. Materials were no exception, she loved their colours and textures – velvet, silk, linen but most of all damask and brocade with their subtle woven patterns. She regretted never being taught to sew, she would have liked to embroider designs with silk and gold thread but as a child she preferred to be out on the garage forecourt with her father or in the shed under a car seeing how it worked, fitting exhausts or changing tyres. *I'm too big and clumsy for embroidery but at least I'm strong.* She smiled at the prospect of using that in the coming months of carving.

For over an hour she luxuriated in fabrics imagining every one at her windows, by a process of elimination she realized that flowers, grasses, abstract patterns were too busy. Finally she found gold damask for the sitting room and pale blue wild silk for the bedroom. With the delivery on Monday and Sofia's bookcase the house would be home and the studio full of promise, the coming winter would be warm and beautiful in every way.

39

A few snowflakes floated in the air when the lorry arrived with the stone, a young man leapt out and ran to let down the back of the lorry where the stone was strapped to a forklift truck. The young man pulled out two ramps and climbed onto the seat of the truck. The lorry driver ran round to guide him down and Oriana led them along the path that skirted the garage to the open studio door. She had pushed the tables aside and erected a platform for the stone to stand on. They worked as a team and the stone was soon in place between two windows. They cut it free and the truck reversed to the door then round by the sink to turn and proceed down the path to the lorry. Both men refused Oriana's offer of coffee and biscotti before departing to leave her alone with her prize.

She closed the studio door behind her and leant against it. *Don't need a 'Do not disturb' notice, nobody's going to interfere, you're all mine.* She couldn't take her eyes off the big block of stone at the far end of the studio standing proud in its space. It was taller than her even without the platform. She walked toward it. *Looks like an actor about to give a soliloquy. Clytemnestra or Macbeth? Antigone or Hamlet? Certainly not Desdemona or Orestes – a freedom fighter, a breaker of barriers, someone expressing themselves, their true nature – that's what's in there.* She walked around it defining the hidden contours of her figure. *Is it deep enough for the bent knee?* She checked the side – *tight but possible – proportions? Start with the head – go big and whittle it down. It'll be bottom heavy – balance it with something in the hand? Use the wall? Maybe.* She walked around it again. *This is bigger than anything I've ever done.* She ran her hands over the porous sandstone feeling the subtle changes in texture with sensitive fingertips. She stood back reassured. *I can cut this, it'll fall to the chisel.* Areas of pale blue grey shone among patches of dark grey. *Light and shade in the stone, maybe I can use that, we'll see.*

She put on a mask, goggles and leather gauntlets then picked up a circular saw. From the top of a step stool she started to cut away the top corners of the stone, rounding in and away to free the head. The studio rang with the whine of the saw and the air filled with dust. Chunks and splinters of stone fell all around. With the head defined the dimensions of neck and shoulders followed. She crouched intent on the person in the stone. She did not want to waste a centimeter of stone. Her figure filled the block almost bursting out. Like a woman possessed she would fight to bring the character to life – her everyman, every woman, empowered by the quest she would happily lose herself in for however long it would take.

40

'I've never seen your cherry tree so full of blossom,' said Sofia looking up into a pink cloud of flowers.
'No I haven't pruned it for two or three years, it's gone mad.'
Oriana and Sofia were sitting on a couple of wicker chairs in the middle of the garden where the bonfire had been. The grass had re grown even brighter green and lush.
'You'll have loads of cherries.'
'Plenty for everyone.'

'Back to jam making.'

'And eating, here, have some.'

Oriana offered her a plate with chunks of fresh bread and cherry jam. Sofia took a piece and tore into it with her teeth.

'Delicious, thanks.'

Oriana settled back with her coffee letting the sun's warmth work on muscles aching from months of hard work.

'Well am I going to see it?'

Oriana shook her head.

'You mean you cloistered yourself away all winter for nothing? The customer doesn't like it? They're not going to pay you for all that work?'

Oriana laughed, 'no, no they like it, you just can't see it yet.'

'How long have we been friends?'

'Longer than a comet's tail.'

'So why can't I see it?'

'I'm having an exhibition, the sculpture is having a grand unveiling, Battista insisted on it and the couple who commissioned it are happy to go along with it.'

'It'll increase the value if your name gets around.'

Oriana nodded, 'I suppose, that's why people seem to be quite happy to lend back old pieces, Francesco is adding some of my studio pieces.'

Sofia leapt up, gave Oriana a hug and jumped on the spot, 'that's so exciting, well done, that's the best bit of news I've had in years.' She turned to the studio, 'You've got to show me.'

Oriana looked her in the eye, 'I want you to see it in situ at the gallery, I need your honest opinion, the gallery's more real than the studio, more impersonal away from all of me that clings to things in the studio. Do you understand?'

Sofia stood still, 'I suppose so.'

'Out of the studio it's full blown, on its own, no excuses, no longer a work in progress able to be altered. It's frightening to expose it like that – I feel like Adam and Eve looking for a fig leaf, nowhere to hide.'

'Come on Oriana,' said Sofia putting her arm round her shoulder, 'Battista wouldn't suggest it if he didn't think it was up to it, he's part of the hard commercial world.'

'There's more of me in that than in my children, I'm nervous, it's as if it's my debut. I need your moral support and your verdict as it happens.'

'This sounds serious, which gallery is it?'

'Aria.'

Sofia whistled softly. 'Wow, the big one, that's impressive. When?'

'Friday, June 6th.'

'Who's going, do you know?'

'Battista's invited people I didn't know he knew. They're coming from all over the country, I can't believe it.'

'New outfit then, can I pass the word around?'

'For the exhibition please do, the opening is limited.' Oriana smiled at her friend, 'your paintings are wonderful, you should have an exhibition.'

'I paint for myself, family and friends – it's enough.'

'I crave authentication, the justification of acceptance. I think marriage eroded my confidence.'

'You'll get it back, your father and mother never put you down.'

'No, my parents made me independent, thank goodness.'

41

The interior space at Aria was all white walls, geometric stands and chrome spotlights on overhead rails. The floor was covered with thick grey vinyl so footsteps were quiet and the surface smooth and clean. Oriana was afraid that her ceramics were not fine enough to be put under this microscope but she had underestimated the talent of the gallery in clever display – a slender pale blue grey urn with a high handle was teamed with a deep bowl of the same glaze on top of a pyramid of shelves. Below it a long rectangular platter in pale green with a design in the same blue grey was placed and another shelf held a straight-sided blue rectangular dish with the same pale green in a geometric pattern. They stood up to scrutiny, in fact they benefitted from isolation although it was difficult for Oriana to accept their elevation. Nothing could ease the knot in her stomach waiting for the unveiling.

It was an alien world and she had dressed to match it in unaccustomed black crepe – a trouser suit and white blouse with pearl earrings and necklace. Her hair was drawn back in a bun and she had bought delicate embroidered pumps instead of boots or moccasins.

Her sculptures were in the courtyard – another immaculate space with the occasional paving stone removed to house a spiky aloe or cactus. Oriana did not like sharp pointy plants but they gelled with the general ambience of the gallery. There were waiters, girls and boys in black and white carrying silver trays of champagne and canapés through a strange assortment of people. The only thing they had in common was that whatever their style and there were lots of them, it was impeccably presented – no creases, no cheap fabrics, all colours were co ordinated, no details left begging – large rings, colourful handkerchieves, bright braces with colourful shirts, dramatic stoles or plunging backs to tailored dresses it was all there and animated, no mouth was still for long fuelled by champagne. Sofia loved it, dragging Bruno to and fro to report approving comments to Oriana and put names to the faces she recognized.

After their tour indoors everyone migrated to the courtyard where Oriana's draped sculpture stood half way down the side wall. The pit of

Oriana's stomach grew sicker, she couldn't take any of the canapés, she sucked champagne hoping to numb her anxiety. The courtyard was packed, voices were getting louder, Battista took Oriana's elbow,

'It's time,' he said with a smile and led Oriana and the couple who had commissioned the work through the throng to stand in front of the hidden statue.

'Ladies and gentlemen.' He had a microphone. The buzz ceased and everyone turned in his direction. 'I would like to introduce Oriana Stella Rossi whose work we have all been enjoying this evening. We can now see her latest work. Oriana.'

Oriana stepped forward, 'the work is called 'Freedom' it was commissioned by Signor and Signora Alberoni from Verona so I will let the new owners unveil their sculpture.'

The couple hesitated for a moment then held hands and stepped forward together. They each took a corner of one side of the cloth, looked at each other and pulled – a swift, dramatic de-nuding. Oriana closed her eyes, her mouth was dry – silence, an intake of breath, the odd gasp and everybody was clapping.

The figure was without gender or race – strong, perfectly formed, without limiting detail. It was surrounded by the remnants of a wall of stone bricks forming a triangle from behind the left shoulder around the back down to rubble before the feet. The right foot rested lightly on a block. The left hand pushed against the middle of its enclosing wall making it bulge and the right hand rested on the few remaining stones behind. Neck and shoulders were emerging in triumph from the ruins. The abstract head, eyes and mouth all curved upward in bliss.

'A Phoenix,' said the owner of the gallery.

'A miracle,' whispered Sofia.

***